Wyoming
Trail

Wyoming Trail

Cheryl Moskowitz

Granta Books

London

First published in Great Britain by Granta Books 1998
Granta Publications, 2/3 Hanover Yard, London N1 8BE

A CIP catalogue record for this book is
available from the British Library.

1 3 5 7 9 10 8 6 4 2

Typeset by M Rules
Printed and bound in Great Britain by
Mackays of Chatham PLC

To my family then and now

ONE

1

I am in a large hall. A beautiful building with high ceilings and long endless corridors. Sounds echo and bounce off the walls, creating a sense of timelessness with no present – only what has been and what might be in the future. There are two people with their backs to me standing at the end of a very large room. It is my mother and my father. They are dressed uncharacteristically smartly; he in a suit and tie and she in a satin shirt-waisted dress with a belt, matching jacket and high-heeled shoes. The shoes make a sharp clicking noise as she walks. The noise echoes and merges with the other sounds in the room but carries with it a faint sense of familiarity. I hang on to the sound of her stepping as though I am clinging to life itself. I cannot see their faces, nor the face of the authority that addresses them, but I know that their task is to walk together down a long corridor without touching and, at a certain point, to separate without faltering as they journey away from one another. The voice that instructs them cannot be questioned. I am an intruder in this place and crouch low, anxious in case I am discovered and taken out, never to witness the final division between the two who made me. I wake shivering. In the night my sister has taken all the covers.

———•———

To me, getting back to the womb has always meant riding in the back of the stationwagon with my ear to the floor, covered completely by our red tartan travelling-rug, inhaling the smell of my own fart, safe in the knowledge that only I know I've done it.

'Who let off that stinker?'

My father's voice always sounded different inside a car. It merged, somehow, with the rumble of the engine and sounded close up and distant at the same time. I used to think it was the sunglasses that made it sound different. My father always wore sunglasses when he drove.

We had been driving all night and soon it would be my mother's turn to take over the wheel. My older sister, Cynthia, lay next to me asleep with the morning sun beating in on her already red face. There were beads of sweat collecting around her temples. Her brow was wrinkled into a permanent frown that had pressed itself too soon into the nine-year-old visage. It made me think of new cement that a tyre has run over before it's properly dried.

'We should stop before we get on the interstate.'

My mother's voice also sounded different in the front of the car. Nicer. She sounded like one of those ladies on the radio that tell you to 'Get on down to Target and home in on a bargain today!' The vibrations of the car and the hum of being on the road enveloped my parents in a sweet, syrupy haze. I loved to lie there with my head just peeping out from under the rug and gaze at the back of their heads, counting each freckle or scar that I could see there. I needed to make a note of every imperfection in order to remind myself of their human and fallible natures.

Things were different when the car was still and they were both turned round to say something to Cyn and I at the back. Like when we stopped for gas or for something to eat at a truck-stop or the Dairy Queen on the highway, or when we pulled over so they could change driving positions and one could put their sunglasses on and face the road while the other reclined in their seat and closed their eyes to the ceiling.

'What the fuck do you always want to stop for?'

My father's voice went into an entirely different register when he wanted a fight. Which, actually, was most of the time. Cynthia moaned deliriously and I wondered whether the change in register had penetrated into her unconscious while she was sleeping.

'For Christ's sake, I don't always want to stop. I was driving the goddamned car for six hours last night without stopping. You've only done four.'

'And it's not me who wants to fucking stop.'

'Oh, stop being such a baby. To get some food, all right? I'm simply suggesting that we stop before we get on to the interstate to feed these goddamned kids so they don't complain all the way through to –'

'You want me to stop so you can say you drove longer. You're such a sneaky bitch. Crap, it's not because of the kids. Crap. You don't want to feed them, you want to feed your goddamned ego.'

'You are such a shit, Leon. Don't worry, I'll give them Fritos.'

'I don't want those goddamned yellow crumbs all over the back. I'll stop when I'm damned well ready – no one's going to starve. Jesus fucking Christ, *who* let off that stinker? Francine?'

'They're both asleep. Leave them.'

'I'm not asleep.'

For some reason when they were fighting I could never resist the temptation to climb right into the ring with them, even when I had the chance to lie low and stay well out of it. I liked the challenge of seeking unwilling defence from my mother and avoiding the wrath of my father. Not an easy obstacle course to negotiate when they were both in this riled state. Their arguments were, more often than not, about nothing. Although to point that out would just have been adding more fuel to the fire.

According to my parents there was always something to fight about. Without a fight, it would have been like giving in or being weak, which would have been a complete disaster. The one single thing they had in common was their value system. Both my mother and my father valued strength above all else. Strength and intelligence. These are good things to value but hell if you should ever show signs of weakness or stupidity.

'What's the matter with your stomach, girl? That is high. Phew!'

'Leave her, Leon. It's only wind.'

Only wind maybe but out of small winds grow great storms.

'Jesus.'

'Open the window then, for God's sake. Who's stopping you?'

I hated the front window being open when we were on the highway. It felt like being slapped in the face by a giant hair-brush. The pages of my colouring book started flapping and an empty Snickers wrapper was whipped up and flew out of the window just past Dad's head. He brushed his ear angrily as though a bee had just stung him.

'I'm cold,' I ventured, knowing it would stir things.

'Shhh . . .' my mother cautioned.

'I don't like the window open. Can't you shut it halfway?'

My father screeched to a halt. Cars behind missed us by inches as they swerved, swinging past on both sides. A whole orchestra of horns hooted their disapproval and shouts of abuse poured through open windows as the speeding vehicles went roaring off into the distance with angry drivers at their wheels.

'Get off the fucking road, Leon. We'll be killed.'

'Get out of the fucking car or I'll kill the whole lot of you anyway.'

'I'm hungry.' The commotion had finally been enough to rouse Cynthia gently from her sleep. Food was always the first thing she thought of on waking.

I grimaced widely at her, trying hard to indicate that it wasn't the best time to be requesting nourishment, but it was too late. Dad had sure-fire reflexes and would have been excellent in combat. He swung round and clapped Cynthia on the head, knocking her over on to her back and sending her legs flying directly into my stomach.

'OUCH!' we both shouted at once and then Cynthia cupped her hand over her mouth and buried her head with her other arm. She was trying not to cry, I knew, but even with her head bent I could see the silent tears forming like boulders ready to fall clumsily and heavily from her eyes. Cynthia spent her life trying to avoid fights and consequently lived in a state of anguished terror most of the time in our house where fighting was more or less constant.

'You folks all right?'

A Wyoming State policeman was peering in the window on the driver's side, his face haloed by the blue flashing light of his car. My father pressed his lips together trying to look intent and shook his head slowly, saying nothing. He was playing for time.

'Sir?' The policeman leaned forward enquiringly. A back-up officer was immediately behind him, his right hand by his side, fingering his holster.

'Gee officer, I'm really sorry to have got you out here. Geez, I just don't know . . .' My father let out one of his wheezy bemused laughs that made him sound like a depressed hyena. 'I really don't know what happened.'

'You don't know what happened, sir?'

'No, I really don't.'

Cynthia and I peered over the top of my mother's head and smiled. I practised making my eyes go big and round as I had heard somewhere that this makes people like you better.

'Are you intoxicated, sir?'

My mother, who was clearly impatient with my father's game-playing and the policeman's line of questioning, leapt in here.

'Not unless Dairy Queen have started putting the real thing in their root beer.'

'Beer, you mean?' The policeman was struggling to understand my mother's interjection.

'No, Coke,' my mother explained sarcastically. The police-man's face lit up. He thought he understood and wanted to share in the cleverness of it all.

'Oh . . . Coke. The real thing. I get it, the Real Thing. Coke is. It's the Real Thing. Coke is. Just a bottle of Coke. Coca-Cola.'

'Wow.' My mother pretended to be impressed. 'You know that off by heart. Do they pay you to say that?'

Despite the fact that he had come up with the slogan, the

advertising connection was completely lost on the policeman who had obviously been trained in literal as opposed to lateral thinking.

'No ma'am,' said the policeman. 'I'm paid to help folks like you out of trouble.'

It was all the time my father needed to come up with an explanation.

'You know, officer. I'm going to go and get my eyes checked. I think this might have been some kind of double-vision thing. I had to brake suddenly because I had a very momentary blackout.'

The policeman was writing something down. His partner was busy flagging the cars into two streams of traffic either side of the blockade we had created in the middle of the road.

'That sounds pretty serious, sir.' He leaned as far as he could into the car and spoke condescendingly across my father to my mother. 'Maybe you ought to be doing the driving, ma'am.'

He pulled himself slowly back out of the car and looked it over disdainfully. Nodding in the direction of our Kansas number plate he drawled, 'I notice you folks aren't from this good state.'

We weren't from the blessed state of Kansas either, home-sweet-home of Dorothy and Toto, but we hadn't changed the plate over since we bought the car two years ago from one of my father's medical students who was from Wichita.

'If you're sick and you want to see a Wyoming doctor, I have an excellent physician I can recommend.' He was bored. He was getting impatient. He was trying to call my father's bluff. Cynthia and I held our breaths.

'I *am* a doctor.' My father smiled sweetly. He hated to be patronized but loved to make other people feel small. Now he was playing his trump card. His crowning triumph. His winning ticket. 'Thank you. I have many contacts of my own.'

The policeman's tone became instantly reverential. Almost visibly he shrunk while my father grew and suddenly it was an honour rather than a duty he was performing. That my father the doctor had caused a road obstruction for no apparent, or for that matter believable, reason was nevertheless entirely forgivable and even perhaps a privilege for the policeman who was called in to deal with it. Now everything to do with this man of medicine, this distinguished person of reason and science, was important. Cynthia and I were noticed then as His children and fawned upon like little angels, prized cherubs that must be checked all over for bruising or possible damage. Apologies and platitudes poured into the car like melted sugar.

'You folks take care now.' The policeman patted the bonnet of the car tenderly as my father rolled up his window to go. The two uniformed men stopped traffic and waited patiently by as my father revved up the engine and slowly pulled away back into the fast lane of the highway. 'You take care now, sir, *Doctor* Weitz, you take care, you hear!' Sir. Doctor. Dr Weitz MD. Your Majesty. As we drove away, the policeman waved to us like an old friend. A loyal subject. I don't know, there may have even been a tear in his eye.

Maybe because it was 1967 or maybe because he looked a bit like Albert Schweitzer, but the fact that my father was a doctor never failed to impress. He used the title to his advantage at every possible opportunity. He was not a doctor of the knee-tapping, chest-listening sort. Or even the listening or visiting variety. My father, as far as I could tell, spent all his working time either in the laboratory cutting open rats and mixing things in test tubes or at home with his boxes of papers in his study where none of us were allowed to disturb him.

He was, I was told without too much extra information, a pathologist. At first I thought pathology was the study of paths. I imagined my father discovering new routes to places. Laying down paving stones and carving grooves through mountain terrain and open desert. I often told people, if they asked, that my father was a pathfinder. It seemed a much simpler and more straight-forward word than pathologist to explain what he did.

It was only after becoming very attached to a white rat called Herbert, which my father had brought home for us to play with, that I questioned the fate of the other rats that my father kept in his laboratory, which so often ended up being pinned on a cork mat and split down the middle with their guts spilling out. It was then explained to me (not by him because my father never really explained anything very directly) by my mother that it was my father's job to test out sickness and disease on animals in order to prevent it happening to humans.

Then, because I couldn't let go of my first image of what my father did, I constructed a rather bizarre picture of him leading sick animals along paths which he had made himself, being cheered and waved at by people in grey overalls with white masks over their faces. These were the humans, I supposed, for whom he was doing it all. I imagined myself as one of them, waving proudly at my father and shouting to get his attention from behind my mask. Though I liked to think of my father as invincible I was always slightly worried in this scenario that my father did not also have a protective mask over his face. Did that mean that he had become sick like the animals and would eventually become part of the experiment himself, pegged out somewhere on a giant cork board in an ether-filled laboratory being poked about with a scalpel by some other pathologist?

'When will we get there?'

Cynthia spoke in a whiny whisper that reminded me of watered-down grape juice. We had been on the road for about an hour after our incident with the police. My mother had taken over the wheel as the policeman had suggested and my father had fallen asleep on the passenger side. Cynthia only dared to ask questions like that when my father was asleep. In fact, not only did she dare to ask them then but she laid them on as thick as the cream on a strawberry shortcake.

'About another eight hours or so,' my mother said.

'Ooohhhhh,' Cynthia whimpered. 'Why? We've been going forever and I'm hot and I'm bored. Can we buy some ice-cream?'

Eating was the answer to everything for Cynthia, but it was true that we had still not stopped for the food my mother had suggested before all the ruction. The suggestion that caused the anger and the anger that caused the argument and the argument that caused the car to stop and the stop that caused the policeman to come and . . . the green grass grew all around all around and the green grass grew all around. When all was said and done I knew it had not been my mother's suggestion about stopping for food and not my fart either that had really made my father angry. I knew, deep down, that Dad and I were allies on this battleground. We shared a feeling of being trapped and a dislike of closed spaces. Funnily enough I never really minded being in the car because, although it was cramped, at least it was moving. But my father, I'm sure, didn't ever like the feeling that there might be no way out. That would fit nicely with my vision of my father as a pathfinder. Someone who had to be free and liked to chart open spaces.

2

Grandma's house was big and green. It had an apple tree and a pear tree in the garden. It would have been one of your ideal 'Grandmother' kind of homes if it hadn't been stuck right on the edge of Pittsburgh, Pennsylvania, Armpit of the Western World. When you were still about fifty miles away from her house you started to pick up the thick tarry smell that had something to do with all the factories and steelworks there. I never took a lot of interest in the industrial goings-on of Pittsburgh. My main interests in going to Grandma's were her attic, and Finger.

Finger, though he didn't live there, was kind of attached to the house. He did everything Grandma couldn't and then some. I think my grandma loved him and I used to tease her about it, although I never really believed she loved him in a romantic way. Finger was about twenty years younger than my grandma and blacker than the smoke that came from the steelworks. He had an extra finger that grew out from the side of his hand like a crow's claw, hence his name. He had a family of his own somewhere but it was hard to imagine him being as important to anyone else as he was to Grandma, who included him in every thought she ever had and most sentences she ever uttered.

'Finger is my life-line,' was one of her favourites, 'he takes me where I need to go and fixes what needs fixing.'

God bless Finger.

'Why don't you drive, Grandma?' I asked her when Finger wasn't around to take us to the department store, as promised, to look for some new shoes for me.

'Oh Lord, I'm much too old to be learning to drive now. I'll leave that to those a lot younger than me, sweetheart. Perhaps when you grow up you'll take me out in your car.'

She smiled and gave my arm a little squeeze and I could see her eyes had filled up a little at the thought of me growing up. She always got a little bit wistful when Finger wasn't immediately there when she needed him. Anyway, I knew she was trying to be nice but somehow logic got the better of me. When I grow up? That was years away.

'Grandma,' I told her, 'when I learn to drive you'll already be dead.'

'God willing,' she sighed, which was another of her favourite sayings, but at that moment I wasn't sure if she meant she wanted to be dead by that time or if she was asking God to please let her live long enough to see me drive. Either way I knew I had placed a curse on the whole thing and I felt sick about it. If the curse was to be borne out, which I was sure it would be, it meant one of two things. Either, the day I passed my driving-test my grandmother would drop down dead in her tracks, or I would not learn to drive until I was very old, if ever. Especially if my grandma turned out to be one of those people that decide to live forever.

Though we always liked going to Grandma's, this was definitely a drop-off of convenience. My parents were going on one of their trips to Europe. They always went by boat because my mother liked boats and my father usually wanted to buy a car from France and you can't bring a car back on an airplane. We were supposed to stay one week with Grandma and then move around each of our other relations on my father's side who, for some reason or another, had all decided to stay nestled quite close to the Armpit. My father had an ongoing feud with his sister and the three brothers whose families we were supposed to be staying with after Grandma's, so my mother had to make all the arrangements herself once we got there. This was not ideal as my mother tended to be quite sarcastic and impatient when she did not like somebody and my father's family were not her favourite people.

'Throw them in a river for all I care,' I heard her saying on the phone to Lorraine, my father's sister. 'Of course they can swim. Cynthia won't go off the high dive but that's just because she values living . . . Well, let them borrow your boys' trunks if you can't find anything else suitable.'

My mother had obviously forgotten to put our bathing costumes in our suitcase, which must have seemed like an absolute disaster for Lorraine who had just paid for a brand-new swimming pool to be dug into her garden. The thought of swimming at her house with her two sons was not pleasant, but the thought of wearing David and Matthew's trunks made me positively wince. Apart from meaning that Cynthia and I would have to go topless, thus exposing my complete lack of development and her rather overripe chesty protrusions, David and Matthew were both about three times our size, width-ways, not height. Having my obese cousins' trunks trailing round my ankles was not my idea of an enjoyable or even tolerable way to swim. I resolved to stay fully clothed at all costs.

The time we spent at Grandma's house went by in a long languorous haze. The summer was oven-hot and steamy with humidity. The fireflies came out in their millions and so did the mosquitoes and crickets. At night, Cynthia and I would hang out of the attic window wearing nothing but our t-shirts, catching fireflies and putting them into an empty cottage-cheese container with holes. Every now and then we lost a few from the holes, but there had to be holes so they could breathe, Cynthia insisted. I don't know why she was so worried about whether they could breathe or not because whenever we got about eight or nine in the container together we would smear them onto the wall inside, like fluorescent ink, writing our names so they glowed in the dark. The effect only lasted for about forty seconds before it began to fade so then we would start all over again. We must have gone through hundreds of fireflies.

The corner store was run by Mrs Shelley who also did my

grandmother's hair. I say 'did' because my grandmother never had her hair cut or washed or any of the normal things you think of people going to the hairdresser's for. She just had it let down, combed, braided and coiled back up on top of her head again like a magnificent serpent. I loved to come and watch Mrs Shelley at work on my grandmother's hair. She had the longest hair I had ever seen, even longer than Barbara Winston's in the second grade, who could sit on hers when her head was tipped back. Grandma's hair looked as if it had never been cut, ever. I imagined it had just grown and grown, turning, over the years, from the copper-red that her eyebrows still were, to the snow-white colour of angel-floss. When it was up on top of her head, she looked like any grandma, the way grandmas are supposed to look, with a tight bun and not a hair out of place. But behind the beaded curtain in the back of Mrs Shelley's shop, she looked like the Snow Queen or a fairy maiden who had drifted in on a sea of magic.

Mrs Shelley sold candy. I guess she sold other things too but candy was the only thing I had ever gone to her store for, apart from the can of black olives I once bought and ate all of myself to prove to Cynthia that I was a sophisticate. The olives made me sick but not as sick as some of the candy we bought from Mrs Shelley and ate all at once, secretly, in our attic hide-out. The 'milk bottles' were the worst. They were made of soft wax shaped like a milk bottle and filled with sickly sweet syrup of varying colours, supposed to be different flavours but they all tasted the same. You had to chew off a bit of the wax to get at the syrup and, even though I knew you weren't supposed to eat it, there was something tempting about chewing all the wax like gum until it was a tight little ball reduced down to practically nothing.

Jason Kearney, a boy in Cynthia's class whose father was also a doctor, once told me that wax, gum, hair, and anything else that doesn't digest properly, all gets caught in your appendix where it stays until there is so much that it makes your appendix burst and you have to go into hospital. I wasn't afraid of my appendix bursting or even of going into hospital but I was terrified of people finding out how many things like that I had already eaten. The olive stones for a start. I must have swallowed hundreds of them.

I wet the bed when I was at Grandma's and I begged her, while she was hosing me down in the bathroom afterwards, not to tell Cynthia, or Matthew and David or any of my other enquiring relations. Unfortunately it had not been the single roll-away with the plastic cover that I had soaked but the big double bed that she slept in together with my grandpa whenever he finally made it home from the bar that he ran downtown. I had crawled in with her in the middle of the night because I was having my nightmare about the witch in the playground again, as I often did on hot nights when I was restless. I didn't even notice Grandpa coming in and getting in beside us. The first thing I remember was Grandma fussing with the bedclothes and bundling me into the bathroom. She had put Grandpa on the sofa with a cover and he was snoring away as though nothing had happened.

'That's what babies do, Francine Jane.'

'No they don't, they get to wear diapers.'

'Do you want to wear diapers?'

'No, I just don't want to have bad dreams.'

'Bad dreams don't make you wet the bed.'

'What does then, Grandma?'

'Wanting to be a baby,' she told me. I thought I understood what she was saying when she said it, but I don't think I really did.

'You won't be the baby forever,' she announced, later on, when Mom and Dad came back from their trip to pick us up with some rather strange news about my mother having a 'junior' inside of her and that we might all have to eat Dad's cooking over the Easter vacation because she might be away in hospital. My father never cooked as far as I could tell, but my grandmother joked about him maybe being able to scramble some eggs if he got desperate. I don't even like scrambled eggs.

Double mattresses are not easy to disguise when you have to take them off the bed and put them out into the garden to dry off. It was quite obvious to Cynthia, who had woken to find the roll-away empty and me downstairs at six-thirty a.m. already dressed and with my hair still wet from being washed watching the *Frost* programme, that something had happened in the night. I told her I felt sick and had gone into Grandma's room where I had vomited all over the bed. Cynthia asked Grandma if that was true and Grandma just shook her head and said that double mattresses were not easy things to wash.

Getting up to go to the toilet in the night, sometimes twice, has always been a regular thing with me. The thing I hate most about waking up when I should be sleeping is having to interrupt a dream. Sometimes my dreams are such good gripping stories that I desperately want to see what's going to happen and sometimes they are so disturbing that I think if I don't get to the end I will just be left with that awful scared feeling and no way to get rid of it.

The dream about the witch on the jungle gym in the playground has always been one of the scariest. She is a lady witch all dressed in black and purple like Hallowe'en witches so I should have known she probably wasn't real. But even so, in the dream she is climbing a tangled maze of shiny metal and rusted iron bars, a bit like the jungle gym in our playground, but much more intricate. I am the only person left out in the playground and she is peeking out of the squares and windows made by the bars, laughing and jeering at me. Her long dress swishes on the bars and makes a noise like wind blowing down an empty hosepipe. All the rest of the kids are in the classroom doing their work, unaware that I have been left out there all alone. I am scared that the teacher will be angry with me for coming back late, and I am scared of what the witch might do if I don't manage to escape. She is wearing a tall pointy hat, a cheap and unconvincing Hallowe'en disguise, which she leads with as she ducks and dives inside the maze. The worst thing about the way she is laughing at me is that she seems to be delivering a message of pointlessness. Her laugh is telling me that there really is no point in doing anything at all. It is the kind of empty hollow laugh that stops you in a certain place and makes you feel as though you will be stuck there forever. If the witch had spoken to me in words, which she never did, I imagined she would be saying, 'Why go back into that school? Any school? What good can they do you in there? Do you really want to go home though? There's nothing for you there either. Where can you go? Who cares? No one cares. Why should they? You're hopeless. It's all hopeless. There's really no point in anything. Ha ha ha ha.'

It's a dream without any real ending. After I figured this out I decided there was really no point in carrying on with it and I might as well get up to go to the toilet. But even having a pee doesn't make the feeling go away. It's a dream of doom I think. A dream about nothing being right. Maybe everybody has them.

'Your father is crazy.' Those were the last words I ever heard my grandfather speak. I don't mean they were his dying words or anything like that, but the last time he said anything to me, the last visit we made there before he died, that's what he said. 'Your father is crazy,' not 'my son is crazy' or even 'Leon is crazy' but *your* father. He'd passed the buck completely by then, I think, and disowned my father. That meant he was ours now, we could have him. I often thought that because of my dad being the doctor, the boy made good, the successful one, he might have been the one they favoured or showered attention on. And it might have been that way if he'd decided to bury himself in the Armpit the way the others had. I guess Leon had decided that leaving was better than staying and whether we liked it or not we were going with him.

'Why's he crazy, Grandpa?' Conversations were nearly impossible with my grandfather. He only very occasionally had something to say and then once he'd said it, that was it. There was no two-way interchange or anything like that. You might have to wait days for a reply to a question like mine. I've waited a lifetime.

Grandpa smoked cigars, which made it easier for him to avoid talking. He was always doing something with his mouth, either licking the tobacco leaf around the edge to moisten it before he started puffing or sifting out the little bits of tobacco that got into his mouth and between his teeth with his tongue and spitting them out with tiny little spurts of air and saliva between puffs. He was either smoking or eating whenever I saw him. He'd be bent over a bowl of kreplach soup Grandma had made him or slurping his favourite breakfast which was matzo crackers soaked in hot milk. The crackers would go soggy and slightly slimy so that the pieces would slither off the spoon almost as soon as you tried to pick one up. Grandpa would bend his head so far over that he was practically inside the bowl and then he would pucker out his lips like a vacuum-cleaner nozzle and just slurp them up.

Funnily enough, even though the sound of other people eating can sometimes make me want to go crazy I never really minded the sound of my grandfather's slurping. It seemed to go with being a grandfather. If that were Cynthia, for example, chewing loudly at the dinner table, I'd start itching all over and have to go and hit somebody.

Patience is something you're born with, I think. And then it grows and develops like any other part of a person. But some people, like me and my father, aren't even born with the tiniest seed of patience, so all we can hope for is for a little to rub off of people who have more than enough for themselves. Grandma was one of these people. The patience in her must have started grow-ing early on and by then it looked like it had just about taken over. There wasn't anything my grandma couldn't wait for or tol-erate about another person. But I've got an idea that patience, if we could see it, is just like a pod or a container. And inside things are just as turbulent as ever. Maybe it's just a matter of time for people with patience like my grandma. Just a matter of time, like with the appendix. One day there will just be too much stuff gone in and the whole thing will burst. I don't want to be around when that happens.

19

3

'Your report card reads just like a machine gun, A-A-A-A-A-A-A', beamed Jackie, my third-grade teacher. I think she was meant to be known officially by us third-graders as Miss Green but I always called her Jackie because she said I could and it was a good way of making the other kids in the class jealous. Jackie had come over to our house a couple of times for dinner and called my mother Alma and my dad Leon so it seemed right that we all called her Jackie. At the dinner table they talked mostly about me, which I loved and Cynthia hated. Jackie told my parents she thought my poetry was excellent and that I really was a very special and sensitive child. Jackie wore glasses and to me seemed pretty old and mature, but I think she must have only been about twenty. The year she came to Peterson Elementary to teach me was her first year teaching anywhere. She said that I taught her a lot about teaching in that first year. At the time I took that to mean that she thought I was bossy and pretty good at telling the other kids what to do, but later on I figured that she meant that *I* was a pretty difficult case to deal with myself and she learnt by having to find new ways of handling me.

I wrote lots of poems in Miss Green's class and she always loved to read them, even if she was in the middle of something else. Sometimes she would sigh like she had just seen a flying saucer or a shooting star or as if someone was rubbing her back in just the place that needed it. 'Ooohhh Francine,' she'd say, 'that's soooo beautiful. Did you think it up yourself?' She always asked me that: 'Did you think it up yourself?' Well, who did she think was thinking all that stuff up and letting me put my name to it? Not Bobby Reinholt who sat at the desk next to me, that's for sure. The one she liked the best was one about the colour of people's skin and how it didn't make them any different inside. I kind of got the idea from listening to my mom talk about Martin Luther King and what he believed in, but to tell the truth I also knew while I was writing it that it was going to make old Jackie Green really sigh her heart out.

We got free rides for every A on our report card at McGlaughlin's Amusement Park over near where we lived. I'd get about eight which was as many grades as we got including for Attendance, but Cyn would usually only get one, for Handwriting. She had really neat writing and knew how to use an eraser to make it so you couldn't tell there were ever any mistakes that needed rubbing out, but she didn't do so well on the other things. Mom said it was because Cynthia found it less easy to be noticed by her teachers than I did and it wasn't just that her work was bad. Mom told Cyn that I spent as much time on my work as on making teachers like me and Cynthia started calling me 'teacher's pet'. Mom and Dad used to have arguments about it because Mom didn't want Cynthia to feel bad about herself and the one thing Dad really couldn't stand the idea of was to have a child that wasn't very smart. I don't think it was so much that Cynthia wasn't smart but she seemed to give up a lot easier than I did.

Miss Green left our school after that one year. Mom said she was going to get married but I didn't even know she had a boyfriend. I was glad she wasn't going to be teaching another class because I would have been jealous if she had found a new girl who wrote poetry that she liked. Even so I was pretty mad to find out that there was someone else in her life she was serious enough about to want to marry. I thought she would probably ask me to be the bridesmaid or at least the flower girl at her wedding, but I never even got an invitation. I wrote a poem about that too:

Miss Green becomes a Mrs but no one misses her
Miss Green gets lots of kisses and like a cat, begins to purr
Miss Green, you have not been, a teacher very long
Miss Green will not be seen because she knows she has done
    wrong
Jackie, you're a fool to leave this school, you know the rules
    and now you've broke them
Is this your way of being cool or just having one big joke
    then?
Now you can get married but don't expect me to be there
A little note from J to F would have shown you cared.

I know it was a bit sulky and when I looked at it later I thought
it sounded babyish too, but I still wanted to let her know how I
felt. It was my first big lesson in realizing that sometimes people
can pretend that you matter to them more than life itself and
then, without warning, those same people can forget they ever
knew you.

'What is Love?' I pondered the question for days afterwards. Is
it when two people can't live without each other, or is it when
you have a tingly feeling about someone when you think of them
even if they don't know who you are or couldn't care less about
you? Is it when you wish someone was your mother more than
your real one? I asked my dad what he thought because he always
liked it when I asked him those kind of questions. He didn't like
having to answer other questions about real things like 'When will
you be finished in your study so we can eat dinner?' or 'What
time is Mom coming home?' He didn't even like answering questions like 'Why are you mad at us?' He said 'Why' questions were
a cop-out because if you thought long enough or worked hard
enough you could usually find out the answer for yourself. But I
figured that 'What is Love?' was just the sort of question he
would like and be willing to answer. I was right.

'If one person who is in love with another goes to a faraway
place so that those two people will never ever get to see each
other again and they still worry and care about what happens to

the other one even though they can't give each other anything then that is love.'

I thought my father must be right because he was a doctor and had been to school and studied longer than anyone else I could think of. Besides, I didn't think my father was the type to answer a question if he didn't really know the answer to it. Sometimes when we got stopped in the street by people asking directions to somewhere, my dad would just say, 'I don't know,' and walk on. When I asked him why he didn't want to help those people he said, 'Why should I tell them where some place is if I'm not really sure myself? Should I make them more lost than they already are?' Once when I suggested that he could have looked on our map which he always had in his pocket, and helped them find their way with that, he hit me. Right there in the street with lots of people looking he hit me on the side of the head, hard enough to knock me over, which took me by surprise. There was a red hand mark on the side of my face which lasted until I went to sleep that night. When I held my hand against my cheek in bed I could still feel the ridges of his fingers etched into my skin.

Dad hit me for lots of things on the spur of the moment like that. Once when Safeway's were giving out vouchers for free gifts with your shopping – one voucher for every ten dollars spent – we traded our vouchers in for a soccer ball. None of us really wanted a soccer ball but it was the only thing you could get for under fifty vouchers. Mom said it was stupid to spend hundreds of dollars buying things at Safeway's that we didn't want just so we could get enough vouchers to get the patio set or the sleeping bags they had on offer. Besides, we already had sleeping bags and the patio set looked stupid. So we got this soccer ball that had a sticker on it telling you how hard you had to pump it up if it went flat and saying it was guaranteed by safety regulations or something like that.

When we got it home Dad asked why we got a soccer ball. 'No one around here likes playing soccer,' he said. He was wrong because I did like playing it in the playground at school and I was the best out of the girls in my class at getting goals. Anyway, that ball sat around for weeks not getting played with and then one day my friend Shirley came over after school. My father didn't really like Shirley (actually he had a hard time liking any of my friends) because once when she was over she had tried to see how bendy one of his records was and broke it right in half. He told me he didn't want her playing here anymore but that was way before Christmas so I thought he would have forgotten by now. Besides, Mom said she could come.

Shirley and I went outside while dinner was cooking and I decided to bring the ball out with us. We kicked it around a bit and then Shirley did this really high kick in the air that made the ball go over the fence into the Jacksons' place. The Jacksons had five kids but they all went to a Catholic school pretty far away and we never really saw them much. The oldest, Brad, was nearly out of high school. He had a rumbly voice and stubble on his face and everything already. He was about six-foot tall and bean-pole skinny. When the ball went over I felt too shy to go and ring on the doorbell to ask for it back. The fence was really high and you had to be taller than Brad to see over it. I could hear some of the Jackson kids in their backyard playing so I figured they would find the ball and throw it back over sooner or later. Shirley and I didn't think about it any more after that. A few days later, I saw Brad walking outside his house with some friends and he had that sticker stuck right on his forehead, the one that told how much air you had to put in and all about the safety. I knew then that he must have decided to keep the ball. I didn't think it mattered much because no one in our house had been all that interested. In fact I felt kind of proud that the seventeen-year-old boy from next door liked our soccer ball enough to keep it. Anyway we didn't pay real money for it, only vouchers.

Later on that night, right out of the blue, Dad asked me, 'Francine, where's that ball we got? I feel like kicking it around some.'

It was pretty late already and I was just about to take a shower before changing into my night clothes. It seemed such a strange thing for him to be wanting all of a sudden like that and I guess he caught me so unawares I didn't know what to say. 'I don't know,' I just said eventually, stalling for time. I was thinking maybe if I could just get into the shower for a moment, by myself, and close the door behind me I might be able to come up with a story about the ball that wouldn't make him mad. 'I'll try and remember where I put it.'

When I came out of the shower, still dripping with the towel wrapped round under my shoulders, Dad asked me again. Only this time I could tell that he was a little mad and that he didn't believe me the first time. 'Francine,' he said, 'I said, where is that ball? The one we won from Safeway's.'

'We didn't win it,' I corrected him. 'We got it free with those vouchers. It only cost us twenty-five of them.'

It wasn't doing any good. He was like a slow rumbling volcano. 'Goddamn it, Francine. Where is that fucking ball? I want to play!'

He'd never played soccer in his life. Well, not in the life I'd known him for anyway. Why now? He must have known I lost it. 'I lost it,' I said.

I couldn't tell him about Shirley or the sticker on Brad's forehead or anything that would have approached a sensible explanation. Not that it would have done much good. His cool snapped and instead of kicking the soccer ball he hit me. When you're wet and you get slapped the red seems to come up much quicker. You could see giant hand marks blooming instantly on my back, my face and my legs and wherever else he could reach that the towel wasn't covering. He was yelling, 'I can't trust you with anything!' and calling me a liar and telling me to leave other people's property alone.

That soccer ball had suddenly become the most important thing in the world to him and I wished then I had been able to ask Brad for it back, or that Shirley had never kicked it over in the first place. In any case I thought I would check my savings to see if I had enough money to buy another soccer ball for my father. In that moment I would have begged or stolen or done just about anything to replace the ball, because even though I was stinging all over from the slapping and he was still yelling, I kept thinking how nice it was that my dad had suddenly felt like playing with a soccer ball that night. He'd never been interested in doing anything like that, with us or by himself. He had always seemed so stiff and embarrassed about running around. I kept hoping my losing the ball wasn't going to put him off ever wanting to do that sort of thing again.

4

Melanie hurtled into our lives like a cosmic shape-shifter. I don't mean she was terrible or evil or had supernatural powers or anything like that, but just the fact of there being a new baby in our house in our family meant massive change.

First off, those couple of weeks before Easter were tough. My mother's absence from home came earlier than everyone had expected, which was a shame because my father wasn't really very good at spending whole days with us. He took us into the lab a couple of times after school and on the weekend which was OK, and we ate in the hospital canteen. I had red jello with marshmallow pieces in it and Cynthia had a tuna-fish submarine sandwich and a bowl of cherries. I didn't want any of the cooked stuff they had there and the sandwiches all had too many extra things in them like tomato or lettuce or pieces of pickle. I liked my things pretty plain but Dad yelled at me for not being adventurous so I chose the jello that had bits in it so that he could see I was trying. On the days that we stayed home with my father it seemed pretty hard for him to think of things to do. He yelled a lot and hit us sometimes, mainly because he felt trapped inside I think. Cynthia and I played out back some and went over a couple of times to see Kirsten and Paula who lived across the street. We couldn't wait till Mom came home.

She had explained to us that she'd waited a long time already for this baby to come, so she was going to go and see if they could help get it to come out at the hospital. Well, I couldn't see how a bunch of people in white coats with masks over their faces and smelling of bleach were going to help get a reluctant baby to come out of hiding any more than we could have at home. I pictured them all there, the nurses, doctors and porters, the whole lot of them kootchy-cooing and begging and pleading with the little thing to come out and face its new life. I could have done a much better job, I knew it, because little kids usually like me. But the trouble was I didn't really care if the baby decided never to come out. In a way I sort of wished it wouldn't. Well, they must have done something right at the hospital because finally, a few days into our vacation, Mom came home carrying a yellow basket with our baby sister Melanie inside waving her arms and legs about and looking just like a little pig.

I didn't know whether my mother was joking when I heard her telling people that Melanie was a beautiful baby and definitely the prettiest out of the three of us. If that was what was supposed to be pretty then I might as well stop trying now because I obviously didn't know what I was going for at all. Bits of her were OK, I guess, like her fingers and toes, but her face just looked like a splodge to me. I liked the way she grabbed your finger when you put it there and her fingernails were pretty incredible if you looked close because they were just like a human's. The other thing that seemed amazing was that she knew how to breathe. I wondered whether there was someone who had taught her that already and thought she must have gone to special classes while she was still in hospital. Her breathing was a bit fast, like she'd been running or something, but other than that she seemed to have mastered the whole thing perfectly. In out, in out, in perfect even breaths. I was kind of proud of her for that. I tried to ask my mother whether I was that young when I first learned to breathe, just to check out if Melanie was going to turn out to be smarter than I was, but my mother looked at me like I was crazy and asked me to move away from Melanie and the little cradle seat she'd bought for her and let my baby sister's fingers go because she probably wanted to sleep. I never heard my mother telling anyone to leave me alone because I probably wanted to sleep. It was always either an order to 'go to sleep' or to 'stop sleeping' because it's time to get up to go to school or somewhere. Never, 'Oh Francine, you probably *want* to sleep.' Not that I would have agreed with her as I can't ever remember an occasion in my life where I would have chosen sleep over whatever else was going on at the time.

I don't think Melanie cried a lot because that's not what I remember going on with her. The first year she was around she was out of the house a lot with my mother who was getting involved in various political things with the Democratic Party. I associated Melanie with a lot of tragic events that both she and my mother seemed part of. It wasn't her who did the crying about them though but my mother, who I would see holding Melanie in one arm and stirring Gerber baby rice cereal with the other, with silent tears coming down both her cheeks. Melanie didn't seem to mind too much so I guess it was like the commercial said, 'A Gerber baby is a happy baby' and she was going to be OK as long as she had her cereal.

I'd never seen my mother really cry before that year. I guess she had at various times before that or she probably would have forgotten how to. Either that or her tear holes would have dried up and got so they wouldn't work properly any more.

Lots of grown-up people say they cried when John F. Kennedy got shot in '63. I was pretty young when that happened but I know that my mom and dad were both very shocked and sad. I was in the living-room helping Cynthia braid pieces of plastic string together to use for shoelaces when there was something on the television about the President. I always liked seeing presidents on the TV because it made me feel patriotic and sort of gooey inside. It didn't matter to me what their principles were or anything like that. I just liked to see their crinkled faces and imagine I was watching God or at the very least the king and ruler of the Western world.

JFK was riding in a big open-top car with his wife, Jackie,

sitting next to him. I always thought it was kind of strange that she had her arm around him and not his around her, but my mother told me later that he was slumped over on to her shoulder not because he was sleeping like I had thought, but because he had just been shot and killed. The presenter on the television sounded kind of panicked and I heard my mother breathe in like she had just stepped into an icy swimming pool. Cynthia and I stopped what we were doing with the plastic string and watched my mother's face. She winced and closed her eyebrows together and stared at the television for a long time without moving or saying anything at all but she didn't cry. I'm sure of it because I was watching her the whole time without blinking. In fact I was staring so hard myself that eventually my eyes began to water just because of the strain of it. I remember saying, 'Mommy, there's tears coming down from my eyes,' and she moved then and came over and put her arm around me. She thought I was crying about Kennedy but I wasn't. I was just watching her.

The first time she really cried, with real tears and that kind of chesty shudder that people have when they genuinely can't help it, was when Martin Luther King got killed, just after Melanie was born. I was a bit older then and I guess I understood a bit more about the way of things and that it took a little more than just being the President to make you a good person. My mom had told me stories about King and how he'd led the protests on the buses and made it so black people could sit together with the rest of us at movies and the kind of restaurants that treat you like you're special. I remembered being with Grandma and Finger at a place we stopped for ice-cream and Finger had to wait in the car because he wasn't allowed to come in and join us at the table. Ever since then I hated the law that could make it so that even on the hottest day some people were allowed to sit in a cool place and have ice-cream and others had to sweat it out in the Buick. I didn't even want my ice-cream then after Grandma told me that Finger wasn't going to sit down with us, so I saved it to take out to him in the car but by that time it was all melted and made the seats of the car messy and my grandma got mad. Mom said she was probably mad about the stickiness in the car and not because of what I wanted to do for Finger.

Martin Luther King died on April 4, 1968, in a hospital in Memphis, Tennessee, after being shot on a balcony. Melanie Rose Weitz was cut from my mother's belly ten days earlier on March 25, 1968 in a hospital in Seattle, Washington. She arrived ten days after she was supposed to and King died long before he should have, and I had never seen my mother cry before either of those two events. Somehow I got it into my head that Melanie was the key to it all. She must be either so evil or so important because she affected my mother in a way that not even my father did, even when he was yelling at her and calling her some of the worst names I can imagine anybody calling another person. Somehow the words from the speech Martin Luther King made the day before he died had got lodged in my head, '. . . Like anybody, I'd like to live a long life. But I just want to do God's will. And He's allowed me to go to the mountain. And I've looked over and I've seen the Promised Land.' I thought maybe somehow those words were also bound up with Melanie and that it meant she was some kind of angel sent by God or some kind of devil in disguise, and that the bit about wanting a long life meant she was here for good and there wasn't any way we were going to get rid of her. Not only that, but she was going to get to go to the mountains before any of the rest of us and Cynthia and I had been asking for years to go up to the Rockies and visit Aspen where our friend Laura lived. Melanie, it seemed, was going to get there first.

Ten days after Martin Luther King died came Easter, which we always got to celebrate as well as Passover because, the way we saw it, we were a little bit Jewish and a little bit everything else. Grandma wished we were a lot more Jewish, but Dad had decided to marry Mom who had never seen the inside of a synagogue and, as far as I could tell, didn't really want to. So from the time it took Melanie to be born, to the King dying and the Lord rising was exactly thirty days. The number thirty has always seemed to represent a complete cycle to me. I think when I'm thirty I will have done everything I need to do. I don't mean I'll die then – I hope not – but I'll have finished what I started anyway. Thirty, the amount of days it takes for the moon to complete a full cycle, the amount of bites it takes me to finish a double-decker peanut-butter and jelly sandwich and the age my mother was when she had Melanie Rose.

5

I think my father had two parts to him. A happy part and a sad part or maybe just a calm part and an angry part. It was always a special treat to see the nice part peeking out from behind the nasty one. In the summer of 1969, along with thousands of other grown-up people who felt young again because of the sixties, my father went to New York for the Woodstock Festival and listened to music, got high with some of his medical students and came back armed with a bunch of paraphernalia for me and Cynthia.

We were into Rickie-Tickie-Stickies, those plastic flower-power stickers that were plastered all over VW Beetles, jeeps and the purple fibre-glass beach buggies that hippies drove. We had psychedelic posters saying 'LOVE' and 'PEACE' covering the walls and ceilings of our bedrooms. We'd both taken off the old wooden doors with 'knock before you enter' signs and replaced them with beaded curtains and chiming bells that jangled as you went in and out. I never wore shoes anywhere except to school and had bangs that covered my eyes enough to qualify me as a genuine 'flower child'.

Dad returned from New York in one of his 'nice' moods. His voice was all soft and laid back and he was using language like 'neat' and 'cool' and 'groovy'. He played records by Bob Dylan and The Doors and introduced me to the Beatles' *White Album* by explaining to me that the song 'Lucy in the Sky With

Diamonds' was really about LSD and acid trips. He said he'd taken acid a few times himself and that it really wasn't true that people threw themselves out of windows just because they were tripping. He said it was possible to have a really 'beautiful' trip but you needed to be responsible about who you were with and how you took the 'tab'. Those few weeks after Woodstock he introduced us to some of his students and especially one called Andrew who came over a lot and played the guitar in the living-room and sang folk songs. Dad seemed really fond of Andrew and would often put his arm around him and laugh softly in a way I could never remember him doing with any of us. They smoked joints too. Little tiny ones they rolled themselves that smelled a bit like the incense Cynthia and I lit in our bedrooms.

One night, after Dad had given one of his 'pot' parties as my mother called them, Cynthia and I went around all the ashtrays and pulled out the ends of the joints to see if there was anything left in any of them. Cynthia had some matches of her own in her room because now she was eleven she was allowed to light the incense sticks herself. We went in there and opened the window and puffed away at the dog-ends of the joints my father and his friends had left. It didn't do any more than make us cough and left us with a terrible burnt taste in the mouth that even our Crest Extra Minty toothpaste couldn't get rid of.

Some of the presents my dad had brought back from Woodstock were badges with various sayings on them like 'Warning – I am Naked Underneath My Clothes' and 'I'd rather F*ck than F*ght'. My favourite ones were 'Save Water – Shower with a Friend' and 'Military Service may be Hazardous to your Health' and there were a couple I didn't understand like one which just read 'PHUQUE' and another which said 'Keep On The Grass'. My father didn't tell me what the foreign-sounding word was but he explained that 'Keep On The Grass' was a funny way of turning a very uptight rule into a more laid-back one. I think I understood then.

We had a 'Show and Tell' session on Fridays at school, when anyone who had something they knew how to do, like play an instrument, or had something interesting to show could bring it in for the rest of the class to see. I wanted to show everyone my badges and the floppy hat with flowers on it that Dad had brought me from Woodstock. Mom had just made me and Cynthia some really cool hipster bellbottoms, too, which I was dying to show off and normally wouldn't be allowed to wear to school because girls had to wear dresses. Dad suggested I go in for 'Show and Tell' dressed up in my bellbottoms and hat and show them that way.

'But I have to *do* something.' I said. 'It's just stupid if I don't.'

'Show them how to roll their own, then,' my dad suggested.

It sounded good but I needed him to do some explaining. He read out one of the slogans from the badges he had brought back. 'A Friend With Weed is a Friend Indeed'. He told me that rolling joints is a friendly thing and something that you do together with people that you like, in company. He said my teachers would know all about it and it might be kind of cool to show the kids how it all gets done. I reminded him that the oldest kids in my class were only ten, but he said we had to learn about lots of things long before we were ready or old enough to do them.

'Like what?' I asked him.

'War,' he said, 'don't they teach you about war at school?'

'Sometimes, I guess.' I had to hand it to him, it was a good example. We were always learning about wars in Social Studies and I was quite sure that it was not because our teachers expected us to go out and fight them.

I went in that Friday with yellow-framed sunglasses on, my floppy hat covered in the badges, a stripy tank-top and my flower printed bellbottoms. I had a little drawstring bag in black velvet with gold and silver sequins sewn on to it. This was the bag I used to carry the 'tea'. 'Tea', my dad told me, was one of the names that was used for marijuana but he thought I should probably use actual tea for the demonstration, the Lipton's variety, instead of bringing in the real thing. He gave me a little box that had some cigarette papers in and a tiny bamboo mat you could use to shape and roll the joints.

I performed the whole thing like I was acting in a show. First I peered round the door of the classroom and looked all around me, lifting my sunglasses furtively. I cupped my hand by my mouth and in a big stage whisper said, 'Psssst . . . anybody seen the fuzz around here?'

A few of my amazed classmates shook their heads blankly and I continued: 'Good, 'cause I'm going to show you how to roll your own. Joints, that is.'

My teacher shifted uncomfortably in her chair. I carried on: 'First you get the "tea". This is good stuff, man. I got it from a friend.' (My dad's script.) 'Then you get the skins and you lay it on, baby. Roll it like this, lick and stick and . . . Magic!'

Some kids were laughing by this time, because they could see that Mrs Edwards was squirming and anyway they'd figured all by themselves that I was telling them about something I wasn't supposed to. After the joint rolling, I paraded round so people could read my badges and finger the finished 'spliff'.

'Can you stay after please, Francine?' Mrs Edwards asked me at the end of the day when we were packing up to go home. I had changed out of my bellbottoms and was wearing a skirt like everyone else so I didn't think she could get me on that one.

'I don't really know to say this, Francine. I'm surprised and a little bit . . . do your parents know about the Show and Tell you did today, Francine?'

How could I tell her that it was my father's idea without getting Dad into trouble?

'Sort of,' I answered a bit non-committally.

'I'm sure they don't,' she reassured herself. 'And I don't want to have to be the one who tells them. Your father is a doctor, Francine.'

Here we go again, the medical ticket.

'He wouldn't want to think of his own daughter encouraging the use of harmful drugs, now would he?'

'No, ma'am.'

'OK Francine. I'm going to keep quiet about it, but only because I think you know better. It was a silly thing to be showing us, now wasn't it?'

'Yes.'

'Perhaps you could think of something sensible to show for next week?'

'One of my dad's rats?' I asked hopefully.

'Perhaps,' she squirmed again, probably trying to work out which was worse: drugs or rodents. 'We'll see.'

But the next week my father said he was going to London, England, for a year on some medical research project and I lost the desire to show and tell anything. When he first told me I thought that the school must have said something to him about my demonstration to the class and Mrs Edward's reaction. I thought he must be either so scared of her or so mad at me that he needed to get as far away as possible. But later I realized that his going had nothing to do with me or my school. I don't think it had anything to do with medical research either. I wish it had because then I might have known a little better what was important to my father and felt just a little less unimportant myself. I wish he had at least given us a reason we could have believed in because then I wouldn't have felt so abandoned.

6

I am wrapped up in a large white sheet. The sheet is pressing in on me on both sides because I am being lifted up high. My body is cocooned in the middle and I am feeling very tight and squashed, but I like the feeling of tightness. When I look up I see that some kind of great bird is carrying me. I try to see the bird's face, to see if I recognize it but then I realize that it is not a real bird. It is a sort of plane. I wish it was a real bird because at this moment I want terribly to look into someone's eyes and see my own reflected there but on this plane, there are none. The sheet is hanging from a long rope which is attached to the nose of the plane. As we fly the rope lengthens and shortens as though it were a thread of silk being spun and retrieved by a spider. Sometimes I think it will lengthen enough to lower me safely to the ground and let me go and other times I think I will be flying up here forever wrapped in this sheet. The tightness of the sheet and the movement of the plane make me want to go to sleep. I try to but I am not sure how safe it will be to really lose consciousness. I wake up. I am awake already.

This is how I remember it. There were no goodbyes. Leon did not believe goodbyes were really necessary. In fact that was the basis for the stalemate that existed between my father and his sister, my aunt Lorraine. He never said goodbye to her when he went off to do his military service before going to medical school. He said that he didn't say goodbye to anyone because it didn't seem either appropriate or helpful at the time. Lorraine said it was a snub and permanently ruined her pride and her feelings about herself as a woman. 'Aunt Lorraine is an idiot,' said my dad.

Just after Dad left, Mom went into kind of a decline. She thrashed around the house for a few days, throwing his papers around and kicking the boxes in his study. She'd yell out things like 'you fucking bastard' while she was doing the laundry even though, as far as I could tell, no one was down there with her. I didn't think she was cursing at the clothes so I figured she must have been thinking about Dad and remembering something or other that she was real mad at him for.

While my mother attacked boxes, Cynthia and I fought each other, wrestling like two mad dogs. With Leon gone I felt weaker, but Cynthia seemed to have found a strength and a forcefulness that I hadn't seen before and she revelled in using it. I don't know what it was exactly that we were fighting about, but it felt as though if we stopped fighting we would both lose something vital of ourselves. I had an idea that we were each guarding a secret that was so powerful and strong we couldn't let the other or anyone else know about it. Keeping a secret needs a constant vigil and sometimes can make you feel like you've been blown up tight as a balloon. I guess that's why we just couldn't stop needling each other. We were each guarding our corner, hoping that the other would be the first one to burst.

'Do you miss Dad?'

'Not telling, d'you?'

'What do you think?'

'I think you don't. I think you're glad he's gone. I think you hate him.'

'I don't hate anyone. I'm a pacifist.'

Cynthia used the word pacifist to get out of a lot of things. She said she was a pacifist and therefore couldn't remove spiders from her bedroom wall in case she accidentally killed them, so I had to do it. She said she was a pacifist so she couldn't sing the National Anthem because it was about bombs and killing people, but really the notes were too high and she was embarrassed about her singing voice. And she said she was a pacifist anytime we were having a fight and I was winning. And even though I didn't believe her, hearing it always made my arms feel weak and I'd have to stop fighting her. What fun is it beating a pacifist in a fight?

About a month after he left, Dad sent me a postcard from a place called Carnaby Street in London with some really cool pictures on the front of it. The message read 'HAVING A GROOVY TIME. LOVE DAD'. He'd written it all in capital letters and I wondered whether he'd forgotten I was nearly eleven years old and didn't have a problem with cursive writing. Nothing came for Cynthia or Melanie. I never saw anything come from England for Mom either, but I figured she must have received a letter and just didn't want to tell us about it. When I received mine Mom got all mad again and said, 'What a shit!' really loudly when she read the message. It didn't seem worth letting her know about my mail at all if it was going to produce that reaction.

Mom started staying in bed a lot more. Not just in the mornings but all of the time. If I came home from school and the house was quiet I knew that Mom would be in her bed and that Melanie was probably by herself downstairs in the rec room watching television with the sound off. It was lucky really for Mom that Melanie would sit still for that long without needing attention. Or maybe she did need it, but had given up on trying because the effort was always greater than the reward. I never knew who to say hi to first. If I went in to Mel, she would want me to play with her and I was never ready for that when I'd just got home from school. If I went in to Mom, which Cynthia usually did, I would have to sit there on the edge of the bed in the dark room with the curtains closed. Cynthia would be busy using her old lady cooing voice to coax Mom out from under her covers and I would be practically choking on the heavy smell of sleep and unhappiness. It's a funny thing about smells, and Mom couldn't smell anything so she wouldn't have known, but they carry the truth in a most undeniable and specific way. Like photographs but even more so. A smell precedes a person. Their fear, their aloneness, their excitement or disappointment. Smells have a kind of music to them with a specially coded message that we read without even thinking about it. If I had bottled my Mom's smell into a perfume I would have had to call it 'Dark Despair with a hint of Mustiness'.

It was the beginning of spring and like all animals in hibernation Mom seemed willing to venture just a little way out of her hole. She started to look, finally, for a ballet class to take Melanie to – all Mel wanted to do these days was dance – and bought some material to make summer dresses for me and Cynthia. I knew I wasn't going to wear mine ever because it was old-fashioned and, besides, the idea of being twins with Cynthia made me want to run a mile. Even so, it was a relief to see Mom doing things again and getting out a bit. She still went into her room when she needed to, retreating to her cave where none of us could really get to her. I tried to sneak in once a day when she wasn't in there and open the curtains wide, just for two or three minutes, so that some real sunshine might start to leak back into our lives.

7

'When you're not feeling well you want your family around you.' That's how my teacher explained the fact that Mom was making plans to move us all to Nebraska where her mother, my other grandma, lived so we could stay with her until the winter was over. I couldn't quite see it myself. If I really wasn't well, the kind of 'not well' that Mom seemed to be at that moment, the last people I would want to see would be Melanie, Cynthia or Mom, who just make me mad and want to fight whenever I'm with them. And I'd rather be anywhere, now, than Omaha, Nebraska, preferably somewhere like Carnaby Street in London, England, where maybe I could have a GROOVY TIME too. Mom was sure, though, that living with Grandma would give her the kind of help and support she needed. She was not finding it easy being a mother to us all by herself. I don't know how far the plans were laid – Mom had only just started collecting orange boxes from Safeway's to pack our things in – when her brother Tommy died in Wisconsin and everything came to a standstill.

Tommy was my mother's youngest brother and my uncle, but I think I probably only met him about twice in my entire life. He was a mongoloid though I don't think we're supposed to call them that anymore. Anyway he had slitty eyes and was shaped like one of those Weeble men that you can push over and they pop right back up again. He was always smiling in every picture

I'd seen of him and I used to think he was a comedian. When I asked my mother if Tommy was a comedian she just pursed her lips and said, 'Not really, honey.' I would have liked to have known him better. He seemed to be the happiest of all my relations. Maybe he knew something the rest of us didn't.

Tommy lived in a special home with other people who also smiled all of the time. I went there once, with Mom and Cynthia, a long time ago before Melanie was born. Tommy knew we were coming and was hanging on the gate waiting for us when we arrived. He was wearing big baggy blue jeans and a red plaid shirt. The gate was swinging back and forth with him on it and he had one foot dangling down, drawing lines in the dirt as he swung. I shouted out to him, 'Hi Uncle Tommy!' and Cynthia told me to shush because he didn't know who we were and we might scare him. But he did know, I'm sure of it. I think Tommy knew a lot more than people gave him credit for.

Tommy was only twenty-one when he died which, even though it seemed pretty old to me, I knew was much too young to finish life altogether. Apparently it was a pretty good age for him to live to 'in his condition'. At least that's what I heard my mother telling someone on the phone. Maybe being a little bit fat had put a strain on his heart or maybe he had got into a accident because he wasn't smart enough to know any better. I don't really know how or why he died because it didn't seem like all that important a question to ask at the time.

Mom left to go to Wisconsin for Tommy's funeral and Katie Simpson, the Nurse from Kansas, arrived to take care of us while she was away. We'd never met Miss Simpson before she walked through our door with bags bulging, ready to stay. My mother had chosen her through an agency that supplied long-term babysitters that would come and live in your house while your parents were away. It sounded like a terrible idea to me. How could anyone whom you had never met before come straight into your house and know what things needed doing and how they should be done? She wouldn't know any of the stuff like Mom letting us have a carrot before bed even after we'd brushed our teeth because carrots were OK. And she probably didn't know that I couldn't have food mixed together like peas and corn in the same bowl. It wasn't that I was allergic or anything but my mind just wouldn't let my mouth eat it if it was all mixed up together. I only really like plain things and I didn't think the Nurse from Kansas was going to approve of that at all. Mom was used to it so she didn't force me.

Katie Simpson was just what we had feared and more. She didn't wear a uniform but all her dresses looked the same. Light blue or sometimes purple with a tight belt around the waist and buttons down from the collar. She wasn't very pretty and she hardly ever smiled. The first night after Mom left she put Melanie in her playpen while she washed Cynthia's and my hair in the bathroom sink. Melanie hated it in her playpen and she screamed the whole time we were washing our hair. Then the Nurse from Kansas made us rinse our hair in vinegar which made my eyes water and my nose sting and smelled disgusting. While we were doing that she went to get Melanie who had by now pushed her head through the bars to try to escape and was stuck there. When Cyn and I came out with towels around our heads, the Nurse from Kansas was putting cooking oil all over Melanie's face and hair to try and squeeze her back through. Melanie had stopped crying by this time and looked pretty limp like she had given up on just about everything. With her hair oiled, all her curls had gone flat and she looked like one of those birds that get washed up in an oil slick. Katie yelled at us to go and get our pyjamas on and by that time Cynthia and I had pretty much decided that we hated her. Melanie probably did too although she couldn't actually say so.

Mom was gone for four days and by the time she got back the Nurse from Kansas had succeeded in forcing me to eat a beef stew with a thousand different things I couldn't identify floating around in it; a vegetable soup with diced vegetables, pasta and beans all in the same bowl; and a hamburger with pickle and everything else on it. It wasn't that she had cured me of my need to have my food absolutely plain but she had threatened me with loss of TV privileges, loss of phone-time with friends and loss of life if I didn't. To this day the sight of a vegetable soup with everything in it makes me want to tip the bowl on somebody's head.

Our move to Nebraska seemed more likely than ever after Mom's return from Tommy's funeral. Cynthia and I were told to sort out all our things into 'take', 'leave' or 'sell' and Mom had more energy than I'd seen her have for a very long time. She labelled boxes and packed crates and transformed messy drawers and cupboards into neat organized storage spaces. It was less than a week after Mom had got back and Katie Simpson had gone that we got a phone call from the Nebraskan Police Department. I spoke to them first and they asked me if I was Alma Weitz née Torval and I figured I was close enough so I said yeah. They said that my mother had just been pronounced dead at the Omaha General following a car accident and they were informing all next of kin.

I don't even have a grown-up voice so I don't know how they thought they could have been talking to the right person, but anyway I didn't think I could ever live with the guilt of stealing my mother's grief from her so I told the policeman on the phone that I had made a mistake and I wasn't Alma Weitz née Torval, I was her daughter, Francine, and would they mind repeating what they'd just told me to the real Alma Weitz. I called my mother to the phone. I couldn't bear to watch the flush in her cheeks from her new-found purpose be wiped away with this one phone call, so I went out to play and left Mom to grieve over the death of her mother in whatever way she was going to.

No one was around outside. It was the sort of time most people were sitting down to dinner or homework and not very often out on the streets waiting to play. I climbed a tree over on the parkway and sat and watched a squirrel hiding nuts away for the winter. When he saw me he bared his teeth and started chattering and all I could think of was Grandma's set of false teeth that she kept in a glass of water by her bed at night. I tried to cry up there in the tree because I thought that's what I ought to do. A kid finds out their grandmother's just died, they really ought to cry about it but I just couldn't. I kept thinking how relieved I was that we didn't have to go to live in Nebraska now and that I wouldn't have to decide whether to sell all my posters; I could keep them on my bedroom wall right where they were.

I went over to the tyre swing that someone had hung a long time ago before the lilac bush had taken over the side alleyway next to our garage. There wasn't really room to swing very high because of the lilacs but you could sit on the tyre and let the flowers brush your face and smell their thick lilacy smell which was what I liked to do sometimes. If I ever become one of those old ladies who smothers themselves with perfume before they go anywhere I hope I choose lilac because that's the kind of scent it seems OK to be smothered with.

I sat there on the swing surrounded by the purple flowers and thought that actually it didn't surprise me that all this stuff was happening to my mother and at a time when she was feeling pretty low anyway. My mother's family seemed to have invented the word suffering. Grandma Torval had six sisters and all of them looked like they had lived through both World Wars on the front line. My grandma, like the rest of them, had the Torval square jaw and a face like painted iron. All of them wore their short curly hair in nets as though they wanted to be ready for action at any time. Grandma Torval also knew all about what it was like to be left alone at home to bring up children by yourself. Her husband, my mother's father, had hung himself on a cherry tree outside their house just a year after Tommy was born. My mother was only eleven. For a long time Mom told me that my grandfather had died because of a sick head and I imagined him with an almighty headache that wouldn't go away and with white bandages tied round his face. If I hadn't developed such a keen interest in death, primarily from watching too many hospital dramas on television, I might never have pressed her for more specific details.

'We found him hanging from a tree.'

'Who did?' I pictured my mom coming home from school and seeing her father swinging back and forth through the branches.

'Grandma did,' she told me with the kind of finality that suggested she didn't want to talk about it anymore. However, I have never found it easy to stop a line of enquiry.

'Where were you?'

'I was inside with my brothers. It was early morning.'

I've invented my own picture of the event, like a movie director who takes the bare bones of a script and builds on it, stretching and pulling at each detail for maximum effect. Being 'inside' I decided, meant crouching for warmth in a dark corner by the stove in a *Little House on the Prairie* type shack. Her brothers, I thought, would have been huddled together on a haystack in a tiny loft while my mother stoked the stove with fresh kindling from the woodpile. I painted in the finer details of the surroundings too. Some bedraggled-looking chickens wandering around a scrappy farmyard littered with old junk and a rusty tractor that didn't work anymore.

She did live on a farm. This much was true. And early morning must have been a time when one or both of her parents would have had to have been up and tending to things. I guess it was my mother's job to look after her brothers in the house, get them up and give them breakfast before they trundled off to school – which I in my film-making style imagined to be a tiny little one-room schoolhouse with a strict schoolmarm wielding hickory sticks and children in pinafores writing their names on chalkboard slates à la Tom Sawyer and Huckleberry Finn.

'Were they asleep?' I asked tentatively, aware that at any moment my mother may just choose to shut down on my line of questioning altogether.

'Tommy was, and Bertrand also. Not Ephrem though. He was with me when Mom came running in asking for a knife.'

'A knife? A knife? Why a knife?'

'Knife' is one of those words which, if you say it over and over again too many times, loses its meaning.

'To cut my father down,' she explained wearily. 'He was hanging from a tree.'

'Dead?' I asked. I was beginning to trespass into uncharted territory, I knew, but I couldn't help myself.

'We didn't know. We thought so. Well, of course probably he was. No one survives that. She tried to revive him. Sent Ephrem for the doctor.'

'Did she slap him around the face?'

'Ephrem?' my mother asked me incredulously. 'Why would you possibly think that?'

'No, my grandpa. To bring him back to life.' I'd never referred to him as Grandpa before. Let alone, *my* grandpa. I wanted to try it out and see how it sounded. It felt pretty good. Sort of complete. Now I had two grandfathers, like I was supposed to.

'No, she didn't. She gave him mouth-to-mouth resuscitation.'

'The kiss of life?'

'I suppose so, yes.'

I bathed for a moment in a warm romantic glow, picturing my grandmother kissing my grandfather with his dying breath. For that moment I did not need to know more. Not why he did it, how they survived after that or even whether they missed him or not. My cinematic picture was complete: my mother in the house looking after her two younger brothers while they slept, her big brother Ephrem running wildly across country hills and jumping fences to fetch the doctor for his dying father, and my mother's mother stooped gently over his sad pathetically slumped frame, tenderly kissing him on his pale colourless lips. I could almost hear the music playing in the background and see the credits begin to roll.

8

Dear Francine,

Well your mother has written to me about the things that have been happening there and it all sounds a bit of a drag. It seems she's not coping very well with things particularly since the death of her mother and I've suggested she bring you all over here for a while. I've changed my plans about returning to Seattle. Why return to a rut when you've discovered the possibility of a paradise? I'm not sure where I'll put you all when you get here but people are so nice and I've made plenty of friends since I've arrived and I'm sure we'll sort something.

London is really swinging at the moment so I suggest you prepare yourself for a wild time.

Love and Peace, Dad.

ps I've just done a mind-blowing course with a wonderful man called R.D. Laing. He's given me wisdom I never knew possible. You can tell your mother from me that madness is in the mind of the beholder. She'll know what I mean. Salutations, Leon xxx

Choosing clothes for the airplane wasn't easy. It was important to look cool, a few years older than I was, and yet be dressed to sur-vive the nine-hour journey without needing to change for warmth or comfort. It was important also to wear something that would meld easily with a European dress code, whatever that was, so that

I wouldn't easily be spotted as a foreigner when we stepped off the plane in London, England. Cynthia had been typically unfussed and complacently agreed to my mother's dire suggestion of wearing a pair of extremely unflattering navy blue slacks with an elastic waistband (supposedly for comfort) and a red polo-neck sweater which didn't stretch far enough down to cover the waist of her slacks. I worried that she would not look thirteen (which she was), but possibly several years younger or, worse still, decades older.

'Oh come on, Cyn,' I pleaded, begging her not to wear the lime-green poncho as well, 'we have to make a good impression.'

'On who?' she asked in her irritatingly nonchalant and smart-alecky way. 'How come?'

'Forget it.' I answered her then, resigning myself to the task of finding a seat on the plane far away from hers for the journey.

Making up for my father's disappointment wouldn't be quite so easy, however. I knew already from his letters what a great time he was having in London meeting all these gurus and everything. He had probably, I imagined, turned into a complete hippy by now. He would be standing at the airport with flowers in his hair, and a long flowing robe or, at the very least, an Afghan waistcoat and tight bellbottom jeans. If he saw his family coming towards him dressed like something out of an early episode of *Peyton Place* he'd probably change his mind quickly about the whole thing and leave us standing there waiting for the next plane back.

Melanie had practically forgotten who our father was, so I think she didn't feel the need to perform in quite the same way. He'd only been gone a year but that was already nearly a third of her life.

We had been waiting in New York for nearly five hours before our plane was ready to go. Mom said we could walk around the city as it was our first time there. I had white jeans on and a leather belt with a peace sign for a buckle. On the top I had a checked shirt and a fringed waistcoat. White jeans were a mistake in New York City. Especially on that day. It had been raining a kind of warm soupy rain all day and the cars were splashing water up from the gutters on to the sidewalks like it was paint. My jeans were splattered from the bottom up and all my other clothes were packed into the suitcases that my mother had already checked in at the baggage counter.

New York gave me a kind of dizzy feeling. I had heard that people were supposed to be real unfriendly there so I started off playing this game of saying 'Hi' and smiling at everyone I passed in the street. I decided to count the number of people who said 'Hi' back. Practically everyone did except this Japanese couple who looked at me with kind of a worried expression and hurried on. But I found out later that 'Hi' means 'Yes' in Japanese, so maybe they thought I was one of those crazy people that answer a question before you've even asked it.

Looking up at tall buildings against the background of a grey cloudy sky has got to be one of the scariest things alive. The clouds move one way and the buildings move precariously the other. Standing at the bottom surrounded by so many unwieldy towers feels like almost certain crushing death. We bought sandwiches in a lunch-o-mat, this kind of place where you buy everything from a machine. You go in and put a quarter into whichever window has the sandwich you want and then a metal claw picks up your choice and a glass door opens and the claw hands it to you. Then a robot-like voice from a speaker on the side says thank you. Mom said we would probably die after eating them because there was no way of telling how long they had been sitting there behind those glass windows or whether the claws ever washed themselves but it was cheaper than buying sandwiches at a deli so we decided to take the chance.

'You can all have one of these,' Mom said, unwrapping some fruit-flavour Life-Savers, in that kind of soft voice she always used at the beginning of long trips. I guess she figured that starting off calm and low-key was the best way to avoid any of us getting really hyper. Melanie couldn't believe her luck and crunched her way through the orange one my mother had given her even before Cynthia and I had managed to put ours in our mouths.

'You're supposed to suck them,' Mom explained, 'so your ears don't pop.'

Figurative language has always had a strange effect on me. If someone says something like that, about ears popping or something, I imagine it happening quite literally . . . *and all at once there was an almighty explosion coming from row 3 seat A where a young girl was sitting on her own without her mother and two sisters who were also travelling on the plane. From the side all that was visible was a crater-like hole where her ear had once been.* It was my first time on an airplane and I had never experienced the sensation of changing altitude so quickly.

On the plane I sat next to a man who wrote children's books. He didn't like sitting next to windows because it made his stomach feel like a root-beer float. This kind of figurative speak I could understand. My stomach felt something like that too. Not from sitting next to the window which the man, whose name was Bernard Gubbins, let me do, but from nerves about going to a strange land to meet a strange dad and face the beginnings of what was bound to be a very strange life. Mine felt like a root-beer float that had been all stirred up so you couldn't tell the bubbles from the ice-cream anymore. It was all just one big, horribly frothy mess.

'Do you like elephants?'

Ordinarily this would have sounded like a fairly odd question coming from nowhere as it did, but travelling at an altitude of 3,500 feet above the Atlantic ocean at a speed of something like 450 miles per hour, it didn't seem an unreasonable thing to be asking.

'Yes,' I said, 'grey ones.'

'Only grey?' Mr Gubbins raised his brush-thick eyebrows in a quizzical kind of way. 'Not purple then?'

'If there was a purple elephant, I would like it.' I didn't want to offend the man, I hardly knew him.

'Let's make one then.'

'Make one?'

'In our heads. You start.'

OK, I thought. My ears were starting to feel pressed like they might implode rather than explode and I wanted to take my mind off imagining what internal carnage there might be if this happened. 'Purple toes.'

'Good. How many?'

'Three?' I guessed.

'Correct,' he said categorically as if he knew about these things. 'Now, my turn. Purple legs, like tree trunks.'

'What kind?' I asked. I was beginning to understand the rules to this game.

'Not saplings,' he said. 'Much too frail. How about oak stumps? Around 100 years old?'

'Sounds right to me. My turn?' He nodded.

After we'd built our imaginary purple elephant the stewardess brought round peanuts and a little carton of milk with a straw in it. Bernard Gubbins had a Punt é Mes in a little plastic cup that moved around on the tray when the plane jerked. After the peanuts we got dinner, or lunch, or whatever you wanted to call it according to the time you left and the time you were going to arrive somewhere halfway round the world where they do things differently anyway. It was hard to tell exactly what it was we were given, but I didn't spend too long wondering about it because as soon as I could see they'd mixed things up together I knew I wasn't going to be able to eat it.

'Do you want some crackers?' The stewardess leant over me nursily when she came to collect my untouched tray of food. 'You might get hungry later.'

'OK,' I said and I was glad I did, because the saltines she brought me formed the basis of the next game with Mr Gubbins.

'How long do you think it will take you to whistle the tune of

Happy Birthday through to the end after you've eaten one of those?' he asked me with the same quizzical brow lift.

The truth is it's impossible to whistle anything for a very long time after eating a saltine cracker, but I only discovered this after betting the little packet of sugar I was planning on keeping as a souvenir from the flight with Mr Gubbins that I could whistle the whole of Happy Birthday within ten seconds of swallowing the last of my cracker. It didn't matter that Mr Gubbins got to keep the sugar though, because he gave me two other things that I could keep to help me remember him and our plane trip to England together. He gave me a signed copy of a book he had written himself and done all the pictures for. The title was long and complicated with made-up words that were as weird and wonderful as the man himself and he gave me a little wooden puzzle of an elephant. Not purple, but it wasn't grey either. It was just the colour of wood and I imagined it to have been carved from the middle section of an oak tree, at least 100 years old.

9

The man standing at the arrivals gate of the airport looked more like Abraham Lincoln than Albert Schweitzer. It seemed incredible that this grave, tall statue of a man could be my father. His eyes were bright and full of purpose and I wanted to hide my own away in case they should appear dull and trite in comparison.

I watched other people reuniting on the ramp ahead of us. Couples, families, brothers and sisters and distant relatives. Their coming together made me think of colours merging on a paint palette or hosts of butterflies landing in a field of flowers. There was a lightness and a strange elusive beauty about the whole thing.

My father still hadn't noticed us or else had chosen not to and my stomach suddenly felt as though it were full of lead. As I watched him surveying the airport with a certain air of grandeur and detachment I knew this meeting would be no flower landing.

Stupidly, Cynthia started waving to get his attention and eventually, when we were only feet away from him, he looked in our direction.

'Wow!' he said when he saw us. 'There's so many of you.'

Whatever my father had meant by that comment, Mom took it as distinct rejection and hostility. She instantly bristled and braced herself to deliver a sarcastic reply but I leapt in there first with something I hoped would be a bit more abating. I couldn't bear for our first encounter on foreign soil to be an argument.

'Yep,' I said, trying to effect some sort of grown-up humour in my quip, 'we're multiplying like rabbits.'

I could tell as soon as I'd said it that it wasn't funny. Mercifully, though, Mom had quietened and everyone else appeared to have chosen to ignore me so my father went on.

'I'm not sure the flat I've borrowed is going to be big enough. It might be floors and sleeping bags.'

'Cool!' I said, trying to smooth things again before they had a chance to get rough, but Mom was right in there before I could even finish that one word.

'Jesus. Leon. Sleeping bags? These kids have just been on a transatlantic flight, for Christ's sake. God damn it, I knew you wouldn't have anywhere for us. God damn it!'

There wasn't really any point in getting further involved. We kids just stood there while Mom and Dad glared at each other and we did look a bit stupid; Cynthia in her poncho and Melanie wearing a paper hat folded out of an airplane napkin which she was calling her 'crown', with two rubber bands hanging from her ears for earrings. I knew before he said anything that Dad would not understand Melanie's desire to be a princess nor would he think it was cute or anything like that. I instantly felt this enormous responsibility to be extra specially pleasing to him to make up for the rest of my family.

'Hi, Dad,' I said eventually, trying to break the icy silence and also aware that none of us had yet really formally greeted each other. 'How are you?' I held my hands out awkwardly to give him a little hug around the neck. He kind of hugged me back and patted Cynthia and Melanie on their shoulders. He turned to Mom then and fixed her with a frozen smile that was kind of spooky.

'How was the flight?' he asked her with little or no interest.

Mom and Dad didn't kiss. I guess it would have been a miracle if they had. She answered his question with the kind of emotionless expression that can only be mastered after years of trying.

'Long,' she said, 'and tiring.'

He sighed. They both did. This was not the cosmic bonding, free love or tender reunion we had been hoping for. This was real home-grown Weitz tension originated in Seattle, Washington, and deposited in a country and place it didn't belong. Had we really travelled all this way just to find out we shouldn't have come?

'You can buy tickets for the train into London from over there.' My father, the expert with practically native confidence, pointed in the direction of a railway ticket counter.

'Gee, thanks,' my mother told him, sarcastically, as she struggled with our bags and Melanie's hand.

'Help your mother, Cynthia!' my father yelled.

'I'll help too.' I took a suitcase from my mother. I didn't want to be conspicuous by special selection.

Cynthia glared at me and whispered under her breath so my father couldn't hear, 'You don't have to. He didn't say you.'

'Shhh,' I warned. I was determined that things weren't going to feel so divided and gloomy already.

'I lost my earring,' Melanie wailed. She was standing in the middle of the airport, refusing to move. One of her rubber bands had fallen off of her ears and she didn't want to leave until we had found it. My father didn't understand. He spoke to my mother, not Melanie.

'Her what? She's lost her what?'

'Rubber band, Leon. She calls it her earring.'

'I'll buy some more rubber bands then, for Christ's sake. That's not so hard.'

He strode off in the direction of a little kiosk that looked like it sold candy, pop and magazines and things. He was there for a while choosing things and he came back with his hands full. They didn't sell rubber bands it turned out, but the man at the kiosk had given my dad a couple of loose ones that had come off some newspaper rolls. Melanie sulked for a bit but eventually accepted these as replacements.

My dad had softened by the time he came back from the kiosk. 'People are so nice and helpful in England,' he told us. It was something I was going to hear my father tell us a lot in those first few weeks. He'd bought some other things for Cynthia and I too. English candy we had never seen before. Everything was odd, the taste, the packaging, the names. Polos. These were 'Life-Saver' shaped mints that came in a roll like Clorets. But the wrapper was green and dark blue and looked like it should contain some expensive perfume or toilet item for a Manhattan bathroom, not candy for kids. 'It's a grown-up sweet,' my dad told us. Sweet was not a term of endearment in this case. It was, I learned, what the English call candy. Apart from Polos he got us two Marathon bars which turned out to be the same as an American Snickers and he bought a sucker for Melanie which the English, apparently, call a lolly.

We went on the train from Gatwick Airport to a huge old station called Victoria. I asked my dad if all the stations had girls' names. He was not in the mood for cute questions.

'Does Piccadilly Circus sound like a girl's name?' he said curtly.

No, I thought, it sounds like a circus, with a fairground and lots of animals. But I didn't say that. I could tell my father was not going to be won over by stupid questions or feigned interest in the place names of this country he had become so attached to. Besides, for all I knew, Piccadilly Circus *was* a girl's name and my father was just trying to make a point.

Piccadilly Circus, it turned out, was another station. An underground station for trains travelling around London. It was also a place but not a real circus ground like I had imagined. In this case, Dad explained later when he had got a bit of his patience back, 'circus' means *'open space in town with streets converging on it'*. He read us the definition from a mini Oxford English Dictionary and I wondered if I had better get one of those for myself in case I had any more trouble with the language.

We were tired, we had heavy bags to carry, and everything felt frighteningly strange and new. But we could not rest, it seemed, until my father said so and he was dragging that moment out for all it was worth as he showed us more and more of his beloved city's centre.

He bought some cherries. There was a lady selling them from a little stand just outside the station. She put them in a brown paper bag and my dad just started eating them without washing them or anything. The bottom of the bag started to go a little purple. He offered me one and I wasn't sure, but I wanted to show him my willingness to be a bit more adventurous with food now that we were in a country where absolutely everything was going to be different. The cherry was sweet and tasted nice. I kept the seed from the middle in my mouth and sucked it until it was completely clean. I thought, if I start saving every stone from every cherry I eat when I'm over here, I could make a necklace to wear when I go back to show my friends.

After Piccadilly Circus and the cherries we went to another place where my father had parked his car and we all piled into it, holding bags and suitcases on our laps because his trunk was full of Indian-looking rugs and blankets. 'For my meditation,' he said, as though that was meant to explain it. Meditation sounded like something he might have been ill with, but after his retort to my question about girls' names and train stations I wasn't about to pursue it further.

His car, *our* car now I guess, was red with a detachable roof. It wasn't a sports car or a Chevrolet or anything like that. It was a small Citroën my father had bought in France, his favourite place to go shopping for autos. My mother said it looked like a Dinky toy and felt like riding in a tin can, but her comment didn't seem to make my father mad like I thought it would. He just shook his head, laughing a little, and said, 'Geez.'

We drove to a place called Barnet. Just a little on the outside of London. There was a tiny apartment my father had borrowed from a friend for us to stay in. I was pleased about that because I had been sort of worried that when we got here there might not be anywhere for us to go. That we might end up being tramps eating cold slices of pizza on even colder sidewalks. But my mother did not seem grateful at all.

'For Christ's sake, Leon. He's coming back on Monday? That's four days away. What are we supposed to do then? You wanna pay for a hotel for this whole menagerie?'

'Alma, for God's sake, relax. The kids don't want to hear you going on like this. You'll make them insecure.'

'I'll make them insecure? I'll make them insecure!? Oh that's great. That's really great. I'll make them insecure. Four days of borrowed time in a cupboard that isn't big enough to wave your arms in is security, is it? OK Leon. We'll go with your brand of safety and assurance. Where are we going on the fifth day, oh Master?'

'To a commune.'

Ha ha ha. We all laughed. Even the clown on the TV screen that watched the little girl playing tic-tac-toe for hours and hours on end without moving, even he was laughing when my dad said that. Let's all go and live on a commune. That's what they do in hippy plays, that's what they do in Bob Dylan songs or Allen Ginsberg poems. People like us don't live on communes. We're from Seattle and I get straight As on my report card. My sister wears bobby socks with her sneakers and my other sister thinks she's a princess and wants to sit on thrones and wear beautiful dresses. We don't live on communes. Not us.

'Have you been drugging the coffee, Leon?

'Yeah, that's right. I put LSD in your coffee.'

He did? Cool. Wait till I tell my friends that my mother has taken LSD. Cool. My mom didn't think so.

'Because I think you're trying to make us do what you want to do without thinking what it might mean for any of us. Where are the kids going to go to school? Just what, exactly, are any of us going to live on. Are there jobs on this commune of yours? Or do we all join in and dig potatoes. Commune with the soil. Get stinking rotten dirty and . . . ouch! For fuck's sake, you bastard, don't you dare hit me!'

Then my mother hit my father and he hit her back and so on and so on until her blouse was ripped down the front, not from lust but from spiteful anger, and my father had little spittle drops in his beard because he was shouting so much. We were supposed to take Melanie off somewhere to keep her away from the fighting. That's what Mom yelled in the middle of the boxing match. My dad gave us some money when his hand stopped slapping long enough to reach in his pocket, and we went trundling off with Melanie between us and ten shillings in a little purse Cynthia had hanging around her neck.

Where should we go? What should we do? How much was ten shillings? I imagined the three of us, lost waifs in a strange land, wandering the streets for days on end until a rich merchant took pity on us and brought us into his mansion and dressed us in beautiful garments.

'Let's get some ice-cream.' Good old Cyn. Trust her to think of food when the going gets rough. Still. It sounded like as good an idea as any.

'OK,' I said. 'Where?'

'A store, stupid.'

'Ice-cream, ice-cream, yay, yay, yay . . .' Melanie had already forgotten about the lions eating each other back at the apartment. Ice-cream, ice-cream would save the day.

'OK, great. Where are the stores?'

'We'll ask someone,' Cynthia said sensibly. I had to hand it to her. When it came to practical logic, she was pretty damn smart.

We saw a man walking his dog. He was carrying a pottery bowl with blackberries in it and his fingers were all stained a dark, bloody purple colour.

'Don't ask him, he could be a murderer,' I whispered. But it was too late. When Cynthia is on a mission not even Jack the Ripper could stop her. That's what I liked about Cyn. Her determination.

'Can you tell us where to find a store that sells popsicles or something?' she asked the man. The man's dog was sniffing Cynthia's behind, but I don't think she knew that.

'I beg your pardon?' He answered in a voice that sounded like Richard Burton in *Camelot*. Thick and velvety and British. 'Popsy what?'

'Popsicles. They're . . . ooh!'

The dog had gone round the front and had his nose in Cynthia's crotch.

'I'm terribly sorry,' said the man. 'Charles, bad dog. Come here. Sit.'

Charles sat. The man looked at us intently. 'You're not from here,' he ventured. 'Are you Canadian?'

'American,' Cynthia answered back proudly. 'We just got here,' she added, even though he hadn't asked, 'Today.'

'Marvellous,' the man said. 'Marvellous.'

'Popsicles are a kind of ice-cream. Sort of. Anyway, it doesn't matter, it doesn't have to be popsicles. Anything like that will be all right.' I tried to steer us back on to the purpose of our stopping him.

'I see, I see,' he crooned. Charles had lain down on the sidewalk by this time. I could see we were going to be stuck here for a while. I wished we'd asked someone else. 'You mean ice-lollies. Or cornets. Wafers, perhaps. You want a newsagent. The High Street. They'll have one. Beyond the common.'

I needed a phrasebook. He'd lost me. Cornet? Wasn't that a kind of brass trumpet? Wafer? I don't think so. What the hell is a newsagent? Somebody help.

'Thanks,' said Cynthia. 'Bye Charles.' She waved politely at the man with the purple hands and his canine companion. Then she took Melanie and I firmly by the hands and pulled us sharply away. It was the gesture of a big sister. The action of someone taking charge, tendering control. Thanks Cyn. Thank you, Cynthia, for getting us out of that mess with Mr Smoothie. He wasn't going to be any help at all with his blackberry stains and his *Camelot* voice. He wasn't going to rescue us or give us shelter in a mansion, some English stately home somewhere. He didn't know the first thing about kids like us. He didn't even know what popsicles were.

Later, while we were still looking for an ice-cream store, we saw two boys about our age, maybe a bit older, sitting on a stone wall smoking cigarettes. They probably would have known about places to buy ice-cream in the area, but somehow they didn't seem worth approaching either. I already had a sneaking suspicion that our American accents were not going to win us huge favour with our English counterparts. Just keep quiet and walk on slowly. Pretend you haven't noticed them. That's the best.

'Oi!' one of the boys shouted in our direction when we had just passed the stone wall they were sitting on. 'My mate fancies you.'

If I'd known what was meant by that statement I might have

been able to muster a reply of some sort, but despite all my mental efforts of quick translation or word approximation I could not fathom the gist of that one. *My mate . . .?* Mates are what wild animals have. To make more wild animals. . . . *fancies you?* Fancy. Fancy is frills, lace, flamboyant colour and design. Was he referring to our clothes, something we were wearing? Damn, why hadn't I brought an Oxford English Dictionary like my father's out with us. It just might have helped.

'Just ignore them,' Cynthia whispered, trying to be brave. 'Just ignore them and keep on walking. They're being stupid.'

'I said, my mate fancies you.' The other boy giggled. His friend sounded angry. 'Oh forget it, you stupid birds. Tarts!'

This was not real. This was not happening to me. We came to a road and across it we could see a row of little country-type stores. Maybe one of them sold ice-cream. Melanie had given up looking and fallen asleep. Cynthia was carrying her on her back. Cars were going pretty fast along this road so we looked for a safe place to cross, but I couldn't see stoplights anywhere. There was a stripy path across the road that people kept walking across. Cars just stopped instantly like some magic barrier had gone up and then they waited until the people got across to the other side. It occurred to me that this walkway may well have been designed by a pathologist like my father. The way it worked seemed to be: you stepped on and cars stopped. Simple as that. Well, it was only a theory but it was our only chance of getting across this death-trap. Cars were hurtling by from every direction and the stores that might have sold ice-cream on the other side were tantalizingly out of reach.

'Come on, Cynthia. We'll cross there.'

'Are you sure? There's no green light.'

'There's no light, period. Except that orange lollipop that keeps flashing away, but I think that's just there for decoration. The cars will stop. You'll see.'

They did. Cynthia, Melanie and I crossed like royalty, holding up the traffic on both sides for at least half a minute. It was the first time since we landed that I'd felt any kind of power.

10

Dad won that fight with Mom but it was probably the last one he did. We took off at the end of that week to do some commune cruising. Well, it was a good way to see the country, I guess. The first one we went to should have been closed down for giving communes a bad name. It was a big fancy house that looked like a castle, only if you looked closely enough you could see that the front part was fake. It was more like a hotel than a commune. As soon as we arrived we were assigned a room in the 'visitor's quarters' and given a number and a key. Our communal duties, we were told, would be assigned to us later after dinner.

Our room was dusty and made Mom sneeze. Melanie found an ant's nest underneath a broken sink unit in the corner and Cynthia said she twice saw a black widow spider running across the pillow on her bed, but I didn't see it. Dad pretended it was all great – he had to, otherwise he would have lost face altogether – but Mom said they hadn't even washed the sheets we were supposed to be sleeping on.

'Well, it's a commune,' Cynthia piped up, practical as ever and trying to be helpful. 'Maybe we're supposed to wash our own sheets.'

We didn't even stay for dinner at the castle place. We turned in our key and left without signing the visitor's book.

The second commune we tried was really only just getting

going. It was a 'baby' commune, Dad said. Hector welcomed us. He was wearing a plaid shirt and ripped overalls. His black hair was kind of all fuzzed up as if he hadn't brushed it for days. He didn't wear shoes the whole time we were there, and I don't think he washed his feet in that whole time, either. One night at dinner I saw him drop some ketchup from his plate on to his overalls and some of it got on his bare feet too. Three days later you could still see the dried ketchup when he walked.

At 'Hector's House', which is what Cynthia and I called the place, it was kind of cool. They had a kids room that was meant for messing up in. Not just leaving toys and stuff around but real messing. If you wanted you could write things on the walls or on the ceiling and it didn't matter whether you used a pen or a crayon that you couldn't erase. The idea was 'to express yourself'. There were big cushions in there that you could jump on and someone had hung a giant kite from the ceiling so it looked like it was flying. You couldn't play with it but it looked good. Hector had two kids: Jenny and Cato, who used to live with their mother in Australia. They had come back to live with their dad, and I guess Hector had decided it would be one hell of a lot easier having kids around the place if they had a room to mess up in.

The other people there were this older couple without children called Sylvia and Peter and a man called Bertie who used to be a marine biologist, which he said just meant that he swam around in a frogman's outfit looking for dead fish. I thought fish floated to the top when they died and didn't think that you would need to wear a frogman's suit to find them. As well as fishing Bertie was great at making bread. Big crusty loaves that were golden brown on the outside and white, soft and doughy on the inside. My favourite thing was to peel away the hard crust from the edges and then squash up the rest until it was a really hard doughball. You could chew on that doughball for ages and it was almost better than candy if you got it just right.

Sylvia was a painter and Peter used to be a teacher in a school before he got too tired to teach anymore. Peter was always reading or talking about reading something, while Sylvia, who didn't talk much at all, spent a lot of time studying the detail of things and then painting something completely different. She had this little easel she carried around with her and she'd set it up in front of something like the fruit bowl on the table and then she'd paint something on her paper that looked more like a battle than a banana. She did that once with me and Melanie when we were sitting doing a jigsaw puzzle. Sylvia came and plopped her easel down in front of us and started watching us real closely like a cat watches a mouse before it pounces. Then she got her paints out and started to paint lines and colours all over the place. When I looked at it after she was all finished I wasn't sure whether to laugh or what. She'd made this mess on the paper – even the walls in the kids room looked better – and she'd called it *Two Sisters at Play*. I hoped it wasn't going to get famous or anything like that because it would be embarrassing to have the first real picture that had ever been painted of you look like that.

Anyway, we decided not to stay at that one either because there wasn't really a school nearby for me and Cyn to go to and the one that Jenny and Cato went to was a private one their mother paid for. My mom said she wasn't interested in boarding school for me and Cynthia. Besides, Hector never stopped trying to work out the house rules and calling meetings to see if every-one agreed with what he had written down and no one could ever agree, and in the end that's why my dad said it was a 'baby' com-mune, because it was still finding out who it was and how it wanted to be. Kind of crawling instead of walking, Dad said, which I thought was a pretty good way of putting it.

So we finally came to rest in the English countryside at a place called Rabbit Hall. This time it was Cressida with a long, flow-ing cheesecloth skirt and loose caftan shirt who glided across the front lawn to make our acquaintance. She seemed to know my father already through a friend of a friend or whatever, and was hugely warm and affectionate with all of us.

'Your children are sooo beautiful,' she crooned. 'They've got your eyes, Leon. Especially this one.' She hugged me to her and

I was reminded of the Jewish family reunions we used to have at Grandma's.

Cressida had long frizzy light-brown hair and wore big hoop earrings which poked out under a brightly coloured scarf she had tied around the top of her head like a Romany Gypsy or a fortune teller. She was a potter and made large unwieldy structures in a little barn by the side of the house where she had a potter's wheel and a kiln. Her husband or boyfriend, I was never sure which, was called Ray. Ray used to drive trains but now spent most of his time taking apart car engines in the back yard of the hall and making them into new things. He had just finished building a 'chariot', which was like a big motor-powered throne on tractor wheels. We were allowed to sit on it and drive it around the grounds of the commune if we wanted. I'd never driven anything before so this would have been a big thrill if we hadn't been given permission so explicitly and freely. Somehow being told we could took the sting out of what might have felt a bit daring and dangerous – even forbidden. Like the messing room at Hector's House.

There were seven permanent residents at Rabbit Hall including Cressida. Jake, who was Cressida's son but not, I found out, anything to do with Ray, was fourteen and had a man's voice and a little fuzz on his upper lip where a moustache was trying to grow. He wore torn jeans that had oil stains all over them from when he had been helping Ray dismantle engine parts. He made my heart beat so I could feel it thudding against the inside of my chest whenever I saw him, and I guessed that must have meant I 'fancied' him.

There was Miranda, a single woman in her late fifties who grew herbs and always smelled of rosemary, and there was another family – Sally, Martin and their little baby Kate who was only a couple of weeks old. Martin was the only one in the commune who had an outside job. He went off on the train every morning wearing a suit and a tie, with his hair pulled back tightly into a ponytail, until he came back at the end of the day and dressed like everyone else. I told Cynthia the suit meant that he made a lot of money and that Martin, Sally and Kate must be the richest ones here.

'But he probably shares what he earns with everyone else,' Cynthia said.

'Really?' I asked incredulously, marvelling at the idea.

'It is a commune, stupid. Like communism? You know, every-one is equal, no one at the top.'

I knew what communism meant. At least I knew what my teachers in America had told me it meant. It meant restriction of rights, opportunities, lowering of lifestyles and no freedom of speech or anything else. I had never made the connection before between that idea of communism and the dream my father was pursuing of free living and new possibilities on these communes. However, apparently my mother had.

'Just how long are we expected to stay in this asylum, Leon?' Mom asked him in one of their usual hushed arguments in the communal living room after dinner. My father was sitting in the lotus position and half-shutting his eyes, which made it easier for him to pretend that he was achieving nirvana instead of fighting. Miranda was the only other one in there, apart from Cynthia, Jake and I who were playing a game of Monopoly in the corner. Miranda was watching television with her eyes completely shut and trying to knit at the same time, so I didn't think she was going to be noticing much.

'We can stay just as long as we want to,' he beamed, radiating peace and inner quietude. 'Ray and Cressida asked if we would like to become permanent members.'

'I've had enough of this fantasy living,' my mother snapped. 'I'm going to find a real house, a real job and a real school for the kids. That's what real people do, Leon. You can stay here and masturbate.'

It was the end of October and neither Cynthia nor I had been to any kind of school since we left Seattle in June. Not that I missed it or anything but I guess Mom was afraid that our brain cells might start to deteriorate.

So my father had to stall on accepting Ray and Cressida's offer of permanency while my mother packed her bags and huffed away from Rabbit Hall like a storm-trooper with a mission. I pictured her ancestors before her, hair piled into nets, ready for action. Perhaps one day I too would be one of these women – leading the way in front of generations and generations of 'Mom' clones, huffing and puffing and waving the flag of struggle, determination and suffering.

We all stayed behind. 'Where would they stay if they came with me?' she spat at Leon.

Where would she stay? Where was she going, even? It turned out that the other members of Rabbit Hall weren't interested in any of us staying if we weren't all part of the package. They had liked the idea of another family unit on the site. 'It helps give internal structure,' Martin explained. I think he must have been in engineering. In Mom's absence, it was pretty clear that we were not brimming with the spirit of family unity. Dad meditated while Cynthia and I fought and Melanie wailed nearly the whole time for her stupid blanket, which Mom must have accidentally packed up with her things and taken with her.

Three weeks later Mom came back and we were all ready to do her bidding. Even Dad, who no longer had the resident's permit he thought he had at Rabbit Hall. So we trooped down to London, a less than solid family unit, where living quarters awaited us. Mom had found us a flat – a house split in two – that had three bedrooms, a big living-room and a back yard the size of a postage stamp. My father's research grant had come to an end and he was faced with the choice of returning to what he knew he didn't want in Seattle or staying to try and find what he thought he did. He chose the latter. Things were still swinging in London. On almost every corner there was a 'head' shop where you could buy beads, posters and cone-shaped incense that burned little holes into table tops. There was Lord Kitchener's Valet, Carnaby Street and a magazine called *Time Out* that listed just about every possible life choice under the sun, a paper called *Oz* and the *Little Red School Book* which you could only buy with all the middle pages cut out.

We set about trying to establish ourselves and make friends with the local crowd of kids who called themselves skinheads and seemed mainly to go about in gangs wearing long coats that changed from khaki green to army blue depending on how the light shone, and big black boots with steel caps on the front of them. Most of them either shaved their heads or had very short hair with wispy bits hanging down at the back. This part of their uniform look was an anathema to me coming from a culture where long hair is worshipped just about as much as the Big Mac. Perhaps the most important thing I had to learn about skinheads was that they truly hated Americans. Bitterly and with a passion. They called us Yanks and thought we were all bastards. The only other race that came in for quite as much revilement from the skinheads were Indians from Pakistan. I thought this must be because the Pakistanis I knew from the new school we had started at had the strongest, sleekest black hair that I had ever seen on anyone and they wore it down in long plaits beautiful enough to make any short-haired person jealous and mad as hell.

At home things were no smoother and no rougher than they had been for a while. Dad wasn't working but still spent more time away from the flat than he did in it. He had picked up fleas from somewhere and they had burrowed their way into his scalp and beard and my mom shooed him out of the side bedroom which was pretty crowded out already with boxes and papers that didn't seem any good to anyone any more. Dad took refuge in our room, the one that Melanie, Cynthia and I shared. My mom had the other bedroom. Dad slept on a mattress on the floor and Melanie, Cyn and I on bunk beds above him.

It wasn't long before the mattress and the carpet in our room were also apparently crawling with Dad's bugs. The whole thing – their marriage, our family life and the life my father lived outside our home where he must have joined company with insects – all began to feel very sleazy and sordid. It became clear that, domestically speaking, my mother was gaining the upper hand at every crack of the whip. My father, she said, had other places he could go and other places, no doubt, he'd rather be.

Mom and him weren't really speaking, amicably or otherwise and there seemed little point in them spending too much time together. Getting pest control people in wasn't cheap, Mom said, and it was going to take some time before we got all the larvae out of the carpet. I'd never actually seen a flea or the worm that it was before it turned into one. Not on my father, his mattress or the carpet in our bedroom. But they must have been there because my mother was insisting on it and I was feeling itchy most of the time.

11

The bathroom door wasn't locked. My dad was shaving, a new image for a new life. I needed to go to the toilet, desperately. Our London flat only had one bathroom.

I know he was disappointed that communes hadn't worked out for us. I figured as a family we just weren't communal enough. Cynthia said that as far as she could tell wherever there was communism there was war, so maybe the plan was doomed to fail. Anyway I'd been trying, since we were back in London, to change all that. Other families seemed to manage it. Meals together, outings, space-sharing generally. In Seattle our bathroom had always been like Grand Central Station with people in and out and not minding each other's business. It could work again.

I was really desperate and Dad was still shaving. The buzz of the shaver was so loud he didn't hear me come in and only saw me when I came into view in the mirror. I prayed to God that whatever I did wasn't going to be too smelly.

'Francine.' He smiled at me, turning like some half-bearded freak. His face was part smooth, part rough, part foam and part flesh. A bizarre sight that made me think of woolly mammoths and guinea pigs for some reason.

'Hi, Dad, do you mind if I use the loo?' I was picking up the jargon good and quick. Those boys on the street wouldn't be able to tell me from a native pretty soon.

'Go ahead,' he gestured grandly. 'Be my guest.'

I hitched my nightgown up and perched on the edge of the toilet seat. My legs looked conspicuously bare and exposed. My father watched my reflection while he was shaving. 'So, how goes it?'

'How goes what?' I asked, never quite sure whether I had picked up on his cryptic nuances correctly.

'Life,' he said in a matter-of-fact, yet esoteric, fashion. At least he wasn't enquiring after my progress on the toilet.

'OK, I guess,' I answered, feeling a little self-conscious in my compromised position though I consoled myself with the thought that soul-searching in the bathroom might be one of the essential components of unifying a family. I tore away some toilet paper from the roll and tried to dab myself without too much display. I got up and flushed the toilet, eager to make my escape having relieved myself and made a small contribution to family unification. My father, however, as smooth-faced now as a treeless plain, wanted to press the matter further. He was preparing, I could see, for a lecture or a sermon. Probably the latter because there were tears in his eyes even before he started.

'Francine,' he said. 'Francine. Things aren't right, are they?'

He pulled me close. I tried to remember whether I had locked the door when I came in or left it open.

'Francine, I . . . I . . . I'm really very frightened.'

There was a sharp intake of breath that came from one or other of us, it was hard to tell, and then a slight splutter like a car engine. It would probably be better if the door was locked. He'd started crying and his nose was dripping. I kept wondering, should I say his name too? Should I be holding on to my father with the same tight grip he had on me? Should I be doing something to put the things that had become so wrong, right? In that rare moment of closeness, what I really longed for was a distance between us.

In fact what I *really* longed for, what I really wanted and hoped for, was for my father to know something, to tell *me* something, to exercise some surety that I could hold on to and rely upon. My head against his shuddering chest started to spin and somewhere I remembered a line about drugged coffee and also a slogan about something to do with saving water by showering with a friend.

Perhaps if I called him doctor. Doctor Leon Father, father. Doctors usually know what's wrong and how to put it right. That's their job after all. Dad. Leon. Doctor. Speak to me of wise things. Speak to me, or let me go.

He laid his hands upon the child and spake in grave tones.

You are a shining light.

The seat of wisdom itself.

You know all things and I look to you for eternal guidance.

No, no. That's not right. I don't know anything. I'm just a kid.

I listen only to you, for in all things you are wise and pure in mind and heart.

You're holding me too tight. You're squeezing the life out of me. Your hand is uncomfortably close to where it oughtn't to be.

Hey. Hey. Hey, little girl. Young lady. How about it? You and me. Let's split this joint, let's take a powder. Let's bound off on a cosmic journey and seek the light in our oneness. Let's cut this father–daughter crap. We are two people on the same journey. Two stars in the universal constellation, two drops in the mighty ocean of life.

'Are you and Mom going to break up?'

Hyena laugh. More splutters. Cobra squeeze.

'I guess she already decided that a long time ago. She wants to break me up.'

'Will you . . . will I see you?'

'You can see me all the time if you want. Come with me.'

It wasn't a question or a command. It was a plea. A frightened, helpless plea.

'Where?'

'Anywhere. Where we go. Wherever we travel to. Who knows?'

Right, well, that certainly sounds definite.

'What about Mom and Cynthia and Melanie?'

'They'll travel too, I guess. To their places. Not places I want to go.'

'Will I go to school?'

I could see my pragmatic line of questioning was beginning to irritate my father, who most definitely wanted to keep things in the realm of the esoteric.

He shook his head and shrugged his shoulders despairingly. 'I guess if you need a system, you'll find one.'

'Oh.'

Was that an answer? Did it mean yes, there will be a school where we're going or not? I needed practical details. This was a crossroads decision. But my dad might change his mind about wanting me if I got too boringly conventional and wrapped up in the specifics. Perhaps he saw the struggle I was having or simply remembered there was a whole section he hadn't told me, but he offered something concrete then. Well, an illusion of solidity anyway.

'There is a Buddhist retreat I've been going to. They live in a small community in a beautiful setting. Their children go to the school at the monastery. You would be most welcome amongst them, I'm sure.'

I looked at myself sidelong in the mirror. My father still had both arms around me and the bathroom door was closed. We looked wrong in that position together. Maybe because I'd grown so tall in the last few months but the picture in the mirror said Man and Woman in love. A couple. *To have and to hold . . . for ever and ever . . . to the exclusion of all others . . . forgive us our trespasses . . . Our Father, Our father . . . Shalom shalom shalom . . . amen.* I pictured myself with a shaved head, going to the monastery school with the other Buddhist children in brown robes, peaceful expressions on our faces.

'You would learn a lot more about life there than you would at the school your mother wants to send you to. But it's up to you.'

Bastard. Bastard. Bastard. Don't leave it up to me. Tell me. Tell me what you're going to do. What is going to happen. Where I'm going next. Who I'm going with. Tell me so it doesn't have to be my decision. So it doesn't have to be my fault. So I can blame someone else and not be left with the terrible burden of a wrong choice.

'I think I'd better stay with Mom.'

He loosed his hold on me and shook his arms limply as though they had been holding something rotten. His lips tightened and he smiled. Not a real smile. His eyes were dry. Not even sparkling. He was flat and dull. Even the smell of the shaving cream had gone away. Perhaps I had made him that way. He turned from me to the sink and began to wash his hands. To get the poison off, no doubt. The awful residue that his holding me so close, so tight, might have left behind. He splashed his face and then dried himself all over with a towel. He handed it to me, damp and heavy, as he opened the door and left the bathroom.

'It's a hard thing to be rejected,' he said as he left. 'Thanks.'

Metal doors slamming shut. Grey prison walls. Restricted visiting time. Solitary confinement. Solitary. Solitary.

I wanted to run after him. It's all right. I'll do it. I'll shave my head. I'll wear a brown robe. I'll denounce my mother and my sisters and their evil ways. Just take me with you. Just look at me again with love in your eyes and call me your wise child. Your special one. Just one more time. Please. Come back.

But I didn't run after him and I didn't say any of those things. I stood there with his wet towel in my hands. With his smell on my nightgown. With his tears in my hair. I stood there, glued to the ground with a huge weight pressing in on all sides. I had done it. Signed my own fate, decided my own destiny. I'd made my own bed and now I had to lie in it.

'Francine, you stupid!' Cynthia yelled from the bedroom. 'Did you do this to my scarf?'

TWO

12

If you stand sideways in a room full of mirrors it's possible to see yourself reflected in an infinite number of different ways and also not to recognize what you see as yourself projected there at all. It is like that story about the three blind men and the elephant. Every possible perspective is the truth. The truth is I was spending most of my time trying very hard not to see or know myself in any shape or form.

It was years since I had seen or heard from Leon. The traces of him had long disappeared or turned to dust. When something is left for a long time, neither dormant nor dead, it transforms itself. It changes from something real into something imagined, or from a material state into that which is wholly immaterial. But even while it is transforming itself, even as it ceases to be of any earthly importance any more, it is collecting a thin film of imperceptible dust which is the only proof that it was ever there before at all. My father, or rather the memory of him, collected dust in this way and I knew from years of cramming my head with trivia that dust is actually tiny particles of dead skin which leave the bodies of the living and come to rest on the surfaces of the flat, the straight-edged and the inanimate. This was how I knew my father was present without him even being there.

Francine Weitz sat looking at Francine Weitz in the small mirror in front of her. The room she occupied was hers in exchange for volunteering herself as a subject in a psychological study investigating the Causes and Cures of Anorexia Nervosa. The room was ten foot by ten foot. An exact square. In fact, practically everything in the room was square. The bed, the chair, the desk, the window, the mirror. Even Francine was square with sharp edges. To be otherwise would be to risk roundness or living a life that wasn't metered and angled with exact precision, control and predictability.

'A Freudian analysis applied today would perhaps conclude that the melancholia we see present has its basis in the losing of a loved object. This loss then, and the incurring sadness resulting from that loss, impels the subject to reinstall the lost object within her own ego, thus giving the temporary illusion of having restored proper balance. However, once installed, the subject experiences a sense of invasion and wishes to devour the impostor, the imagined loved object, and thus the object is regurgitated, spat out, aborted and got rid of and the subject is once again forced to feel the emptiness of that loss. The result then is the illness you see here. Whilst this perspective may provide us with a possible understanding of the causes which drive this particular patient's condition, it does not provide her or us with the notion of a cure. Let us proceed then to a medical model. I would like to propose . . .'

Why I ever let myself get into this I don't know. I'm sat here like a still life on a slab, being scrutinized, minutely observed and finally drawn out as something that doesn't nearly resemble who

I think I am. Not nearly. What good are Freud's ideas or anyone else's for that matter? It is not a loved object I am throwing up and flushing down the loo every day, but a bucket-load of assorted items from Sainsbury's. I don't really feel like sticking around to hear what else he has to say on the subject, anyhow. I'm feeling very cold in this room, almost a kind of death chill, despite the fact that the lecture-hall is filled to brimming with live warm pumping medical students and not a cadaver in sight. I've always thought I might like to see a cadaver. It's not a gory wish; more a curious one, I think. I'd like to look at the face of a dead person who knows (or doesn't) that they are about to be cut up in the name of science. A worthy sacrifice of course but not one, I suppose, that anyone would go leaping into. God, I'm cold. I answered an ad. They were looking for young, intelligent and articulate women who were starving themselves, or bingeing, and would be willing to be the subject of study. It's not all looking and prodding and poking. They do ask me questions too and they seem genuinely interested in what I have to say so I guess that's something. They don't give me enough to wear in these Show and Tell sessions though. I guess they want the students to see how thin someone like me really gets. All the finer details. It's the same with cadavers, it's never enough just to look at the face.

When I'm with Mr Eccles there is no one else who watches. His office is a kind of haven from that other very public display. Mr Eccles likes me to free associate. I can't get the idea of Eccles cakes out of my head. I don't think I've ever had one, but I know what they are. They're usually the last thing left at the bakery at the end of the day when everyone has bought the nice stuff. There's a tray of Eccles cakes, most of them slightly squashed with stuff oozing out, a stale jam doughnut or two and loads of those granary rolls that break your teeth when you bite into them. Why do they make so much stuff that never gets eaten? Maybe they give it to the homeless at the end of the day but, let's face it, even if you're out sleeping rough and haven't had a meal for weeks you're not going to be overjoyed to see a tray of squashed Eccles cakes and hard granary buns coming your way. I imagine most people living on the streets for any length of time would steer clear of bakeries at closing time.

What he does is he stays silent for ages and then every so often grunts a bit or coughs and clears his throat just to let me know that he is there. I don't mind that he doesn't say much. If I were him I wouldn't either. I mean most of it would be lost on me because I'm sure the sort of conversations he likes to have would be impossible for me to follow. I can't be entirely sure he manages to follow my train of thought very well either but he's there and he doesn't say much, which means I can say just about anything I like. If I want to.

Free association basically means you say what pops into your head. It doesn't always work like that. Sometimes you plan for ages what you want to say and it comes out all rehearsed and planned and ordered but then what usually happens is that you start to free associate about how weird it feels to be saying something that is so carefully scripted and the process all clicks back into gear again. I'm not sure what good it's all doing but it keeps me away from food and toilets for at least an hour every day.

The first time I came to see him I sat up in that chair over there. I don't really like to sit and face anyone for too long, because you start to see all sorts of things in that other person that you either need to comment on or just keep to yourself which is practically impossible. Sitting facing Mr Eccles for the first time I couldn't help seeing that his eyebrows were kind of separated when they were really the sort that should have met in the middle. I kept wondering whether I should ask him if he plucked them and if so why? I thought, if he plucked them then that would mean that he wasn't really happy with himself the way he was and he'd decided to change things. Or maybe he thought other people would be bothered if he had those kind of werewolf tufts that come together on the bridge of the nose. But then who was he trying to protect by plucking – himself or them? Or maybe he didn't pluck. Maybe he used that kind of leg cream like Immac or maybe his hair was just receding and had started to fall away in quite unusual places. The best conclusion I could reach without asking was that he had a kind of brow alopecia. This particular fantasy really helped me to like the guy. If someone had such a lot of problems of their own that their eyebrows were beginning to fall out and they were still willing to sit there and listen to someone else's woes, then they must be alright.

To stop myself scrutinizing his facial hair, and to move things on a bit, I told him about a dream I'd kept having.

'It's a dream about a banister,' I said.

I was sure he must have heard thousands of dreams being talked about, much stranger than mine, so I couldn't figure out why he was looking so perplexed.

'What's that on your forehead?' he came out with finally, leaning forward a bit in his chair.

As I've said, it was not in keeping for Mr Eccles to ever say very much at all, but to volunteer a question like that which could have been mistaken for a kind of chatty inquisitive interest was highly unusual even in those very early stages of our relationship. I wanted to reward him with an answer, but I was not at all sure what he was talking about. Perhaps he had mind-read my thoughts about eyebrows and he was asking about mine. I put my fingers up to my face to show willing. I could not feel anything out of the ordinary.

'That grey film,' he said at last, 'or powder. Is it make-up?'

I realized then what he must be talking about. Fortunately I have become skilled over the years in answering such questions in a way that does not involve too much personal disclosure. I replied as clearly as I could without giving too much away.

'It's ashes,' I told him.

'Ashes?' he repeated.

'Yes,' I said.

He waited then as though he expected me to say more.

'Burnt ashes,' I offered, but it was clearly not enough for Mr Eccles.

'Have you been in a fire?'

The man was obviously seeking an explanation.

'No, no. It's just something that I do. A habit, you know, like flossing.' I could see the analogy wasn't good but I was trying to edge things off track for a bit.

'Would you like to tell me about it?'

Rhetorical questions do nothing for my own patience. What about my dream? I wanted to say then. Who's sidetracking now? I thought we were supposed to tell about our dreams, get in touch with the unconscious, move things along a bit. What did the ashes on my face really matter? Ah well, I could see he wasn't going to give up.

'OK,' I said finally. 'I write things down on bits of paper. Then I burn them and rub my face in the ashes. I usually wash but I obviously missed this time.'

'What?' he said.

I thought at first he hadn't heard me. Either that or he was so incredulous that anyone could do such a thing, but it turns out that he was asking me what kind of things I wrote down on the pieces of paper. I could see that we weren't going to get very far on the subject of banisters for a while so I told him about my burning rituals. I told him how I write down things that I don't want any more. Friends, moods, people, choices. It's a kind of cremation. I write them down and then I burn them. He wanted some examples. I said, for instance, I could write down *anger* and then burn the piece of paper I'd written it on, anoint my forehead and, hey presto, lost tempers would be a thing of the past. I could see that he wasn't impressed. He wanted a more specific example.

'What did you write down this morning?' he asked me.

At this point I felt as though I'd been manoeuvred into a corner. Checkmated, so to speak. When you're asked a question so directly it's hard not to imagine that the person asking it has the power to know whether the answer you give is true or not. Besides, anyone with his training is bound to be able to read minds a little. What I wasn't sure of was what he would do if I never answered him at all, or if I tried to squeeze out of the corner with a lie. I remembered that song my mother used to sing us before Christmas. About Santa Claus.

> *. . . He knows when you are sleeping,*
> *He knows when you're awake*
> *He knows if you've been bad or good*
> *So be good for goodness' sake . . .*

I never liked the idea that someone so jolly and round and supposedly benign could be threatening little children with this Big Brother-type mentality. Just to test the water, I'd tried being fairly disobedient for a whole week before Christmas and then staying up all night before the big day. I still got presents but I can't remember whether I liked them or not. Perhaps if I tried to pull the wool over Mr Eccles's eyes now there would be nothing but coal in the bottom of the stocking for me.

'I wrote Leon,' I told him.

'Leon?'

'Leon. It's my father's name. I wrote his name down on a piece of paper and then I burned it.'

'And rubbed your face in it?'

Yes, yes, yes, Mr Eccles. Now can we get on with that dream?

'About my dream . . .'

'Ah yes, your dream,' he said. 'About banisters.'

'*A* banister. It's a dream about a banister. There's only one. The other one is missing.'

'I see,' he said. This is a more typical example of Eccles-speak. I figure it must be part of a shrink's training to say 'I see' when maybe they don't see anything at all, or perhaps very little. It's a good tactic though because it keeps the whole thing ticking along.

'Yes, you see,' I continued, 'I dream about a stairway that should have two banisters, only it doesn't.'

'Go on,' he said. More encouragement and at last we were off the subject of ashes.

'That's it,' I said. 'It should have two banisters only one side is missing. There's only one. One banister to hold on to.'

'What do you think that means?' he asked me. 'What is the significance of the missing banister?'

It was nearly the end of the session. I could tell because he'd glanced at his watch twice and sat back in his chair the way someone does when they're almost ready to take a break. With so little time left I didn't really feel able to compose the kind of answer he might have been looking for, which was a bit disappointing.

Neither of us said anything for the next couple of minutes which felt like an interminable length of time. However, silence is another thing shrinks are well trained in. I started studying his eyebrows again and he straightened up some papers on his desk until he told me it was time to stop. Time already and we'd only just managed to get started on this banister conundrum.

The thing was, I had this dream a lot so I did kind of hope to get it sorted. Still, there was always next time, I suppose. Mr Eccles and I were going to be seeing a lot of each other.

13

This time last summer I was staying alone in the London flat while my mother and my sister Melanie were away visiting relatives. Cynthia was living in Skye with a part-time Mormon named Mike, I had a job in the summer sales at Harrods and Alma's pot plants needed watering. Cynthia didn't want to leave Mike or Skye to flat-sit for Mother so it was a suitable arrangement on all sides.

I didn't mind staying anywhere if I could be on my own. Undisturbed I could play out my starving/bingeing rituals without fear of interference and without the need to fabricate endless lies to cover the tracks of my self-destructive behaviour. With the run of the flat for the summer I could actually set myself some routines and intimate some air of normality about my existence.

I rode the bus each day to work and home again to the flat in north-west London. I was keeping a diary to fill in the gaps between working, bingeing, starving and sleeping and I found it helped to give me a sense that my life was still a full and intense experience. One grey morning after I had waited more than the usual fifteen minutes for the bus and was shivering underneath my several layers of jumpers and overcoat, despite it being the beginning of August, I decided to buy a bar of chocolate. A Kit-Kat to nibble on the way to work. I had already agreed with myself that this would be my week's ration for anything that contained more calories than a carrot and, consoled with this, I put my purchase in my carrier bag with the newspaper I would pretend to read at break time, and boarded the very late and crowded bus. Actually I was glad it was crowded and hoped that in the absence of my own padding, the mass of people huddling together in close proximity might give me the sensation of being well-covered.

It's a funny thing about extreme fatness or extreme thinness. Both seem to merit extra attention in the same way that being elderly or infirm does. Even though I was probably one of the youngest of the commuters that morning, I was offered a seat before many who looked greatly more in need.

My usual impulse was to refuse such an offer as I knew that standing up required more energy than sitting down and would therefore burn up more calories and be a greater safeguard in the long run of my mission to disappear off the face of the earth altogether.

However, so as not to hurt the feelings of the kind-looking grey-suited gentleman who offered it, I took the seat next to an oldish woman who was wearing at least as many layers as I was. The difference between us must have been that I had a home and she didn't, but still I recognized myself in the pointy features and cavernous eyes that stared out from the tattered scarf she had pulled around her weathered face. I smiled at her, more in comradeship than for politeness. Her smell, though strong, was no less tolerable than the choking concoction of expensive perfumes I'd had to put up with working near to the cosmetics department at Harrods.

Gingerly I took the Kit-Kat from my bag because I had already promised it to myself and so to alter my plans now would have been unbearable. To avoid feeling self-conscious I imagined that I had achieved my ambition of becoming totally invisible and proceeded, undisturbed, to carefully peel away the membrane-like foil that covered the chocolate-coated wafer underneath. I laboured over this task as if it were a job that took not only dexterity but a great deal of skill and patience. It was a good ten minutes and several stops of the bus before I finally brought the semi-opened bar to my lips for a first taste of the forbidden fruit that lay within.

Having endured the entire display from the start, the woman next to me had reached the end of whatever patience she might have had. Her temper burst like an infected boil from her very centre and she grabbed the Kit-Kat from me and flung it to the floor of the bus.

The extra calories it must have picked up in dirt quotients on its way down already made it more than I wanted to sample, but it would have been impossible to retrieve because then she stamped it into the grooves of the London Transport floor slatting with the split toe of her grimy street-worn boot. She began to spit at me and to shout insults that I could only half make out in the thickness of her tone and anger.

'Bitch!' she yelled. 'Dirty skinny bitch. You're ugly. You ugly, dirty, scummy bitch. You pig!'

Everyone in the bus was watching except for the driver who was safely tucked up in his cab at the front. Everyone was watching and waiting for my response to the woman. I couldn't say anything. I didn't feel angry. I didn't even really feel embarrassed. I just felt a little sick and found-out. I figured the woman must have been an agent sent by God or some other higher power to spread the truth about my horrid ugliness. Perhaps she had secret access to my diaries and knew the truth about me that way. For whatever reason, to me, her outburst seemed completely justified. I couldn't even say I wished it hadn't happened. I was relieved in a way that she had taken the Kit-Kat from me, because if I still had that in my hand or had eaten any more of it than the microscopic crumb I had already swallowed I probably would have needed to throw up right there and then. And if not throw up then suffer the agony of having gained several imaginary pounds.

Outside it had started to rain. The next stop wasn't mine but I got off anyway. I walked the rest of the way to Knightsbridge, which was probably another five miles from where we were. I got in to work around eleven. I was two hours and fifteen minutes late and soaking wet. My P45 was already waiting for me in Personnel.

I stole a silver spoon on the way out and then I went to Hyde Park and lay down on the wet grass for a good while. A woman with a shiny trenchcoat walked by with a little girl carrying a pink umbrella. The woman gave the girl a few coins to drop onto the ground where I was lying. I wanted to shout after her that I was only on my coffee-break from Harrods, but that would have been a lie because they had given me the sack already.

The rain stopped eventually and the sun even poked out a few times from behind the clouds. A few office workers turned up around lunchtime and I watched them eat their sandwiches and eavesdropped on some of their conversations which were mostly about other people they worked with. I walked around a bit and strolled up and down Park Lane a few times, remembering the games of Monopoly I used to play with Cynthia.

Cynthia always won at Monopoly but that was only because she also nearly always cheated. It was not the kind of cheat you could throw her out of the game for, but the annoying kind of cheat that got right under your skin and made you want to strangle her. Cynthia hid her money, the five hundreds mostly, from very early on in the game. She'd put the carefully hoarded pink notes under the board or sit on them so it was impossible to know she had them and then anyone playing would figure that she must be nearly broke. That always made me feel sorry for her and I would deliberately try to land on her property or sell her things of mine if she needed them, just so she felt a little boost and would want to stay in the game. Then, just when things were getting tough for everyone else, Cynthia would pull out her stash and say, 'Oh gosh, I didn't realize I had this. Wow, I think I'll buy some hotels please . . . on Park Lane.' I always wanted to kill her then.

On the way home I rode the bus standing not sitting. I figured it's best not to take chances. I thought of a few slogans I might use for making some badges if I ever got round to it. 'Stand, Don't Sit – It Saves Meeting People', 'Warning – I am a Tramp Underneath my Clothes' and then one that I was sure I'd seen somewhere already . . . 'Life's a Bitch and Then You Die'.

14

Practically before all else, they asked me about love. Did I love, was I loved, could I love? We all agreed it's not an easy concept to talk about. Particularly in the early stages of knowing someone. This was only our second Show and Tell session, the first being yesterday and almost purely an introduction. Background, names, that sort of thing. There are eighty students taking part. Eighty students, two professors, a couple of technicians (for setting up the OHP, moving tables and chairs, switching on slide projectors and so on) and me. Otherwise we are completely alone. The students have to take their own notes and write up their own observations. Then the whole thing will be collated into a report. I will be given a bound copy for posterity.

While the students get on with their paperwork, I stay in this room. It's the kind of room you might expect to have been designed by a prison architect. There are no windows apart from a small one for ventilation above the hand basin. There are no jutting walls or alcoves. Everything is completely plain and flat but that suits me at this particular moment in time. I am trying to lead a life with as few complications as possible. Which brings us back to love.

After a brief presentation given by one of the professors, the floor was given over to the students. One of them, a short stocky bloke with a freckly face, raised his hand and asked if he could address a question directly to me. The other professor, who hadn't spoken yet, said we had to start somewhere.

The student, whose name turned out to be John, stood up. 'Have you ever loved someone?' he asked, looking directly at me.

I was a bit thrown as you can imagine. I thought they might start by asking me about my eating habits. How often did I starve, how often did I binge, that sort of thing. Maybe even more practical things like, what order is the best to eat things in to make sure it all comes back up in the end. I didn't expect things to get quite so esoteric so quickly but I didn't want to leave him floundering so I thought I'd better have a go at answering John's question.

I could see the two professors looking a bit worried. I suppose it's only natural to want to protect the subject in an investigation. If the subject cracks the whole experiment is shot. Professor Cherry, the small round one with stiff hair, reminded the students that questions to me should be of a practical or physiological nature, and not an emotional one. In other words, the 'hows' and 'whats' of my condition could be discussed openly but the 'whys' needed more careful, more discreet and discerning handling. I was there to provide the nuts and bolts of the plot, a kind of 'Confessions of an Anorexic'. The more complicated bits, underlying motivation, deep-seated reasons, causes, unconscious processes, etc. were more up for grabs and certainly not expected to be spelled out by me. In fact, to be honest, I think Drs Cherry (the round) and Wilhelm (the tall) believe that the anorexic themselves can't possibly be aware of *why* they do what they do or they wouldn't be doing it. Fair enough, I suppose.

'Well, I'm not a virgin if that's the kind of love you're talking about,' I told John, bringing the question quite nicely, I thought, on to a practical basis.

He said that he had been thinking of that kind of love but also about it in other forms. After that I was stuck. Another student, with a bright green cardigan and a ponytail, whose name-badge said Amanda, told John that he should be more specific especially when using such a general and non-specific concept. They argued for a while about whether it was possible to arrive at a single and non-emotional definition of the word 'love' and while they argued I kept getting snatches in my head of something my father had once declared on the subject and was trying hard to remember exactly what it was he had said. Something to do with being away from someone, and still caring.

When they'd stopped bickering long enough for me to get in there, I asked John if he might be thinking of a kind of love that could be defined as a spiritual togetherness which can be sustained through physical separation. He looked like he needed to go and lie down and think about that one, but I could have saved him the trouble I suppose by simply answering his initial question, 'No John, I don't think I've ever experienced anything quite like that.'

By this time the general discussion had moved on to libidinal states and the question of whether certain levels of starvation may dampen or heighten these drives and whether or not bingeing can be seen as a substitute for the sexual act itself. Dr Wilhelm said that it was too early in the life of the Project and that not enough trust had yet been built up between all those participating for anything more than a cursory look at this topic for the moment. I guess that means that he plans to return to it later. A mousy-looking type asked meekly from the corner how I felt about being a woman, but Dr Wilhelm came down on her like a ton of bricks before I could even acknowledge the question. Feelings are not to be discussed unless, of course, they are of a straightforward physical nature like the question of temperature which incidentally has improved some since yesterday. After I'd shivered through the entire morning they finally agreed to let me put on a few more layers and to shut the windows around where I was sitting.

After the break, one student with large round red-rimmed glasses, who looked more like an advertising executive than a trainee doctor, asked me whether I'd ever shoplifted. She came right up close to me and I thought she was going to pull out a little Instamatic.

When I said yes, this started a discussion from the floor about the links between deprivation, starvation and depravity. Some of them seemed genuinely shocked at my admitting such criminal behaviour. I just let them get on with it. I'll read the reports when they're finished.

The truth is, the main things I have taken from shops, apart from the silver spoon from Harrods, are items of clothes and food that I would never have chosen to buy in a million years. I once stole twelve scotch eggs and a packet of pork pies from a crowded supermarket, but as I have never seen anyone at the check-out with either of these two items I have to conclude that I was the first person to shift their scotch egg and pork pie stock, albeit without paying, for a good long time.

I have also taken clothes from small boutiques and larger department stores but I always choose something that looks as though it's bound to end up in the bargain bin or be unsold and given away to charity like the Eccles cakes. I take whatever it is into the changing room with a few other items and stick it on underneath my own clothes. I'm so skinny that no one ever notices if I'm wearing an extra layer or two but sometimes, if they're being strict with those plastic discs that tell how many things you went in with, I hand the shop assistant back the clothes I was originally wearing and walk out with the stolen ones that still have the price tag on. When you're handing something back and the shop assistant is saying, 'Were any of these OK?' and you're answering, 'Not really, they all make me look too fat', and she's shaking her head sympathetically, working out how to tell you that not even wearing a large rubber ring could make you look fat you are such a wisp of a thing, then no one notices much what you hand back and what you go away with. The last thing I stole like that was a pink and orange nylon blouse with a pocket shaped like a pineapple. I have to admit that this particular garment was so garish that I needed to wear it inside out so as not to bring attention to myself, but that's how it's done mostly.

The girl with the glasses, however, didn't want to know how I shoplifted – she wanted to know why. And as I've said before, they're not supposed to ask me that. They have to draw their own conclusions with the evidence provided, otherwise it wouldn't be Science.

Some of them don't even know my name. They call me the patient or the subject or 'Miss A'. You can't blame them, though. There will be a Miss B or a Miss C in another few weeks, after my part's over, being moved into the lecture hall and subjected to the same third degree. I know you have to be strict with controls and all that, but I hope they throw a party at the end of it all so we can all get to know each other a bit more personably. Anyway, I shouldn't complain. I am being paid a bit, and my accommodation is free. It's not for long and it's better than selling handbags in Harrods. In fact I didn't actually ever get to sell a handbag because they moved me down to packing after my first day on the shop floor. Some well-fed Turkish woman, who was probably the wife of a sultan judging by the huge entourage she had in tow, decided to complain to the management about my skeleton-like appearance. She said she found it offensive and that the sight of me was going to give her children nightmares. The 'customer is always right policy' was enforced on this occasion and I was moved down a floor to the basement to work in packing.

The one with the red-rimmed glasses is certainly persistent. She caught up with me after the Show and Tell session, when I was on my way to see Mr Eccles. She was panting a bit and she had her notepad out with pen poised.

'Why do you think you have the compulsion to steal?' she asked me breathlessly, looking around her to make sure she wasn't being watched. 'Is it connected for you with being hungry?'

This was outside my agreed contact time with the students or the Project and besides she wasn't supposed to be asking me questions of this nature, but I didn't really see the harm in telling her what I thought.

'No,' I said, 'it's not exactly to do with being hungry. It's about getting away with something. Getting something for nothing.'

'Is that what you think you are?' she asked me. 'Nothing?'

Her approach was nothing if not direct and I wasn't sure what her chances were of succeeding in general practice with that kind of boldness, but she certainly had a way of getting to someone. I didn't mean to but when she asked me that, I cried. Something in me just opened and started to leak out. You see, I'd never really thought of it that way before – something for nothing and me being the nothing – but she was right, that's exactly how it was. Something for nothing and the something always turned out to be nothing anyway. If it was food I was stealing then I would binge it and bin it in one way or another and if it was clothes I'd stick them in the bottom of my drawer or the back of my wardrobe and never look at them again.

I nodded and looked up at her with wet eyes, expecting to see compassion come flooding out from those red frames. I thought she might even wrap her strong student-doctory arms around my pathetic and bony shoulders and hold me until the crying stopped, but her head was bent over her notepad and she was scribbling away with the kind of determination and intent that not even compassion can break through. It made me feel a bit better anyhow to think that at least I had provided her with something.

15

Today I am a thin line walking in space. My hope is that by the end of the day either I will get smaller or the universe will have expanded enough to render me undetectable.

Cynthia got married yesterday. I didn't go because Mike, the man she married, has lots of family and Cynthia was worried about there not being enough room. I don't take up much but I'm not entirely invisible. Not yet. Besides, I was having my last session with Mr Eccles before he disappeared off on his summer holiday. It would have been a hard choice to make between the two.

My part in the project has finished and I have had to give the room back. It's funny to think of a shrink on holiday. I wonder if he possesses a pair of swimming trunks.

I'm writing a letter to my father. Or rather to my mother's solicitors to pass on to my father's solicitors, as no one seems to have an exact address for Leon. There is not a lot else to do and, besides, I have a message I need to pass on to him. Yesterday, after leaving Mr Eccles, I went back to the flat to see if the key still fitted. Everyone was out, at Cynthia's wedding I presume. The key did fit, that was one thing, so I went in and made myself a cup of hot water as you do and while I was sitting there sipping away the telephone rang. I didn't think it was going to be for me but I figured that whoever was ringing might appreciate a message being taken.

It was someone who was looking for Leon. That's strange, I told myself. Only a day ago Mr Eccles had brought the subject back up.

'When is the last time you have seen your father?' he asked me.

I have to admit, I'm a bit hung up on grammar at the moment. I don't know why, exactly. I think I'm trying hard to keep things in their proper perspective. I was momentarily confused by his question. When *is* the last time or when *was* the last time? Have seen or saw? It was hard to work out whether Mr Eccles had just had a long day and was muddling up his tenses or whether this was some involved and clever tactic to bring everything from the past back into the imperfect present. I wanted to say that the last time was when we were in that bathroom together and I was just a little kid and he was being reborn, but there is a time which feels more recent than that.

It took me ages to find the telephone. They've moved everything since I was here last. The caller spoke before I had a chance to say hello.

'This is . . . Leon?'

The mention of my father's name worked like electricity through my body. Something fizzed and my head felt light and my fingers jelly-like. It was like the feeling you get when you stand too near to the edge of a cliff or a high balcony. The handset felt heavy in my hand. I was afraid that I might drop it. My voice when I finally replied was groggy and thick.

'I'm sorry . . .'

I always feel terribly sad when someone rings up out of the blue and straightaway says someone else's name like they expect it to be you. And when you have to tell them that you're not that person or, even worse, that you don't even know who or where that person is, you feel like you're stranded there with that stranger on the telephone and neither of you will ever find the person you are looking for, and that you will never again be able to answer someone's call with a simple, Yes, it's me.

'Leon, please. Leon Weitz. He is at home?'

The person ringing was called Sal. Sal Greenburg. It must have been short for Salman or Salamander. In any case he was an old man, a dying man, a desperate man who said he met my father on the boat coming over. I conjured an image of Jewish immigrants and wide-eyed Eastern European children staring through ship portholes as the sight of new war-free land approached them, but in fact what Mr Greenburg was referring to was my father's trip to England seven years ago. Mr Greenburg was now alone and in hospital. He was calling up old friends.

'He's . . . I don't know where he is.'

I felt wary at first of giving anything away although there was really nothing I could have told. His voice was crackly, with the frail brittle quality of old dry leaves. I was afraid that one of us might break. 'I'm sorry. I haven't seen him for quite some time.'

'You are . . .'

'. . . his daughter.'

'His daughter? Really? Leon's daughter?'

'Yes.' I was trying to read the surprise in his voice and began to doubt myself that I could really be Leon's daughter or anyone else's for that matter.

'His daughter . . . so,' the voice laughed weakly. 'So, he has a family. So . . .'

'I haven't seen him for quite some time,' I said again. I wondered, as Leon's daughter, how to justify the years of non-communication between us. 'I'm sorry.'

'It's a pity,' said the man. 'It's a great pity. I like your father very much. He is a good man. A wonderful man. I would have liked . . .' His voice trailed off wispily in fragments, like the last snowflakes of winter dissolving into thin blue air.

For a few moments there was the kind of stillness you get when someone famous has died and they fly the flags at half-mast and no one is allowed to speak for a whole sixty seconds. Mr Greenburg obviously felt it too.

'He's not . . . is he? Is he . . . is your father . . . all right?'

Maybe because I had such a fragile hold on life myself or because we shared in the same confounding search for a man we had both once loved, but at that point I felt this man's reaching and desperation becoming my own. I lied in an attempt to reassure and to breathe some longevity into the fading voice which already seemed so doomed.

'No, no, he's fine. My father is very well. He's been away, that's all. I'll pass him on a message if you'd just like to tell me where he can reach you.'

'Yes, yes,' said the man, reaching for the life-line that I offered him. 'Yes, that would be good. It would be so good to hear from him, from Leon. I would so like to see him once more, to speak to him. I am so pleased to hear that he is well.' The voice spluttered weakly. 'And that he has a daughter.'

I had to work things through in my mind quickly. The hope of my reaching Leon before this man took his dying breath was practically nil. I would have to go as his proxy. I needed more information. It was good to have a mission.

'So, Mr Greenburg, where can my father get hold of you?'

'Sal, Sal. Call me Sal. You can tell him (cough) that Sal Greenburg called. He will remember. It was he who spoke the first words to me when I was such a stranger and he, maybe not so much. (excessive coughing) He knows much, your father. It's true, eh? He is a wise man with many gifts to offer. He is . . .'

Old Sal broke off then to go into a paroxysm of wheezes, coughs and spluttering. Long passages were not good for Sal. I felt the need to help him out.

'Yes, yes, Mr Greenburg. My father is a very good and wise man who knows much. I will certainly tell him that you called and that he can find you in . . .'

Now all I needed was the location from him. C'mon Sal, this is your cue.

'Orchid Ward . . .'

Bingo.

'. . . like the flower. I'm in the (cough) in the (cough) . . .'

OK Sal, take it easy, I got that first bit.

'Orchid?'

'Yes, yes, at St Leonard's.'

I scribbled it down on a piece of paper.

'I'd (cough) I'd be very grateful, (cough) if it's not too much trouble (cough) if you, if he —'

Sentence unfinished due to severe coughing seizure. I waited till it was quiet enough for me to speak.

'That's fine, Mr Greenburg. Sal. I'll tell him. Orchid, like the flower. I won't forget.'

I had to find him for Leon's sake. To say goodbye properly. The sand was running out. Orchids. They are the huge open-mouthed flowers, aren't they? Like babies crying. Shouting out in bright terrible colours. Oranges, reds, purples. Purple, the colour of mountains. The colour of bravery. Hope. The colour of death.

16

'Perhaps he is the missing banister. Your father, Leon. Perhaps he is the other rail you wish to hold on to but can't.'

Yes, yes, I believe you might be right, Mr Eccles. I really think the analysis might have worked on this one. Leon *is* my missing banister. That is what I needed to tell him in my letter. That is what I needed to let him know. Perhaps that would explain why I even tried to become him for a while. Otherwise, you see, I might just have slipped and never stopped falling. Like Alice down the rabbit hole. Only she found Wonderland at the end of it all.

I dressed in black. It seemed appropriate and besides most of my clothes were black. I liked the neutrality, it made me feel less conspicuous, less likely to be questioned, or accused. A mere speck on the landscape, a moving dot, a floating orb with no colour and no design.

It was the first day of pure unclouded sunshine there had been that entire summer. I was so used to a feeling of permanent cold that it was surprising to feel warm, almost too warm, on this occasion. I sat upstairs on the bus. From this height I could see everything. The sounds, sights and smells of a city always seem to waft upwards and it becomes possible to observe and absorb things with a kind of totality from a position which is above rather than below. That is why people who have been to the top of the Empire State Building say they have seen all of New York, whilst those who have just ridden on the subways still regard it as a vast, confusing jungle.

There were crowds in the West End. Mostly shoppers, bustling with carrier bags and large holdalls. Traffic was moving slowly and the bus had come to a virtual standstill. We were surrounded on all sides by black taxi cabs inside of which agitated passengers looked at their watches and mumbled abuse at the already harassed drivers. I moved to the front of the bus and opened the window at the side, which did little to mitigate the closeness or the heat but opened up the airwaves to sounds below which had been previously muffled. Amidst the general background of hooting cars and angry voices, the cutting jangle of tambourines and little bells like Santa's sleigh filled the top portion of the bus. Not a soul sat with me in that slow-moving gallery. It seemed so odd that the world outside could feel so busy and crowded while I was surrounded by so much empty space and for a brief moment I felt as if I might be more than just a shadow in a dark corner. I wondered if it were possible for the colour black to merge imperceptibly with the transparency and light that surrounded it.

The tinkly bells and tambourines turned out to be Hare Krishna devotees dancing in cotton loincloths and flimsy cheesecloth gowns. As they whirled and swayed to their self-made cacophony, I sucked on a sugar-free mint and thought of Sal Greenburg dying in the middle of it all.

None of the thousands of people on the streets below could possibly have known about my mission to take Leon's place, to complete this circle of lives meeting then parting and meeting once again, and yet I felt sure that I was being carried along by a kind of procession. An entire city had turned out to help me send Sal Greenburg on his way with a sense of roundness and completion.

When I'm in crowded places I sometimes get the feeling that if I look hard enough into the hordes of people around me I will see my father standing there looking for me with the same intensity. But I know, also, of course, that even if he was standing

there and looking for me at that moment he would have missed
me. I had become too thin. A line splitting air, that was all. If I
turned sideways he would not even have noticed a gap in the
horizon.

> *Follow the fold and stray no more*
> *stray no more*
> *stray no more*
> *Follow the fold and stray no more*
> *Follow, follow the fold*

Another sound pierced through the others. It was the brassy
music of seaside proms, upbeat and melancholy all at the same
time. Trumpets chorused with trombones and there was the insistent hooting of one lone tuba. I sat in my place above with the
angels and watched. It was the Salvation Army, Sally Army.
Sal's Army. Of course. He had sent them. It was his sign, his
message, calling me forward, onwards. 'I'm coming Sal,' I whispered, as the bus finally found an opening and moved forward
leaving the troops and the tuba behind. Don't worry. Hang on
just a little longer. I'm coming. I'm coming.

The hospital was a large old building separated from the rest
of London by a double set of wrought-iron gates. Orchid Ward
was on the third floor but before I made the journey up there I
stopped for contemplation in the hospital chapel. It was no more
than a tiny crypt with a little alcove for lighting candles. There
was a metal box that looked as though it might once have stored
syringes, with a slit cut where donations for the candles could be
put in. I put in whatever spare change I had left in my pockets
and took three. I lit the first one for the dying man upstairs and
prayed.

> *Our Father who art not here . . .*
> *forgive us our trespasses . . . forgive me for trespassing,*
> *forgive me, forgive me Sal Greenburg*
> *forgive me, Father*

I lit the other two for my grandmother and Tommy. It was tempting to stay and watch to see which one went out first but duty was calling me so I carried on up the next two flights to Orchid Ward which turned out to be a long row of beds partitioned off by folding screens, converging on a rather tiny little central desk behind which there was nobody sitting. I would have to pick Sal Greenburg out for myself.

'Francine?'

A voice that must have travelled light years to get here called out to me from behind. I cannot be recognized, I thought. Not in black. Not as carefully inconspicuous as I have become, have so carefully made myself. Maybe if I just slip sideways out of my casing now.

'Francine, is that you?'

The voice sped up. Rocket ships have never travelled so fast. I turned around. It was Leon.

'Dad . . . I . . . you're here.'

'Yeah. Hey, Francine . . .'

This man, this big man whose shadow I had become, leant forward and tried to hold me. I was reminded of our bathroom, with its cracked tiles and mirror that needed washing. I was reminded of the flat and home and the place where I could be alone and apart and away from all this sickness and noise. I hunched my shoulders and turned to one side, needing desperately to dodge his hug but trying to make it look as though I was suddenly having to huddle for warmth. The truth is, a shiver like a ghost had gone right through me the moment I realized it was him.

'He phoned me, your friend. I was going to . . . anyway. You're here now. That's great.'

I turned and ran, escaping the grasp of his hands and the urgency of his voice.

'Francine, wait! We could go for a coffee. I'd like to . . . Francine! Francine!'

The third time he said my name he sounded angry. That was the last thing I heard before I made it through the double doors at the end. But it didn't matter anymore. He was there now so I didn't need to be. I wanted to shout loudly out of the hospital windows into the streets of London below. I wanted to jump up and down in slow motion and wave my fists in the air like they do in the Olympics when they have won a gold medal. I wanted to say to the world that couldn't see me that I had achieved both my missions today. My short-term one of bringing my father to the man who needed him and my eternal one of escape. He wouldn't have been able to hold me anyway. Even if he had tried. I was only a wisp. There was nothing to hold on to. He was better off going to see Sal Greenburg. He was at least something concrete. Someone he could touch and be touched by. I would go back and savour the last hours of privacy I had in the empty flat and try to work out how to make a thin line disappear down to absolutely nothing.

17

What about your mother, they said. It was our last Show and Tell session and just about every boundary was being contravened. My mother, I asked. What about her? Who is she, they asked. She's Alma, I said. She's my Alma Mater. Which of course I knew, because she had told me so herself, refers to a place of past learning and is also Latin for Bounteous Mother.

The thing is, it was true. Alma hadn't had a look in, really, to any of these Show and Tell sessions so far. Not one. But I thought that must be something to do with my inability to give or receive or even recognize bounty these days, however it's dressed.

'The anorexic part seeks to be like the father while the bulimic side wants to possess and then get rid of everything to do with the mother.' That piece of wisdom came from the one with the red-rimmed specs who I have since found out is called Sally. Sally is full of little gems like that.

'Do you want to devour your mother? Do you want to disempower your mother? Do you want to compete, do you wish to possess, do you want to defeat, cause upset and distress, would you, if you could, discard all that is good and annihilate the one that you came from?'

Howard, who I think really wants to be a DJ rather than a doctor, made that up as a kind of rap. There's a few of them, the students that is, who have this theory that it's all to do with the

Mother. That a person only starves or stuffs themselves to either get back at or replace the missing maternal link.

I have to admit that I've never really thought about Alma as a link, missing or otherwise. Links join things together. One part to another part. Links need other links to make a chain. Links are interdependent pieces of equipment which are virtually nothing when they're on their own. This was not the case with Alma. To Alma, the only value in being dependent is that it might be a necessary period that precedes independence. A 'link' in Alma's book is a dangerous concept. Alma links herself to no one and wants nobody linked to her. At least, that's how it seemed to me most of the time growing up with Alma.

'Maybe your denial of food to yourself is a way of rejecting your mother? Perhaps you wish to reject anything she stands for or supplies you with?' Professors Wilhelm and Cherry didn't care anymore. The students could ask me just about anything they liked. My part in the study was virtually over. Ten more minutes, then the wine and cheese farewell do and the initiation of a new subject. That's how it is with modern science. Easy come, easy go.

She tried to give me pills once, I rejected those. It was when we were still in Seattle. Long before Leon left for London, but maybe as far as Alma was concerned he was already gone. Melanie was only a baby – I don't even think she could walk. She gathered us all together, Melanie, Cynthia and I and she asked us if we wanted to have some candy with her. Now that was pretty strange for a start because Alma hates candy on the whole. I mean she sometimes let us have some but she almost never, ever ate any herself. Except for something called a New Orleans praline which is a kind of sticky toffee with nuts in it. The 'candy' she was wanting us to try was actually an assortment of brightly coloured capsules and pills she'd collected together from her current supply, various past prescription bottles buried away in the back of our medicine cabinet and God knows where else. It was a pick and mix that would have sent all of us to the top of Sugar Candy Mountain before we could say Tootsie Roll if we'd actually agreed to take them. Mom was pretty upset at the time. I never really asked her what it was about exactly, but she had been crying, you could see that, and she had a kind of vague faraway look in her eye that made me think she'd probably tried a bit of the assortment herself already before calling us all together. Leon wasn't there; I guess he may have been away or at the lab or in his study where he usually was.

'That's medicine, Mom,' I told her, stating the obvious, but at that point I thought she genuinely might not know.

'I know, honey,' she said. 'It will make all of us better.'

Cynthia licked one but luckily it was one of the capsules with an outer casing that tastes like glue and she spat it out again. Mom offered us some lemonade to wash it all down with, but I told her that I preferred not to take medicine of any kind until I saw whether I could get better all by myself. I said if she had any real candy I'd be glad to help her eat it. She kind of came to her senses then and started crying, a lot. She threw all the pills away and said she was sorry over and over again. The thing was, we never really talked about that again, then or since. Cynthia's forgotten all about it and thinks I made it up as a way of explaining why I'm always so suspicious about any of the food other people try to get me to eat.

That was the last time and maybe the only time Alma ever suggested we do something together, entirely, as a family. Without Leon, of course. But he was the link she would have considered eternally broken, or never really ever there at all.

'Do you ever want to be a mother yourself?'

Rose, who I'd hardly heard speak two words since the project began, decided to come right out and ask me this just seconds before Dr Cherry pulled the cord on the whole thing. I'd always kind of suspected that Rose might be anorexic herself, she was so tiny and thin and scared-looking. She could, of course, have just been scared but she had those kind of eyes I recognized, like dark alleyways that warn you not to go in too deeply or you might never come out.

Before I could answer, Dr Cherry spoke.

'I'm afraid that's all we've got time for. So I'd just like to say thank you to Miss Weitz on behalf of all the students, Dr Wilhelm and myself and wish her well in whatever course she chooses for herself.'

I wonder if Rose ever had any children.

18

January 12, 1977

Dear Dad,

*Well, it's January and the start of a new year which always gets
me thinking about change. There is lots I want to do differently
and lots I wish I never did at all. But there is also some stuff
that I have wanted to do for a long time but just haven't got
round to. Writing to you is one of the things that falls into the
last category. I think about you a lot. An awful lot actually.
Too much, probably, than is good for me. When I'm thinking, I
kind of hope you might be thinking about me sometimes too. But
it doesn't really matter, either way. I know you must be busy
doing whatever you're doing.*

*I don't know where you are, I mean literally, I don't have an
address or anything. I guess you might have thought it was easier
not to lay tracks, make a clean break, that sort of thing.
Anyway, that's why I'm having to send this letter via Mom's
solicitor so I'm sorry that it is coming through such scary and
official means.*

*I'm eighteen years old now. I know, hard to believe, isn't it? I
wish I felt as grown up. I'm at university which feels pretty
good. I'm studying English together with Psychology so I'm on
the other side now though I've had my fair share of being the
subject. It's kind of helped me to think about things in new ways*

111

and I even went to see a shrink myself as part of the build-up. Actually quite a lot has happened since I last saw you. Oh, by the way, I'm not counting that brush we had the year before last. I was kind of freaked seeing you there. I mean I'm glad you got there alright and how was your friend? Sal? Did he get off OK?

What I mean is quite a lot has happened over the years. I've been pretty sick. I guess you could tell that when you saw me there at the hospital. Not sick so I've been lying in bed doing nothing, but sick so I haven't really been living life like I wanted to. I've had anorexia which means I've been starving myself but I also tried out this thing called bulimia which means I eat a lot and then puke it up everywhere. Not a pretty sight and both states amount to the same thing. I've been pretty wasted. Anyway, like I said, it's a new year and I'm at university and I'm trying hard to change all that. It's not easy and I'm having to really work at ways of keeping my mind off old habits.

It feels weird not knowing where you are or how you are although I guess you're real well because I can't imagine you not being. I'm not really sure what I want to say in this letter because it's not really like having a conversation, is it? I mean, I just get to talk and you have to listen (or throw the letter away and not read it, I guess) and I don't know what you're thinking about any of it.

Anyway, I'll just start. I think I probably need to see you again. Nothing heavy or anything like that but I have this kind of gap in my left side if that makes sense. I feel we kind of left things unfinished and I'm not sure if you blame me for that. It's like a surgeon had cut part of me away in an operation and forgotten to put it back. Does that make sense? I know that if you'd wanted to see me, or any of us, you could have done it so I guess that means that you probably don't.

It's strange to think that it's because of you that we came here in the first place. I feel pretty English now which is a kind of scary thing to say. Not that I don't like English people or anything like that but it makes me feel like I haven't got a beginning or a starting point. As Alex Haley might say, I'm searching for my 'roots'. Grandma doesn't write to me anymore. I guess she feels that you're her son and she doesn't want to split up her loyalties now that we're split up as a family. I'd like to know how she is and stuff so if you are in touch, maybe you could tell me.

Anyway, I'm happy to meet wherever or whenever you say. I could come to where you are if you want. I don't have a very big room at University and I don't really have anywhere else I could invite you so maybe it's better if we got together on neutral ground. God, I'm making it sound like I'm planning on having some kind of huge confrontation. I don't want it to be that, honestly. I just need to put my side back in place. I just need to find some way of starting to feel whole again.

I don't mean to put the burden of responsibility on you. I'm the one who got myself sick and I've got to get myself better, I know. I think it's too crazy to prattle on any more than I already have. I'm not even going to go back and read this letter through or I probably would never send it.

My address is at the bottom of the page. There isn't really a phone number as I'm in University accommodation so just write and let me know how I can contact you. That's if you want to. Oh, I mean I hope you do. Anyway. That's all for now, so I'll see you. I hope. I love you. I think. I miss you. I know.

Francine.

Waiting for a reply to a letter is nearly as bad as waiting for Santa Claus to come at Christmas time. First of all you don't know if he will come and secondly you don't know if you'll like what you get if he does. I sent my letter to my father at the end of January via Watkins & Peters of Camden Town. I figured there might be some delay what with the solicitors forwarding it on to another address, possibly not even in this country. (Mom suspected that Dad wasn't on this side of the ocean anymore as all the correspondence she had tried to have through her solicitors with his recently had taken an awfully long time, and they seemed to be in cahoots with an American firm anyway.)

By the end of April I was still waiting with no word whatsoever. I thought about ringing Watkins & Peters to see if they'd received the letter in the first place and to try to get some kind of idea of when they might have sent it on, but I couldn't quite bring myself to make the phone call.

At first, I let a lot of my coursework slip. Since January I'd gone into a kind of 'on-hold' mode of operating. I didn't start anything new, nor did I finish anything I had already started. In April, however, when the crocuses came up and they shipped the swans into the moat that surrounded the refectory to impress any prospective students looking around the university, I got sort of swept up into the kind of spring fever that makes you want to put things into action. I decided to go all out and put a major part of my energy into my studies. I was doing a class on science fiction at the time and we were supposed to explore, through a kind of narrative, the idea of utopia.

With all my waiting and not-knowing I thought that my utopia would be a world where there were no mysteries. A mind that knew everything, all the answers, so there would be no mistakes. I set about constructing that world inside the walls of a short story. It started with a girl, Diana, who was waiting for a letter which would tell all her exam results. The letter was late and Diana couldn't do anything else except wait. Her entire life was on hold. Everything stood still, in wait for this most important bit of information. The information that would determine her future, so Diana thought. Well, there is a certain point for everyone, a breaking point, where the waiting becomes too much. It becomes so unbearable that one has to find some way of dispersing some of that knife-point anxiety. Some way of releasing oneself from the tenterhooks . . . the hooks of Tenter.

At this point in the story I decided to invent another character. A huge monster-god called Tenter who had terrible claws, hooks, for fingers and hands. This monster-god would get people in his grip so that they thought they would die from mental suspense or anguish. No one had ever found a way to release themselves from his hold. No one, that is, until Diana.

Diana has a most cunning plan. She decides to make use of the mental imprisonment she is experiencing, rather than suffering at the hands of it. She decides to delve deep inside her mental regions and start, from the very beginning, to go through everything she knows, stopping only when she comes to something she does not know and then not going any further until she knows that too. Her aim, of course, is to outwit the monster, Tenter, by making everything in the world knowable so that no one, ever again, will be at his mercy. She has to go right back in her mind to start this process. Right back to when she was first born. Even before. Right back to the moment she was first conceived. The very moment the sperm first reached the egg that was going to become her. She follows the process through in her mind, every detail, making absolutely sure she knows at every point what happens next. How it happens. She goes on that way until she is born and leaves her mother's body. Then she opens her eyes as a newborn child might and begins to try to know everything that is on the outside of her as well as what is on the inside. Inside Tenter's prison she searches for tiny details, a fly on the wall. She examines its wings, its legs, the way its two antennae move like a blind man's white stick searching for obstacles and boundaries to its path. She looks at the walls, their colour, their texture, the places where the paint peels. Places that expose another layer, another colour underneath. She begins to know the history of the room through its layers. Cracks, chips in the plaster, dirt, dust, the way dust clings to itself and becomes like a fuzzy blanket over smooth surfaces. The way a spider spins and re-spins its web and then lies in patient wait for its victims. The way it wraps the fly so slowly, tenderly and meticulously before devouring the mummified corpse in one sitting.

Diana is determined to know everything. Tenter is doomed. No aspect of her own life or the life that goes on outside will go unfathomed. It is a long task. A life-long task, perhaps even longer, and it makes any other task seem pointless. Who cares now, anyway, what Diana's exam results are going to be? What does it matter anyway? Diana will one day know everything there is to know. She will not be constrained by the grades on an examination paper and the limits imposed in a world governed by a value system constructed of imbalance, injustice and unrealistic expectations.

I got good marks for that paper. My tutor, who was a Marxist, liked it because he said it was really a treatise on dialectical materialism. I hadn't intended for it to be anything more than a way of dealing with the waiting time for myself but that is the way with writing – it is not always read the way it is written.

Writing about Diana helped time to pass more quickly and, before I knew it, it was the first day of June and another summer was looming.

I got my mail through a pigeon-hole in the student union building. My usual routine was to check it on the way out to the refectory, which I only ate in on Thursdays when they did vegetable curry.

On this first day of June I'd run out of Ryvita and there was no one around to borrow any from. I knew they did it in individual packets in the refectory so I decided to go, and I popped in to check my mail situation on the way. The semester was coming to an end and most internal mail had stopped coming. There were no more lecture lists till the autumn term and the University newsletter SPARK had already printed its last issue before the summer break. The pigeon-holes are spread across the entirety of one wall, split up into the letters of the alphabet and further subdivisions beyond that. Like the set of encyclopædias we had in Seattle that were too heavy to ever get shipped over. The first hole was Aa–Ack (Aardvark to Ackerman presumably) and it went on like that till it got down to Zu–Zy (Zummer to Zymmer? I guess they figured no one had a name like Zzaszmann or just plain Zzzzzz or, if they did, their post would find them anyway.) My correspondence could be retrieved from the hole in the section marked We–Wo (Weekes to Wolstenholme or something like that).

There was nothing else in there so it was easy to spot the long parchment-yellow air-mail envelope with my name and an

American stamp and postmark on it. For some reason I decided when I saw it that I had waited five months so I could wait a little longer, and I went to get my Ryvita first before opening it.

Back in my room I sat on the edge of the bed and opened the letter with the back of a teaspoon. I wanted to do it like they did in the movies. Whenever there is something important in an envelope, they never rip it open like you want them to but they use a pearl-handled knife or a letter opener to slowly cut away the top of the seal while suspenseful music plays in the background.

There were a few pages inside, I could tell that. He'd used onion-skin to write on so it hardly weighed anything. Four pages, it looked like, maybe three. I unfolded them and began to read.

Dear Francine,

Your letter reached me via the messengers you chose for me. I didn't open it for a few days thinking it was another court summons administered by your mother. She seems determined to keep me constantly under siege with her demands for more and more of my possessions. I suppose I have to thank her in a way, Francine, because through her grabbing attacks I have begun to see the evil in possessing anything at all.

I live in California as you can probably tell by the return address. I have been here long enough to know that it is a climate and people that will suit me for a long time. Perhaps for the rest of my life, who knows?

I have carried your letter around with me for several weeks now. It has felt somewhat like a ghost in my pocket. I do not wish to cast you alongside your attacking mother and sisters in the old life that haunts me and won't let me be at peace in my new surroundings. But that was a kind of fear of mine when I first received it.

Perhaps I should tell you a bit of what I have been doing. I, too, have been learning. In the University of Life which is perhaps not as constrained as the walls you find yourself in. You say you have found a shrink and I worry that you might be referring to a way in which your perspective is ever narrowing instead of widening. In California I feel as though I am on the Western Frontier. Pioneering ever more wide open spaces. It is perhaps the most exciting time I have had in my entire life.

I am in love with a man. He is a very beautiful person with great stores of wisdom. I want so much for you to meet him and understand what beauty there is to be found in a loving relationship. His name is Michael. I have showed him your letter, which I hope is all right, and he has recognized a sadness in its tone. He tells me I should see you. That it may be healing for both of us.

I cannot leave my present surroundings. I have found a home here and it feels too unsettling to journey from it. I can make myself available to you here, however, if you are able to travel in order to meet. My living space in Palo Alto is simple and I am unable to lavish you with expensive meals or plush surroundings. You can join me, however, in the enjoyment of my friends and my new life here and I'm sure that I can find a place for you to stay. As it happens, the woman-identified-woman who I share this house with and for whom I am a tenant, will be away for three weeks at the end of August. She will be climbing mountains in the Himalayas and I'm sure she will have no objection to your using her home for discovery while she is away doing the same.

I do not suppose I feel qualified to 'put your side back' as you put it. I am not sure if what you mean is that you wish to take a part of me away in order to complete something about yourself. I have already said that your mother is stripping me dry of my material possessions. I feel that my spiritual self is something that cannot be raided quite so easily. Nevertheless, I am happy to help you on your search to find whatever it is you feel you lack. There is an Instant Enlightenment course which will be running in the area for three days from August 29. If you wish me to reserve a place for you on this course I am happy to do so.

Let me know of your plans.

Felicitations,

Dad

19

In love with a man. I guess that meant my father was gay. I felt kind of pleased about that. There was enough of the term left to gain membership into a few of the societies and groups I had felt unable to approach previously. I thought having a gay father would score me a few points with some of the more radical organizations. I went along to an open meeting held by the Gay Society, with the title 'Are You a Gay in Straight Clothing?' First there was a speech given by the president of the society about how important it was that he had found the courage to come out during the second week of his first term at University. He was making the point that coming out had been the permission he needed to become absolutely who he was and to achieve absolutely what it was he wanted to achieve. After coming out, he had changed his subject apparently from Molecular Science to Humanities. He was likening being in the closet to wearing the wrong set of clothes. Becoming gay is just like changing your wardrobe, he said. It feels great and you look better too.

I raised my hand to speak in the meeting afterwards. 'I have a gay father,' I said. 'So I think I know about what you mean by changing your wardrobe.' They all nodded appreciatively. I'm glad they understood because I didn't. I just wanted to find a way to be accepted.

'Do you want to come out at this meeting?' A dough-faced first year looked at me with evangelical eyes. 'I'm Cindy.'

'Hi Cindy,' I said. 'No, it's all right, thanks. I'll wait. I'm seeing my dad this summer, that might give me strength.'

Strength for what I wasn't sure. I felt a bit like a heathen amongst the faithful and Cindy seemed sorry that there wasn't going to be the kind of religious awakening she'd hoped for at this meeting. At least not provided by me.

I tried the Women's CR group next. Consciousness Raising is a term I struggle with. If you raise your consciousness does it become something else? Lofty thoughts, perhaps? I've always imagined consciousness to be something very grounded. Earthen, low down somehow. The idea of raising it seems like kind of an anathema to me. Something not quite connected. Flighty, off the wall, out of this world. Perhaps that was just me being frightened of being found out as someone who has a very low consciousness as opposed to a high one. But I went anyway because it seemed to be the thing that the more sophisticated and popular women students did with their leisure time.

They were deep into a discussion about whether it was all right for a feminist to wear make-up when I arrived. I wasn't wearing any so I wasn't in danger of being ostracized for that. Eventually the discussion turned its way around to men. Boyfriends and fathers to be specific. One woman, Miranda, who appeared to be the leader or at least in charge of that particular meeting, said that you could usually tell what was unresolved about a woman's relationship with her father by her choice of boyfriend. What if you don't have one, I thought. A boyfriend, that is. Does that mean that your relationship with your father is fully resolved or not at all?

I was surprised that any of the women here admitted to having boyfriends anyhow. It seemed a dangerous ground to be treading given the emphasis placed on absolute independence and women's supremacy.

'My father is a homosexual,' I explained. I couldn't really think what to say after that. I guess they were all waiting for me to talk about resolution, or tell them about some boyfriend or other.

'That must be terribly difficult, Oedipally speaking,' one short woman with glasses commented.

A red-haired woman called Marlene cut in vehemently. 'The Oedipal Complex is Freudian and therefore misogynistic,' she yelled. 'Having a gay parent makes you more politically aware whatever your relationship with that parent is like. It has to.'

I felt good about that. I liked to think of myself as an aware person in any sphere. So far both meetings had made me feel profoundly unaware so I welcomed this last suggestion and tried to wear it so it fitted. I straightened my shoulders, trying to look like someone who was politically aware, and then I said, 'I'm going to meet up with him in California this summer. We're seeking some kind of resolution in our relationship.' Some of the women clapped and others shook their heads in apparent dismay.

Those who clapped seemed to be encouraging the visit. Those who shook their heads were suggesting, I guess, that seeking resolution was an impossible quest. I suspect that those who felt it was impossible probably thought that resolution with any man was a fairly unlikely happening, gay father or otherwise.

However, having made my announcement publicly on two occasions in two separate society meetings, I felt I could not really renege on it now. I checked out flight times and availability with the student travel agent on campus and tentatively reserved a seat on a plane to San Francisco leaving on August 15. That would give me plenty of time once I was there to limber up for the Instant Enlightenment course if I decided to do it, but somehow I didn't think it was going to be necessary.

20

How does that song go, 'I left my heart in San Francisco'? There must be other words to it but for now that's the only line I can remember. The plane's just three hours away from landing at London Heathrow and I've got everything I took with me safely stored as hand-luggage next to the blankets and headsets over-head, yet I can't help feeling I've left something vital behind. I got on to an earlier flight back than I had expected. It was not that I had anything particularly that I needed to get back for, but the truth is I really felt it was going to be impossible to stay. I've got no one to blame but myself.

I got this seat through standby so I didn't have much choice about where I sat. I'm in the middle seat of three, sandwiched by a man in a dog collar on my right in the aisle and a middle-aged depressive named Marjory on my left by the window. It's Marjory's birthday, she told me, and she especially chose to fly on this day because she wanted to make the day shorter. We left San Francisco about 9 a.m. their time and we will be arriving back in England just before midnight Greenwich Mean Time, so old Marj will have spent practically the entirety of her special day on an airplane with nothing but me and a couple of Martinis to celebrate with.

'I hate birthdays,' Marjory told me. 'Always have done, always will.'

Marjory has a son in San Francisco and a daughter in Leamington Spa. She lives alone in a two-bedroom flat in Pimlico and works for the council. Her son is a lecturer at Stanford University but she seemed so bored by his work and indeed with everything to do with America that our conversation came to a kind of dead stop when I showed any interest or tried to tell her why I'd just been over. The man in the dog collar has been plugged in for most of the flight to his headphones which he has tuned to number 8, the Melody Channel . . . I've said 'excuse me' to him a couple of times (probably interrupting some burgeoning Bacharach number), when I've needed to get out to the toilet, but apart from that our conversation has been practically nil. I would have liked to say more. In fact I have spent a good deal of the flight composing a speech in my head which takes the form of a kind of confessional.

Being raised an agnostic Protestant Jew I have never really had the opportunity to sit in a real confessional box and tell my story, although this is what I have often longed to do. I think perhaps had I had this option open to me I might not have needed to expurgate myself in so many other bizarre and ritualistic ways.

I don't even know whether this man next to me goes in for all that hushed whispering behind the curtain stuff but I like to think it might at least be possible to hand him my speech in written form if I manage to finish it before the flight is over. What I really want to know is whether or not what happened during my stay with Leon in San Francisco could constitute a mortal sin and, if so, what I could expect the ultimate outcome to be. My speech starts like this:

Airplanes always make my mouth go dry. And they leave me with an empty feeling. Like a little place has been carved out of my stomach . . .

It's true, for a start, and I think it has rather a poetic ring to it. It also goes some way towards explaining the feeling I went to San Francisco with in expectation of meeting my father after so many years of silence on both sides.

The rest of the speech I haven't really written. I just have a running commentary I can't get out of my head of the way things happened. If he takes off the headphones between now and the time we hit English soil I might just run it by him.

Airplanes always make my mouth go dry. And they leave me with an empty feeling. Like a little place has been carved out of the pit of my stomach, so when I got off at San Francisco Airport my first thought was for something to eat. I'd slept through breakfast on the plane and had to make do with a tiny packet of peanuts and some orange juice in a little plastic cup with a foil top which tasted like liquid paraffin.

Baggage collection took hours, which is another reason why I put everything into hand-luggage for the journey back. They'd managed to route the bags from our flight down to the carousel where the arrivals from Moscow were currently waiting, and we got all the Russian luggage. I wouldn't have minded going off with a couple of shawls and a Matroschka doll, but by that time they'd cordoned off the collection area. Then two airport officials argued at length about whether it would be easier to redistribute the bags or the people collecting them, and when luggage and rightful owners had been reunited it was about twelve noon San Franciscan time. Two hours and fifteen minutes after the plane had landed.

After that, getting through customs was easy. All the officials, including the one that frisked me, told me to 'have a nice day' and I told them that I intended to try and have a nice life from now on.

I had sent my father details of my flight arrival time but with all this delay I thought there was little chance, even if he had decided to come, that he would still be waiting. There was nothing confirmed about our meeting, so my plan was to go off and change some money, grab a coffee and a doughnut, phone him and brace myself for the reunion.

After Jeff (it said so on the friendly 'I♥CA' name badge he was wearing) had stamped my passport I went through into the Arrivals Lounge. And I was thinking – here's another bit of poetry for you, Mr Clergyman: *A native returns to her homeland, only she has become a foreigner in her absence.*

I looked around for somewhere I could change money. I needed it for coffee and a phonecall. God, would I remember how to put a dime in? Was it before the pips or after the pips? Were there any pips? Do you dial straight or put the money in after? I hoped someone might have had the decency to write a list of easy-to-follow instructions inside the phone booth.

'Francine!'

Déjà vu. I was back in the hospital looking for Sal Greenburg. It's a long story, Mr Clergyman, so I won't bore you, but it was the feeling that before I could disappear I had been spotted. If I could have gone backwards through customs and got Jeff to unstamp my passport, I would have done that. I wanted to shrink down to nothing again and be a non-person. Francine, unseen. I looked up. He was there. Just a few yards away with a young man. An Adonis. A blond god. My father had his arm around the younger man. He waved at me with the other. Adonis just smiled. I tried to swallow and choked slightly on the dryness. I wished my mouth didn't feel so stuck together, like a deflated balloon. Puckered rubber that would have to be peeled apart before it would work again.

I managed a slight wave, too, but that was all. I felt a little silly and imagined we were being watched by television cameras (you will perhaps think it was God's presence I was feeling) and that somewhere a brass band was about to begin a fanfare. America is the land of gesture and open display. You'll know this, of course, having just come from there. I had forgotten all about it. I had lost most of my skills in this area. I was out of practice.

The two men moved towards me like a slow-build action movie. I had no choice then but to stay where I was and become the third point of the triangle. We hugged, a three-way embrace with a child, a father and a stranger and it was hard to know which was which.

125

'This is Michael, Francine. He's my . . . friend.'

Michael radiated a halo-like glow. I don't know if you have personally witnessed similar visions. Blue crystal eyes shot laser beams through me. A fresh sweet smell of men's cologne or aftershave billowed towards me from the open neck of his starched white cotton shirt.

'Hi Francine.'

He took my limp hand and squeezed it, smiling his angel's smile. A soft melting squeeze. My mouth felt wet again. I could swallow.

'Hi.'

It was hard to know who I should be addressing or what exactly I should say. Leon seemed similarly tongue-tied. We stood there inanely for a good few seconds before he managed an entry.

'Plane late, huh?'

There may have been accusation in his tone. It would have been understandable. After all, I had kept him and this friend of his waiting the whole morning for me. I offered up my weak apology.

'Luggage delay, sorry.'

Michael touched us both, trying to connect a circuit.

'No worries, hey. Leon's been telling me airport stories to pass the time.'

Leon touched Michael's hand and smiled drippingly. I laughed nervously, trying desperately to remember if my father had ever had occasion to tell me stories to tide over a given period of tedium.

'Michael and I were thinking about picking up a bite to eat. Wanna join us?'

Leon had softened over the years, there was no doubt about it. Or perhaps it was just with Michael that he was relaxed in a way I had never seen him before. He reached out to pick up my bag for me and then smiled at me too. I remembered how hungry I was feeling.

'Sure,' I said. 'That would be great.'

We went to a Harvey Johnson's. Nothing special though there were thirty-three flavour choices of syrup to put on your stack of pancakes. I chose bilberry because it felt quite English and I was just easing my way into all of this. We didn't talk much during breakfast. Michael smiled a lot and I couldn't help wondering if he'd been paid to do it and Dad asked me things like how was the flight and wasn't the view of the Bay Area as we came in just the most stunning thing I had ever seen? He was anxious to show off his new-found home and I was anxious to do whatever I could to preserve the lightness and good mood he seemed to be in, which was so different than the way I had remembered him. I enthused about what I had seen of San Francisco so far which was mainly the airport and the highway but Leon seemed pleased. Michael paid the bill. Dad kissed him again. You'll be wondering, like I was, Mr Clergy, about the concept of relative love. Love that is relative to its surroundings and love that ought to be present through being a relative. In any case it was hard to tell where genuine affection was really located.

In the car on the way back from the restaurant Michael and Leon were making plans. How should we three spend the next couple of weeks together? Where should we go, what should we see, how much time could Michael get off from his job and his studies? When should they show me the Hot Springs? The Hot Springs, I believe, are a kind of Californian Lourdes equivalent. Pilgrimages are made and miracles take place.

Michael worked nights as a security guard for his father's building firm while he spent his days finishing off his degree in Personal Studies. He'd managed to negotiate time away from both. I wondered, did Personal Studies mean he just studied himself all the time? I could obviously see how it could be an attractive pursuit, particularly in his case, so it wouldn't have surprised me, but it did seem odd as with so much in America that such a subject might carry qualifications. Perhaps, though, with all the individual atonement and inward reflection necessary, your own theological training might even be considered a form of Personal Study, Mr Clergyman.

My visit with my father turned out to be a visit with Michael *and* my father. It occurred to me on more than one occasion that Dad might have engineered having Michael around so much because he was a bit nervous of being left on his own with me, but the truth was, I began to be as glad as my father that Michael was there. He fed me compliments constantly. He took my hand somewhat cornily in restaurants and held it under the table, while I tried to cut steak one-handedly with the other. He stood close to me whenever and wherever he could, grabbing opportunities to hold me around my waist, helping me down stairs or steering me through doors or whatever. One evening, while we stood, all three of us together, after a concert looking out over the San Francisco bay and watching the lights reflected on the water, he stroked my hair with a kind of tenderness I had never known before and whispered to me that he thought I was truly beautiful. Many of his touches were quiet, unseen and hidden, deliberately I guess, from my father who may have begun to feel his prized possession drifting from him.

This is how it was, Mr Clergyman. I had come seeking my father in hopes that he might fill up some aching void in the centre of me and here I was beginning to ache for the man he said he loved. His lover? By now, I really wasn't sure.

Thou shalt not covet thy father's lover. Was that ever one of the Commandments handed down to Moses on that high hill in Egypt? Did they have problems like that in those days?

The Hot Springs trip was planned for the beginning of the second week of my stay. We drove up together in my father's car. Michael insisted that he and I sit together on the back seat, so he could point out sights along the way to me, he said, and Leon seemed happy enough to do the driving. My father tried his best to keep himself entwined in our conversation but it was not the words we were saying that threatened to exclude him. A new circuit of secret energy flowed between us on the back seat of my father's French car. Michael had one arm draped across my lap and his fingers wedged easily between my thighs. He held my hand with his free arm and steered it to a place on his own lap

128

where I could feel the heat of his flesh radiating through his clothes. Once, when we stopped and my father left the car to get directions, Michael moved my hand to rest on the warm mound that had grown hard and insistent inside his jeans.

'You did that to me,' he said and kissed me gently on the lips. It was a raindrop kiss, a velvet brush, like the rustle of trees in a darkened wood. When Leon came back we were both pink and flushed.

'I'll open the windows,' he said drily. 'I got some candy for us to have on the way.'

He threw two packages of Reese's peanut butter cups and a Three Musketeers bar onto the back seat. He opened a Snickers for himself and began to eat it noisily.

Michael moved slightly away from me and leaned forward in his seat. He began to rub my father's shoulders. Gently and slowly he pulled him back and seduced him with his touch. My father melted into Michael's kneading hands. He groaned with pleasure and leaned his head to one side to kiss the top of Michael's arm. Michael stroked him at the base of his neck and said teasingly, 'I'd better stop or we might never get there.'

My dad laughed drunkenly. He spluttered with unashamed joy and looked over his shoulders to address us both. 'I love you,' he said. 'Both of you.'

Michael kept his hands off me for the rest of the journey but later, submerged in the blood-warm water of the Hot Springs, they found no limits to their exploration.

21

It is not that I had no idea, Mr Clergyman, of the consequences of my actions. It's for this precise reason I need you to hear me. My father loved Michael, I think there can be no doubt about that. So that's as sure as maybe. And I wanted my father's love. Well, that's a way of seeing it, isn't it, Mr Clergyman? The question is, was I wanting Michael as a way of getting closer to my father or was my growing desire simply disguised aggression or a perverse longing? Revenge or repair? Sweet or sour? Holy or evil? Whatever it was, Mr C, I didn't want it to stop.

The Hot Springs are hidden away in the Californian valley on the Nevada border. Only from the mountain approach were they visible and from there the Springs glistened invitingly like a little circle of paradise.

The ring of azure blue sparkled like a sapphire under the dazzling gaze of the late summer sun.

My father and Michael had visited the Springs before, several times it seemed. When we'd parked the car they proceeded together in familiar camaraderie and took off all their clothes, urging me to do the same. There seemed to be a generally accepted code of undress here and we joined several other nude bathers in the warm, gently bubbling, slightly sulphurated water. We stood as a threesome together holding hands. I kept my gaze fixed on people's faces and the scenery around me and my neck stiff as I tried to avoid looking down beneath the surface of the water where I might catch a glimpse of Michael or my father stripped of any armour or mystery.

After a while Leon moved to a favourite spot and sat on a ledge with his head leant back on a rock. He closed his eyes and was either sleeping or had begun to meditate in the deliciously warm pool. Michael pushed me back against another rock at the other side of the Spring. He leant his body against mine pushing his tongue into my ear and slowly running his hands up and down my back and round in front to the flat of my belly. The sulphur in the water made it soft and slippery and his hands felt like silk against my skin.

'Lean back,' he said, whispering in my ear through the moist wetness his tongue had left and the strands of my hair that had been soaked by the water.

'I can't,' I said, afraid that my father would come out of his reverie and want to join us.

'You're so beautiful,' he whispered again and glided his hands around the front, the back and every part of me.

'So are you,' I said.

We were the Beautiful People, glorying in our splendour in the Californian sun and the warm waters of the Hot Springs. So you see, Mr C, it was hard to know whether what I was doing with Michael was very right or very wrong. Perhaps you might have been able to lessen the confusion if you'd been there. You could have given me some wise words to meditate upon.

> *forgive us our trespasses . . .*
> *lead us not into temptation . . .*
> *Our Father . . .*

Our father, for it felt like he was part of us both now, woke from his sleep about an hour later. Michael and I were talking to a couple from Fresno who came up to the Hot Springs regularly, they said, for medical reasons. He was a painter and she made pots and they both thought Michael and I were newlyweds because of the way we were all over each other. Apparently, they told us, the Springs are a popular place for honeymooners. Michael said he would never believe in marriage.

Leon came and put his arms around both Michael and I and pulled us close together.

'I feel so lucky,' he said. 'So lucky to have people I love here sharing this with me.'

We stayed in the water about half an hour more until the ends of our fingers and toes had puckered beyond recognition. Then we sat on the side wrapped in blankets and ate oranges and cream cheese bagels. The couple from Fresno joined us and offered round some wine they had bought locally, made and bottled in this same valley. The wine, the sun, and the luxuriant warmth of the Springs themselves left me light-headed and unable to speak with any real coherency. I was happy to be left out of the conversation altogether. Michael dozed and my father spoke about Hindu philosophy with the painter and the potter who, it turned out, were both Buddhists. I closed my eyes, half-listening, and dreamt about Greek gods and being cast into the midst of a burning fiery furnace.

22

It was not my first time. That was with a man who sold fruit outside Kentish Town Station. I asked for oranges and we ended up
rolling in them in the back of his truck after he'd packed up his
stall for early closing day. He had nice eyes and I figured it was
better to break the ice with someone I didn't have to see again if
I didn't want to. There are loads of other places to buy fruit from
and I was sure he wouldn't miss my custom. In any case, I'm not
looking for absolution on that one, Mr Clergy. Wasn't it the Bible
anyway that said 'By their fruits ye shall know them'? I remember reading that in a *Watchtower* leaflet given to me on Victoria
Station by a Jehovah's Witness. I was eating an apple at the
time. So in Palo Alto it was not my first time in practice, but
maybe in my soul it was a progression from the citrus to a less
acid state of being.

On the way back from the Hot Springs Michael drove and my
father sat in the front seat with him. It was a relief to be on my
own in the back and be allowed to drift in and out of my dreamy
state without interruption. When we arrived at the house a few
hours later I felt rested and full of energy. Leon lit a fire in the
living-room and opened the french doors on to the patio where
there was a flood-lit swimming pool shaped like a tear-drop. He
lay, curled like a cat across the breadth of the fireplace. I made
cocoa which we all sipped while staring at the flames. Michael

133

reclined opposite my father and I sat apart, separate, wearing a dressing-gown I'd borrowed from Leon. Hugging my knees to my chest, I willed them into coupledom and savoured the feeling of being on the outside again, free and alone with my own thoughts.

Stolen waters are sweet and bread eaten in secret is pleasant.

I love swimming at night. Everything – the stillness, the sensation of water on flesh, the exhilaration – is exaggerated in the dark. Michael and my father were deep in conversation, planning a Sumerian Philosophy course my father wanted to structure for Michael's university. I finished my cocoa and slipped out the french doors to the back by the pool. I left Leon's dressing-gown in a heap by the side and dived, head first, into the deepest part of the pool. I swam underwater for as long as I could, pretending to be Esther Williams. The cool water of the pool was a contrast to the blood warm waters of the Hot Springs. The full moon shone like a beacon from the black sky overhead and I basked in its light as I dived and swirled in the water below.

Michael and Leon were still deep in conversation when I got out, dripping. I put my father's dressing-gown back on and tip-toed through the living-room, trying not to leave wet footprints, on my way to the bathroom to get a towel from the rack. Dad looked up and smiled as I went past.

I felt very little, Mr Clergyman. Like a small child. Happy and with no responsibilities. The two men's voices talking filled me with a sense of safety and security. Perhaps you, yourself, lend this feeling to your parish as you serve them with a sermon. I sat in the bathroom with Leon's robe around me, burying my head in a freshly laundered towel. It had his smell on it. Everything in the house did. It was the smell of pine forests and damp midnight air.

I must have fallen asleep, Mr C, because the next thing I knew, Dad was peering round the door asking if I was all right and saying that he was going to bed. Then, out of nowhere, he thanked me.

'Thanks,' he said. 'Thanks.'

He stuck out his arm and put it around my shoulder, pulling me to him.

'Thanks,' he said again.

'For what?' I asked.

Perhaps I have not explained my position fully in relation to my father. This is, possibly, because I was very unsure at that moment what precisely my position was, but suffice it to say I did not feel worthy of his thanks.

'For being you,' he said. 'I'm going to bed. Michael can let himself out. Goodnight.'

'OK,' I said. He looked old. More like a grandfather than a father. 'OK, Dad. Thank you for today. Sorry if I . . .' I called after him before he shut the door. 'Goodnight.'

I listened to his footsteps echo down the hall and the door of his room close as he went into it. I took down his wet robe and put it on again and went to look in the living-room. Michael was still there in the same place that I had left him.

Lead us not into temptation but deliver us from evil . . .
Sweet, sweet, sweet are stolen waters.

There are times when it is better to rise up and outside of an experience, even if it feels like it might be one of the greatest things that has ever happened to you. That is because everything that is great has a sharp edge to it and someone, somewhere, is bound to get hurt. The further you can be away from that when it happens, the better.

I am in no way justifying my position here, Mr C, but only letting you know that I had moved into a place of spiritual exaltation where earthly consequences appeared to hold little matter.

'Nice swim?' Michael caught my hand as I walked back into the living-room towards the fire and pulled me down to where he was reclined.

'Yeah,' I said. 'It was. It was wonderful.'

'Your father is a brilliant man.'

'Yes,' I said. 'Yes, he is.'

'He's a brilliant man to have produced such a beautiful daughter,' he said. 'And a selfish one for having kept her hidden for so long.'

'I wasn't hidden.'

'You were for me.'

Michael started kissing my finger tips and worked his way up on the inside of my father's robe to my face, neck and eyes.

'I'd like to stay the night here, with you,' he said. 'Is that all right?'

I didn't resist, Mr Clergy. Not really. 'Wouldn't Leon mind?' I asked him, hoping for some clarity on a situation which had become far too blurred and incestuous already.

'I'm not asking Leon, I'm asking you. Would you like to stay with me? I want to explore you, all over. I want to love you, to make love to you.'

This is what I had come seeking, Mr C. Maybe not in this form and not intentionally from this man but I wanted to be explored, to be known. I really, really wanted to be loved and at this moment in time I thought he was connected enough to my father that he just might do.

'OK,' I said. 'OK. Um . . . here?'

Michael led me to my father's study where Leon had set up a futon mattress for me on the floor amongst his papers. He laid me down on the makeshift bed and pushed the dressing-gown off my shoulders and then away to one side. I thought about telling him the gown was wet and belonged to my father and really ought to be hung up properly in case it was lying on top of something important, but he had already unbuttoned his shirt and the top of his jeans and moved my hand down to where I could feel inside of them.

'Did I do that too?'

'You sure did,' he said.

He licked his finger and circled it round, easing it up inside of me where it got even wetter. He moved his head slowly down across my breasts and my belly using his tongue like a surgeon's tool, probing all the time as though he might find something new, something uncharted with this method.

'Mmm,' he said, as if he were eating an ice-cream sundae. 'You taste so good.'

It may not seem relevant to you, Mr C, to be graced with all these details, but this whole experience was a kind of revelation for me and like any revelatory experience it is the tiny details, the inch by inch eventfulness of the thing that shines so extraordinarily brightly in the final analysis. We were both completely naked now. Michael had pushed the door closed but a crack of light still shone in from the hallway. The curtains on the small window at the side weren't drawn either so the room was practically half-lit by the hall light and the brilliant glow of the moon outside.

Michael sat up so I could see his face. He asked me if I liked what he was doing.

'I want you to teach me what to do,' he said. 'You have to tell me what you like and how you like it being done.'

'I like everything you're doing,' I said. And it was true, Mr C, I did. Everything felt right except for this awful feeling that it all might be so wrong.

I didn't hear the door open, neither of us did. Michael had gone from licking the bottom of my feet to taking me on a guided tour of my own body, proving that up until now, in myself, I had been living as a stranger in a strange land. Now he lay on top of me and answered my question, 'Does it feel OK to you?' with a metaphor I think I shall never get out of my head.

'Francine,' he said, 'you could turn on a pencil.'

Pencils write messages. Shade in detail. Draw out plans and symmetry. The figure I saw was just a loose shadow next to our clamped and shiny forms in the centre of the ghostly lit room. A silhouetted giant with slumped shoulders holding his wet robe across a limply crooked arm.

'I think you should go,' the vision spoke.

There were no muscles in his voice, nor in the shadow I could see standing there. There was only dejection, a defeated, deflated balloon.

Michael struggled with his clothes, pulling on his shirt and jeans over his naked body. It spoke again.

'I think you should go now, Michael,' my father said. 'I'd like you to go.'

'Leon, maybe we should talk.'

I was trying to imagine how we might now try to put into words the measure of what had happened, which of course is what I am trying to do with you, Mr Clergyman, in the hope that I may understand it better myself. Does one begin with the justifications or the accusations? I curled myself around tightly like a snail retreating into its shell. My skin was sticky with our lovemaking.

'I'd rather you just went.' My father's voice cracked.

The moonlight reflected magnificently off a round, pearl-shaped tear that I could see rolling silently down the side of his face. A thousand lifetimes of pain and hurt were contained in that tiny sphere. We were three points of a very separate triangle now. Three points that had no lines of convergence. Michael took his keys from the mantelpiece above the fireplace where the embers were still burning. The jangle of metal against metal cut through the stillness of the night and the gentleness that had gone before.

'Goodnight, Leon.' Michael reached out to put a hand on his rounded shoulder but my father flinched to avoid his touch.

'Francine,' he nodded in my direction. It was a formal, slightly awkward acknowledgement. An apology of a farewell.

I stood behind my father in the shadows of the darkened house watching Michael walk down to his car where it was parked on the drive that seemed to be fully lit by the bright night sky. I wanted to yell to him, to beg him not to leave me alone with my father's sadness and anger. I wanted him to stand trial with me, if there was to be that kind of hearing. I wanted a bit of his hair or a piece of his clothing, anything that would have kept us connected for just a little longer.

My father stood by the doorway in silence watching Michael fumble with his keys, sit behind the wheel and turn on the engine. When Michael switched the headlights on my father had to shield himself from the brightness. He covered his face with his arm as though he were being attacked. When Michael's car was gone my father turned slowly to face me. I braced myself for a physical onslaught but none came. My father's lip quivered and the lone tear was joined by a shower of others dripping from his nose and his chin. I willed him to say something, anything, Mr C. It was the worst torture, to be left alone with his silence.

The FASTEN YOUR SEAT-BELT sign has just come on. Marjory is asleep or has passed out from too many Martinis, and the man next to me on the other side has just removed the strip from his neck which I had foolishly mistaken as an indication of his godly stature. It turns out (he has now unplugged himself from channel 8 and its sugar-coated medleys long enough to have a conversation) that it was not a dog-collar at all that he was wearing but an 'aura-sensitive shock absorber' (ASSA), prescribed for him by a mystic healer in the Golden Gate City to help him overcome his fear of flying. The trick is, he told me, to reduce worry, anxiety and stress by wearing this paper strip across your Adam's Apple, which absorbs negative vibrations emanating from your aura, while listening to relaxing music. It's not quite the same as being told to say five Hail Marys and repeat the Lord's prayer through a couple of times while listening to hymns on a church organ. But both might work, I suppose, assuming of course that you are a believer.

23

I went back. I had to. I hate loose ends. Unfinished stories, unanswered questions, unresolved differences. Besides, you know what they say; if you fall off a horse you should get straight back up again and ride.

Leon had left the house belonging to the mountain climber. On her return from the Himalayas she had turned her place into a lesbian separatist community and headquarters for Women on Top of the World (WOTOW), an all-female expedition party set for the North Pole. My father had been turned out.

I re-entered Leon's life, or he mine, in the more luxurious surroundings of Nirvana. Located in the swish section of San Francisco, Nirvana was the name given to the palatial home of his newfound lover, André, and André's dying wife, Nina.

I had not even told Alma of my plans for a second visit. She would have discouraged me like she did the first time. 'You will not find what you are looking for,' she told me. I didn't know what I was looking for, exactly. But I knew I had to keep on looking.

As for my sisters, Cynthia and I hardly spoke any more, ever. She was so busy in Skye now that she had reproduced herself twice over with newborn twins, Katy and Tom. She was apparently wonderful in her maternal role, but somehow it seemed I was destined never to communicate effectively with mothers. Melanie was still at school. Homework and taking exams had become her raison d'être. Melanie attended to her schoolwork like Cynthia attended to her babies and, though it meant she got good grades in everything, it made her pretty unreachable on any other level.

Going back wasn't easy or, I suppose, really necessary. It would have been possible to live my life without ever returning to San Francisco. I tried to tell myself that there was little point in re-establishing contact with Leon or trying to lay down roots in a city where people had their dogs holistically massaged and their budgerigar's horoscope charts drawn up. But at the back of my mind I was worried that if I didn't finish what I'd started I might never know if having a father was really possible or if one should actually look to the stars for any answers at all.

Following the night of the swimming pool, I had cocooned myself for a short eternity in a Holiday Inn near the airport while I waited for a flight back to England to become available. In my hurry to leave, I had forgotten vital things like my passport and my toothbrush which I had to return to the house to get. I found my father standing out back by the pool, quiet and monk-like in a black cotton dressing-gown (not the one I had soaked). His eyes were bloodshot and I guessed that he had not eaten or slept for days. When he saw me, he spoke quietly but his words reverberated within me like a thunderbolt in a canyon.

'You have taken the only thing I ever loved and now you are going to deprive me again by your going. I have already cried a small pool of tears but it is only the beginning of the ocean I still have to weep.'

I thought about what he said for most of the following year as I sat my way through final exams and contemplated my future. Going to find Leon the first time had been my quest for clarity, for completeness, and now I found myself swimming disjointedly in a sea of guilty confusion. He said I had *taken* the only thing he ever loved, which I guess by implication meant I wasn't it, but it seemed odd then that my leaving of him would be experienced as deprivation rather than good riddance. Perhaps he needed a daughter as much as I needed a father and Michael was the red herring, the unknowing decoy placed there in the middle of it all to put us both off our tracks.

Leon and I didn't exactly stay in close touch during the year after I left Palo Alto. After a conspicuous silence on both sides I finally wrote Leon a casual letter in the spring saying I was going to be in San Francisco again and wondering whether I might look him up. After several rounds of mail-forwarding the letter eventually found him at his new address and he wrote a similarly casual reply inviting me to join him where he was living with his new 'family' for as long as I wished.

The idea that in this short space of time since living like a misfit with his lesbian mountain-climbing landlady and unrequited love for Michael, Leon had found not only a new home but 'family' as well, filled me with an oddly wistful sense of admiration and curiosity. It struck me that, whatever our differences, one quality that Leon and I shared was a commitment to renewal. Maybe not so much in the sense of complete change, but a willingness to rebuild, start again, try out and experiment. In a sense, my returning to see Leon once more was a kind of experiment. I needed to test out validity, compatibility, and to find out whether it was possible to produce a compound from such disparate elements as we had become. So this re-establishment of contact was about as close as I have ever come to performing a scientific act in the name of my father. I figured, if nothing else, Leon the erstwhile doctor would appreciate my concerted attempt at trying and testing even if the results yielded unworkability and combustion.

Once again, despite where it had got us last time, my father met me at the airport together with the 'man he loved'. Fortunately, I felt sure at this first meeting, there was little likelihood of the same carnal wanderlust occurring as before. André was a small rotund man shaped like a barrel. Besides which, the relationship between Leon and André was definitely consummated. I had no desire to be consumed by it as well.

André had small dark mole-like eyes that bulged slightly from his rather rounded forehead. His hair, or what there was left of it, was soft and babylike. It covered the back of his head like the greyish down of a new-born duckling. There was an air of a Jimmy Cagney gangster movie about him but the man also had a saintly presence. His large wet lips were stuck together like two garden slugs, while his small smooth hands had the gentle quality of a wise man or a healer. The vision of André standing next to my father made a comical but touching tableau. The small Buddha resting alongside the tall totem pole.

'Francine!' my father called to me from across the airport lounge.

Time may not mend all things but it seems to seal over cracks and blur some blemishes. It was as though nothing untoward between us had ever happened. He hugged me close to him and I smelled the same father smell that never seemed to change with time.

'This is André.'

'Pleased to meet you.' I surprised myself with my terse formality. I had wanted to sound more genial.

André responded with a smile that grew and spread over his face like an oil spill, showing me a perfect set of pearl-shaped white teeth. I wondered in the silence that followed what the odds were that they were all false. My father interrupted my perusal of his lover's mouth by suggesting a move from the airport lounge. 'We have the car downstairs. Shall we go home?'

That seemed to be the cue for a gross and openly public demonstration of affection between André and Leon. I watched, along with the rest of the general airport milieu as Leon leaned down towards André while the little man craned his fat neck upwards and they both puckered their lips, stretching them outwards as if they needed to go that extra distance to finally meet and make a loud showy kiss. André's brow was beginning to sweat from the exertion and he wiped it with his handkerchief while he made wet smacking noises with his mouth and little hums of appreciation directed towards my father. My father grinned broadly and equally wetly and I had to turn my head away quickly, worried in case I should see them both begin to dribble from the sides of their mouths.

We walked down to the car park where Nina, André's wife, by either mishap or convenience I supposed, sat waiting in the back seat of André's gold Mercedes. Nina's whole body crackled with a kind of Miss Havisham fragility. She had dry porcelain skin that you could practically see through and a bluey-white complexion completely devoid of any signs of rosiness or health. She had no hair that I could see, her head was covered with a sewn turban made from Liberty-print material. I should have been honoured that she had been part of the welcoming party at all. Nina, I discovered, rarely ever left her house to go anywhere. She felt happiest, she said, inside her own home where she could be close to her washing-machine and television. Her body was riddled with a cancer which doctors had told her should have squeezed the life out of her some months ago, yet she seemed remarkably unperturbed by the harbouring of such a deadly inhabitant.

It was not easy to make sense of the rather bizarre relationships juggled within this threesome. André, I decided, was the Sugar Daddy, lord and ruler of the manor; Nina, the attendant mistress and house-servant; and Leon, the prized and adored concubine enjoying the comfort and luxuries provided by André and his money.

Nirvana was shaded on all sides by sycamore trees and protected by iron railings and an entryphone. Once inside, Nina made us iced tea in the kitchen which was adorned from ceiling to floor in dog-related décor. There was no evidence of a real one anywhere but that, I learned later, was because Nina's days were numbered and neither André nor Leon were prepared to take responsibility for a pet after she had gone.

'I used to have a Queen Charlotte poodle named Nancy,' Nina told me as she collected an assortment of vitamin pills which she put into little piles by Leon and André's glasses of tea.

'Love you.' André dabbed Nina on the cheek with one of his wet puckers.

'Love you.' Nina responded with a slightly drier kiss on André's forehead. Then she moved over to where my father had just sat down. 'Love you, Leon,' she said and kissed him gently on the brow as well.

'Love you, Nina,' my father told her and then they all chorused in my direction like a leaking honey-pot, 'LOVE YOU, FRANCINE. LOVE YOU.'

'Thanks,' I said, sitting down with the rest of them to pills and tea. Tea and pills. I was back in San Francisco.

Later, when my father and André had gone to 'pick up some shopping' I sat with Nina while she folded their boxer shorts and ironed their shirts. The television was on as it seemed to be constantly in any room Nina spent time in. It was an afternoon soap set in the emergency room of a hospital. We watched two road accidents and a life-saving operation while Nina ironed and folded and watched, with an expressionless stare, the screen in front of her.

'How long has Leon been here with you both?' I asked her during a commercial break so as not to interrupt any involvement she might be having with the plot.

'About six months,' Nina responded with that annoying habit some people have of nodding their heads profusely when they answer your questions, even when they haven't been asked anything that requires a yes or no answer.

'Oh,' I said. 'He and André seem happy.'

'Yes,' sighed Nina with a complete absence of emotion. 'Yes, they are. I'm so happy for them.'

'Yes,' I said, not knowing how else to respond. 'Yes, I am too.'

In fact, sitting there with Nina in Nirvana enveloped by the soft strobe-like glow of the television and the clean dry smell of starch and freshly ironed clothes, I knew very little of how I felt about anything apart from being slightly anaesthetized by the strangeness of it all. Whether this triangular unit of which I had become a fourth point was an idyll of harmony or a recipe for disaster, I could not be sure. I sat with my not knowing and stared with Nina at the pictures on the television screen.

Mercifully the drama ended with only one more accident, involving a bicycle and a guinea pig. Nina asked me during the next commercial break if I had brought a winter coat with me as part of my luggage. It seemed a strange question, especially as it was just the beginning of September and still deliciously warm outside. I said that I had brought some jumpers but I really didn't know how long I was going to stay and whether I even needed a coat.

'Would you mind if I bought you one?' she asked me then. 'Please. Would that be all right?'

'Sure,' I said, sensing that it might be rude not to accept her offer, but also with the feeling that regardless of whether or not a coat would be useful to me this dying woman had a need to get me one. There was something I recognized that was similarly tenuous and uncloaked about both our situations. Nina was holding on by a thread to a body that had gone beyond its capacity to be looked after. My ticket to be here was laced with the same lack of guarantee and uncertainty. A coat like an embrace might hold the two of us together just long enough for us both to gather the strength to let go.

24

Nina was very close to her washing-machine. It occupied a good deal of her mental and physical space. It was a front loader and after the washing powder had gone in she had to be on standby to give it a little extra boost if it looked like the water wasn't sudsy enough. Then, two wash cycles later, the conditioner needed to be added. There was an automatic dispensing compartment in the machine that could have saved her the trouble but Nina said she preferred monitoring it by hand. Then there was the business of unloading. There were some items, like André's perma-pressed trousers, that had to be removed before the spin cycle or they would get creases that Nina said even her ironing couldn't get out. The other clothes had to be taken from the drum immediately and shaken, as vigorously as Nina could manage, when the spin cycle finished or they too could be wrinkled beyond repair.

With such constant domestic demands and preoccupations, it was impossible to see how Nina might find the energy or the time to buy me a coat. I did my best to reassure her that it really wasn't necessary and in any case I could wait for however long, but Nina was adamant that we would go together to buy the coat before the week was out.

The opportunity presented itself a couple of days and four loads of washing later. André went to London with an ancient Chinese weaving loom to auction at Sotheby's and in view of

147

André's pending absence my father had booked himself into a week-long retreat in the Redwood Forest. He asked me if I wanted to go but I thought I needed time away from them both and besides there was probably going to be no other time that Nina would be freed enough from her household chores and attendant responsibilities to make the coat trip with me. I declined my father's offer, saying that I had decided to stay home at Nirvana with Nina.

That first morning on our own we both slept late and arrived simultaneously at the breakfast table at around eleven o'clock. Nina had more colour in her cheeks than I had seen since I arrived. There was a noticeable gap on the table where André and Leon's cereal bowls should have been and where their glasses of juice usually stood with the pile of pills beside them. Neither Nina nor I ever took the vitamins. She, because she finds the tablets hard to swallow and me, because like Alice in Wonderland I've always been suspicious of things that come in little bottles.

'I'd like to take you to visit my hairdresser, too,' Nina said between tiny nibbles of dry toast. 'He's very good and he could cut your hair for you, if you think you would like that, that is.'

I wondered if I was taking the place for her of the poodle dog she was no longer allowed to have. It was as though some deep and maternal urge had been awakened in her and she now wanted to preen and cosset every part of me. I allowed myself to be petted. It had been a long time since I had been receptive to anyone's mothering.

'Thanks,' I said. 'I'd like to meet your hairdresser. I'd really like that.'

André had taken the Mercedes to the airport and left it there in the car park and my father had taken his car, a red Citroën 2CV, up north to the Redwoods, leaving Nina and I without transport. That didn't really matter, however, as Nina wasn't keen on driving and I didn't have a licence. We booked a taxi to pick us up the following morning at ten. The plan was to buy the coat, have lunch in the restaurant at the department store and then taxi over to Mel's, the hairdressers, for a two o'clock appointment. It was important to Nina that we be back home by four for the start of *As the World Turns.*

With a new energy Nina set about the house, dusting shelves and shining cutlery. For the first time ever she let me help her fold the laundry. In the evening we sat together in her bedroom and she showed me pictures in an old photograph album she kept hidden away.

'You had loads of hair then.'

It was only while looking at photographs of her younger, healthier self that I realized how much of a toll her illness had taken on her whole appearance. The hair on her head had gone, but so had the hair from everywhere else. Her brow, her eyes, the inside of her nostrils; everywhere completely denuded of even the tiniest fuzz.

'I could sit on it,' she said proudly.

'Amazing.'

There were several photographs of Nina in the embrace of a younger man who was not André.

'Who's that?' I asked, sensing that he might be the reason behind the secrecy of the photograph album.

'His name was Larry,' she told me. 'He flew planes. We flew planes, together.'

'You worked on the airlines?' I asked, trying to picture Nina as a stewardess.

'No, we flew little planes,' she said. 'Little planes for fun. The kind that only have room for one person in the cockpit and one passenger. They were very little planes. Just Larry and the plane and me, together in the sky.'

She told me that she had known Larry from the time they were both fifteen years old. He was reckless, with a boundless and passionate zest for life. She was quiet and gentle with a determined longing to look after the hurt or injured. Their relationship had been discouraged by her parents who were keen for their children to concentrate on studies rather than romance. Nina went to university to study Humanities. Larry pursued his love of aircraft and got a job as a traffic controller in a local airfield and began to learn the rudiments of flying planes. When term breaks and working holidays permitted they would see one another and he took Nina out on short flights in borrowed planes. It was during her second year at University that André came and began to run the Theology department. Nina was inspired by the new professor's teachings on love and religion and decided that nothing was more important than to be with the person she knew she wanted to spend the rest of her life with. With the blessing of her teacher, André, for whom she had just finished a paper entitled 'Love and the Holy Union' she wrote to Larry and proposed to him. He accepted immediately.

To appease her parents they planned to wait until after her graduation for the wedding. They were to celebrate their engagement immediately, however, with a fireworks display at the airfield where Larry worked, and he'd arranged, as a surprise, to perform a little air stunt of his own: spelling her name in the air with a stream of coloured smoke.

I knew what Nina was going to tell me before she had even started the story. I imagined it in my mind like the synopsis of a corny film script:

1) Childhood sweethearts bound together by love, lust and passion, separated only by the higher expectations of society (*character notes*: Puck and the Madonna)
2) Togetherness temporarily interrupted by the pursuit of individual goals and supposed gains
3) Courtship continues despite the boundaries and constraints on both their lives
4) Enter priest figure who bestows his blessing on the pair
5) Togetherness restored and future plans made
6) Togetherness permanently halted by the cruel hand of fate snatching the free spirit from his gentle bride once and for all.

'Did Larry . . .'

Nina nodded through tears, fighting to regain her former grey and neutral composure.

'He got the letters OK but he wanted to try to do a heart around the whole thing,' she said earnestly, and then neither of us could keep a straight face. The image of Larry, like some comical Biggles, diving in circles with his little plane spelling out his love for the bride-to-be below, only to fall from the sky, goggles and all, suddenly felt funny beyond words. It was almost as absurd as Nina marrying André, a homosexual university lecturer in religion who was twice her age. Nevertheless both were true and both, tragically, happened.

25

The store was called Lacey's, no doubt an attempt at being the West Coast's answer to New York's Macy's. The ladies' coat department was beautifully laid out with elegant displays of mannequins modelling coats with matching scarves and gloves and pretty plastic faces that reminded me of how Nina looked when she wasn't aware of people watching her. I hadn't had a winter coat for as long as I could remember. Mostly I wore jackets, usually scruffy ex-army versions bought from the surplus store or sometimes thick blanket-type garments made from woven material that looked like the kind of rugs old people keep in front of their hearths. I wasn't used to the soft subtle colours and style of the cashmeres and silken-lined woollen wraps I saw hanging on the racks around me.

'Try some on,' Nina said. She could not disguise the excitement in her voice.

'OK,' I said. 'Which ones?'

Nina motioned to the coiffured shop assistant to come over and help us choose. I watched with admiration as this sick grey woman took complete control in way I had never seen before. The shop assistant listened as Nina explained that I had recently come over from London, England, and had omitted to pack a winter coat. She said I was used to European fashion and design and wanted something stylish and flattering to keep me warm for the coming months. The shop assistant nodded attentively and looked me over quizzically. I suppose she could have been silently measuring me up for size and type in order to help me find the perfect coat to best match my needs, but I suspected she was probably more likely to be wondering how someone supposedly so cultured from across the waters could look as unkempt as I did.

'We have some gorgeous tartans,' she said. 'From Scotland, England.'

Nina looked at me expectantly. I shrugged. 'Ummm, OK,' I said.

The sales assistant was not comfortable with my lack of enthusiasm. She got a determined 'must try harder' expression on her face and took another stab. 'Or some Burberry's, some Trenchard's . . . or, madam, perhaps you would like to try our latest . . . the camel-coloured cashmere straight in from Paris?'

Well, I was intrigued. What colour, exactly, is a camel? Are they all the same colour? Is there really such a thing as camel colour? Did she mean 'caramel' maybe? Was I to cloak myself in sticky toffee? In any case, the idea of camels and winter coats appealed to me. There was something of the desert in camels and something of the Antarctic in winter. Vast, open, barren opposites. The hot and the cold, the refined and the plain, the sick and the well.

'I'd like to try the camel cashmere,' I told the lady. She and Nina both beamed.

The shop assistant scuttled off to bring me back some coats in different styles and sizes but all in camel-coloured cashmere. Camel, I discovered, is the colour of Bambi. A light fawny brown. Cashmere is the softest and most inviting wool I have ever come across. Just touching it with your fingers makes you want to rub it against your cheek and bury your face in it. The one I liked best wrapped around like a dressing-gown and tied with a sash. Two silky ribbons from the lining fastened it on the inside, and a long belt pulled the whole thing together on the outside with Scarlett O'Hara tightness. I didn't think I would actually wear it but I thought I could live with it.

'I'll take it,' I said. The shop assistant and Nina could not contain their delight. The shop lady must have thought she had read me expertly and catered to my European tastes exactly. She looked flushed and pleased with herself like a person who thinks they are in line for a promotion. Nina was pleased because she had achieved her mission. The waiting and the agonizing were over because now we had found it, the winter coat that she could buy for me. None of us had looked at the price tag.

'Four hundred and fifty-eight dollars?' Nina repeated with momentary disbelief when the shop lady told her.

'What's the eight for?' I asked. Everyone ignored me.

Nina began to fish in her handbag frantically. I started to untie the inside ribbon on the coat. No one could be worth spending four hundred and fifty-eight dollars on just for a coat, surely, could they? I stared at the floor uncomfortably. A packet of Marlboro thins, 20's, dropped out of Nina's bag, spilling cigarettes on to the carpet in front of me. She snatched the box up quickly. She obviously did not want me to know they were there. Maybe the Marlboro's, like Larry, were a secret, something she kept private, inside of her, only for herself. At last she had found what she was looking for in her handbag. She pulled out a brown paper envelope and handed it to the shop lady, as I held out the cigarettes that had fallen.

'André doesn't know,' she cautioned me as I gave them back.

I didn't think he did.

'He doesn't know about the money either,' she said. She turned to the shop assistant who stood unsurely now with the brown paper envelope in her hand. 'There's five hundred in there,' Nina told her with all the poise, authority and directness of a confirmed outlaw. 'Would you mind counting out my change for me?'

We watched together like Bonnie and Clyde at a bank robbery as the woman took a wad of bills from the envelope and shakily put them on the counter. There was an assortment of ones, fives, tens, twenties and fifties. I felt for one moment the triumph my sister Cynthia must have known when she revealed her hidden

154

stash in our games of Monopoly. The shop assistant squirmed with discomfort as she counted out each bill. It was clear she longed for her normal sort of customer who bought on account or paid with a credit card. After checking the notes anxiously for counterfeits, she finally conceded she had been given enough of the right kind of money. I stood next to Nina, safe and warm with the coat draped around me.

'Won't madam take the coat off, so I can wrap it?' the poor woman pleaded.

'Yes, of course.' I fumbled with the ribbon I had been trying to untie before. It had knotted itself into a tight wad and wasn't going to give easily. I pulled the top part of the coat off my shoulders and tried to pull the rest down with it over my hips. I had forgotten how tightly the ribbon was fastened around my waist and although there wasn't a great deal of difference between my hip and waist measurements there was enough to force the stitching on my almost-purchased four hundred and fifty-eight dollar camel-coloured cashmere coat. The knotted ribbon ripped from the lining, leaving a gaping hole exposing the cashmere underneath. The shop assistant gasped and Nina laughed.

'There's no bringing it back now,' she said. 'Do we get money off for damaged goods?' she added. It was wonderful to see her so animated and full of life.

'I'll carry it like this,' I said when I'd stepped out of the coat feet first. 'No need to wrap it up, thanks.'

'It's regulation,' the shop assistant said, close to tears, as she took the sorry-looking garment from me and started to lay it on some tissue paper on the counter.

'Oh, OK, thanks,' I said. Nina and I laughed some more.

The shop lady wrapped my coat in tissue paper and put it in a large rope-handled Lacey's bag. Then she gave Nina back her change of forty-two dollars. 'Tax is included in the price of the coat,' she explained as she handed back the change.

'Thank goodness for that,' Nina said. We had club sandwiches in the fifth-floor restaurant at Lacey's. Nina had a black coffee and I had a cranberry juice with ice. The lunch bill came to $8.39, leaving us exactly $33.61 to get to the hairdresser's.

'I can charge the bill at Mel's to André's account,' Nina explained to me in the taxi as we left Lacey's with my torn cashmere coat safely tissue-wrapped in its bag. 'Usually I can only shop where he's got credit.'

'Where did the money in your purse come from?' I asked her.

'My ring,' she told me. 'The ring André bought for me when we got married. It was too big for me after I'd had my first operation and started the treatment. I lost a lot of weight then, so I didn't wear the ring anymore because I was afraid it would fall off. André offered to put it into the bank safe for me, but that seemed silly, to let it be locked away like all of his other treasures. I sold it. Pawned it, actually. I could get it back, if I ever had the money or if I ever wanted to, that is. I could get it back so it's not necessarily gone forever.'

But I could see in her heart that it was. Nina had traded in her ring from André which held no value for her anymore, for a cashmere coat for me which obviously did. I reached in and felt the wool of the coat like velvet against my skin. I clutched it close and felt my wrist pulse beat with an urgency and life against the strong rope handle of the brown Lacey's bag.

26

There was once an exiled girl – a princess – who had been forced to roam unguided and alone for many years. Because she could not be his, she had been placed under a spell by a great magician, whose curse had been that everything she came into contact with would become unfamiliar. The princess wandered alone in forests she was destined never to know or be able to fathom. Eventually she was met in her wanderings by a small bird with a bald appearance and bright eyes, carrying in its beak a piece of parchment inscribed with strange writing. The bird explained that what it carried was an invitation for the princess to come to a tower belonging to a nearby king. Grateful but apprehensive, the princess followed her small featherless exegete to a clearing, a welcome respite from the tangle of trees and undergrowth, where there stood a magnificent tower of antique splendour. The princess was led to a small room at the top of the tower. The room was bare apart from a single bed, a small table and a book with scripture of the same type the bird had carried. Though its dimensions were small and the only view from it obscured by a metal grille across the window the room was pleasant and afforded the princess what she had not had for so long – a quiet, protected solitude.

For a while the princess was content just to rest and do nothing. She had lived her life as a nomad for so long that it was like a sigh of relief to find herself in some place of permanency. Being in the tower awakened something very old and very primitive in the girl and she lay there for many days, still and unmoving, basking in this sense of returning to a place where she had once been. Though it was he who was responsible for her being there, the king was unnerved by the presence of the princess in his domain. Every day he walked the distance from his castle to the tower and stood at the bottom, sometimes for hours, wondering what he should do about the young lady who now dwelt there. He, like everyone, knew of the magician's curse and, because of it, knew that the distance created by the tower between himself and the princess was a necessary part of their intimacy. To attempt any closer form of contact would render him forever a stranger in the young girl's heart and this he could not bear.

If he could not take himself to where she was and be with her directly, the king decided he must send gifts in his place. Again he enlisted the small bird's help and asked it to carry up fine ribbons and bits of silk, small jewels and ornaments and endless poems, odes and sonnets which he wrote himself in a language he knew the princess could never understand. Each of these things the bird placed in her beak and travelled up with on a current of air to place them gently through the metal grille of the window and into the room where the princess lay. Eventually the gifts, though small in themselves, began to crowd the room and the princess felt she might lose her view altogether or even the ability to breathe if anything more were brought to her once so simple abode. The king knew nothing of the crowding and continued to send his gifts as substitutes for himself.

The princess knew that the only way she would survive was to escape the tower and risk her blind wanderings once more. The king's gifts had taken away her ability to think or experience herself as anything more than an inanimate object like all those that had been bestowed on her. She longed for human contact but knew she could not ever love and be with someone at the same time.

Her means of escape came to her in a dream. The bird, she thought, must be an exile like herself. In her dream she met with the bird as one would meet with their own reflection in a pool of water. 'We are the same,' the bird had spoken and, looking in the bird's bright eyes the girl could see that it was true. 'Yes,' she said, 'though you are bald and my head is burdened with hair.'

The bird cocked her head knowingly to one side and seemed to smile as she told the princess, 'Unburden yourself.'

When the princess had cut and torn away every single hair on her head there truly was no difference between herself and the bird who had brought her to this place. In her waking as well as in her dream the girl shared every feature with the small delicate creature, including her size which, unfettered by feathers, could slip easily between the spaces of the metal grille and fly free back into the depths of the forest from which she had come.

Dear Alma,

I thought I should write and tell you how I'm getting on. Well, I'm in San Francisco staying with Dad and . . . a couple of his friends. One of them is a woman called Nina. She's a great woman, Mom, you'd like her. I've told her all about you. She bought me a coat and, wait for it, persuaded me to get my hair cut. Short!!! There's hardly any of it left. I'll send you a photograph when I get around to it.

Dad is fine. He's busy, you know, involved with lots of things. He's off on a retreat at the moment. He loves the life out here. I don't think he would ever go back to England. He still says he did us a favour by getting us over there though. Funny how things turn out, isn't it?

Well, that's about it, I guess. I'm fine. Oh, did I tell you my period started again? After all these years. Isn't that amazing? It means I'm better. Well, getting there. I've put on lots of weight. I'm not fat but you know, just regular. Normal. How I should be. So that's good, isn't it?

Dad's other friend is called André. He's an art collector. Amongst other things. You'd probably like him as well. Well, maybe not. So how's everybody? Tell them I said hi. Hope you're OK too. London feels like a long way away. I could sure do with some tea-bags and some Marmite. Maybe you could send some when you get a chance. Bye for now,
    Francine.

After I'd read the letter through I went back and crossed out a few things. The bit about Leon and England for a start. That would just make her mad. Then the stuff about Nina, and André. If they're friends of Leon's, she's really not going to be interested or sympathetic in any case. Then I thought twice about letting her know my period had started back up again. It's not that it's not important. I've been aching for it to come back for years but what with Cynthia having the twins and all, she might feel I'm trying to hog some of the limelight. Anyway, when I was real thin and it was a miracle that I didn't stop breathing, let alone menstruating, she always seemed so furious and blocked for something to say. Well, you know how it is, if someone is deliberately making themselves ill, forcing the life out of their body by their own volition, then it must be pretty hard to know how to respond when they complain of the side-effects. It could be, of course, that Mom was just scared, but whatever the reason I didn't think it was worth stirring the whole thing up again. It's different with Nina. She hasn't chosen, she didn't make herself . . . Actually, maybe it's not all that different with Nina and me. Maybe we're more alike than I think.

Anyway, by the time I'd finished with the crossings out, the letter read, *Dear Alma, Please send me some Marmite and some tea bags. Francine.* I decided not to send it in the end.

My father came back from the retreat wearing a halo of tranquillity. André came back from London looking puffed and exhausted. I wondered at how often their lives, like their physical appearance, took on this unbalanced state of equilibrium. They needed time together, I figured, to reconstruct some of the

160

former semblance of order. Their's was not a love that worked in absentia. Nina went back to her washing-machine and television and looking after the men. I began to think about a future for myself that might not involve any of them.

Apart from the coat trip to Lacey's I had not really ventured far from Nirvana. Alongside Nina I had settled into a fairly quarantined existence within its pristine quarters. It was just as rare for us to leave the house as it was for someone from the outside to enter in. So when Roy, the television repair man, came to breathe new life into the vertical tuning of Nina's window on the world, it was the breath I also needed.

Roy was about my age and came from Los Angeles. He said he didn't want to end up a bum on Hollywood Boulevard so he'd come to San Francisco to make good. When he arrived Nina was watching the rinse cycle, André was asleep on the sofa and Leon was out taking a walk. I asked Roy if he wanted a soda or a glass of tomato juice, the two things we always had lots of at Nirvana. Roy went for the soda.

'So, you English?' he asked me.

'Kind of,' I said. 'I've lived there.'

'Cool,' said Roy. 'You going back?'

'I don't know,' I answered truthfully. 'It kind of depends.'

Roy nodded like he knew what I was talking about and that made me feel like I did.

'It depends whether I decide I can look after myself,' I explained.

'Things a bit psychedelic here then?' asked Roy, nodding in the direction of the snoring André.

At first I thought he might be being sarcastic but then I realized that in a way he was right. I was existing in a kind of psychedelic haze where nothing felt entirely real or tangible. It wasn't just Nirvana that made me feel like that. The previous nineteen years had something to do with it too. I wondered if Roy had a way of seeing when people, like televisions, needed their pictures adjusting.

I did not want to leave San Francisco altogether but I knew I had to move away from Nirvana. The irony of the house's name had only just dawned on me in its entirety. Nirvana is a state of absolute perfection which only the holiest can ever hope to attain. Even the most determined and devout of mortals can spend many lifetimes in its pursuit. To arrive at such a place at the beginning of a journey rather than at the end of one is to deny everything that may go beyond it. I liked this city and I wanted to make a go of it, however difficult it might be, on my own. As I had used up most of the cash I came with and I didn't have a ring like Nina's to pawn in order to get any more, I started to investigate other ways of making the money I would need to pay for alternative accommodation. I went around the little arty shops and cafés on Fisherman's Wharf and asked if they needed anyone. I came close to getting some part-time work in one of them, a gift shop called Blue Moon. The snag came when they asked me what my star sign was and I told them I was a Gemini.

'Oh God, I'm sorry,' the woman of indeterminate age with poppy-red dyed hair and dark purple lipstick told me. 'We already have a Scorpio and a Leo working here. I don't think the karma would be that good if we had a Gemini too. Sorry.'

It soon became apparent that to be eligible for a job in this city I should be prepared to vary my birth chart and have a flexible ascendant. My accent, which had become almost completely anglicized, was not helping much either. The Americans have too much respect for the British to want to employ them.

'Celebrate your differences,' Leon told me when I was discussing my day of job-hunting that evening at the dinner table. 'Be unique and you'll never have any competition.'

It seemed to make sense while he was saying it but later, when I thought about his advice, I realized it was totally unworkable in the real world. If you were really so different and special that there was no one else like you then you would be irreplaceable. Accepting someone irreplaceable into your workplace, home or life, is too great a risk for anyone. I could see that my dad and André tried to make a virtue out of being different but I wasn't sure it made them valuable to anyone except each other, perhaps. I would have to think about the charting of my future as a displaced national in this country very carefully.

'Do you want to see Golden Gate Park, Francine?' Leon asked me on one delightfully warm October afternoon.

'Sure,' I said, 'I'd like that.'

'Good,' said my father. 'I have to stop by the cleaners and pick up André's suit for him, but then we can drive over to the park and take a walk.'

It was probably the first time we'd been alone together since my arrival. Of late, conversations with my father had taken on the same syrupy blandness that enveloped the rest of the household. Lots of tender nothings and empty endearments but no real words of any meaning being exchanged by anyone. Not that I relished major intensity or a confrontation about anything in particular, but I felt we needed to make a real point of contact somehow. A walk in the park seemed the perfect way.

'What do you think of André and Nina?' my dad asked me when we entered through the golden gates. 'Nice, huh?' he answered for me before I could speak.

'Yeah, nice,' I echoed as I didn't really feel I had been left any other option. 'Too nice maybe,' I ventured, wondering if I was sticking my neck out just a bit too far at this early juncture.

'Too nice?' he asked.

'Well, you and André . . . you don't seem to . . . well, I guess it seems that you don't really know each other all that well. I mean . . .' I desperately searched my father's face to try and tell whether what I was saying was going to make him erupt with anger. 'I mean, you're so busy being nice to each other.'

He was silent for a few moments, kind of looking at the trees and beyond with a sort of wistful expression on his face. Finally he spoke. 'Geez, Francine,' he said with that kind of wheezy laugh I remember from years back. 'How'd you get so wise?'

He wasn't being sarcastic. I could tell his sarcastic voice. It had the cutting edge of a meat cleaver. This was soft and gentle and a little bit sad like he had lost something.

'How did you ever grow up to see things so clearly?' he went on, shaking his head and still looking into the distance.

For some reason I thought of Miss Green then. My third-grade teacher who sighed about my poetry. I wondered if she'd have expected things to turn out like this for me. Walking here in Golden Gate Park with my father who I was only just beginning to know. I hadn't written a poem in years. Miss Green is probably a grandmother by now.

'It's only because I love you.' I went through the words several times in my head before I actually spoke them. I was worried about them coming out wrong. Too corny or insincere. I don't think I have ever said this to anyone without it being through some kind of formality or jest. I stopped walking and looked out to the same distant point my father had his eyes fixed on and repeated what I had said.

'It's because I love you, Dad.'

The thing was, it was true. True in the way that Leon had explained love to me all those years ago. If two people live totally separate lives, maybe even in separate countries on two opposite parts of the world, and they still worry and care about what happens to the other, then that is love. Something like that.

'I love you too, Francine.'

For that brief moment in time, nothing, but nothing else, mattered any more. I was cocooned, wrapped up, safely contained in the surety of my father's love for me and mine for him. Golden Gate Park was beautiful. Never had I heard birds sing so loudly or so clearly and never had I seen people's faces shine so brilliantly in the sunshine.

On the way home in the car we talked some more. He asked me questions like I was the guru and he was the disciple.

'Do you think I'm being false?'

'The relationship is stifling,' I said. 'It's based on pretence. The pretence of André's marriage to Nina. The pretence of your child-like dependency on André. The pretence that he could be a father to anyone.'

Leon liked that last bit. Questioning André's ability to be a father obscured any doubt there might be over his own. He sat straight and tall behind the steering wheel, growing with an ever-increasing sense of superiority over the man who kept him and the dying woman who saw to his needs.

'You're right,' he said. 'I'm going to be more real.' He let one arm leave the steering wheel and reached out affectionately to ruffle my hair. 'Hey,' he rumbled softly, 'thanks for helping me to be me.'

Somewhere inside I felt I might be betraying Nina and André somehow by having this discussion with my father. Something about biting the hand that feeds you. But I was too drunk on my father's appreciation of me at that point to give it too much thought or worry. We arrived back at Nirvana like two rebellious teenagers high on life.

Nina eyed us suspiciously and asked where André's suit was so she could hang it up.

'Oh yeah,' my dad giggled. 'I left it in the back of the car.'

'Seems like you got high on the fumes,' said André with expert bitchiness. 'The dry cleaners can't have aired it correctly. I'll have to say something.'

My father and I burst into giggles again and exchanged a knowing look.

'Sorry,' Leon said as he went back out to the car, still giggling, to fetch the suit.

When he was out of sight the whole thing suddenly seemed less hilarious and I went upstairs to my room to look through the classifieds again under 'Rooms Vacant'.

27

For a short time I was my father's guru. Bhagwan Francine. He looked to me for guidance and 'wisdom', he said, to help him be 'true to himself'. This kind of truth did not go down well in the André household. Leon started to speak his mind which turned out to be a much more critical discourse than the kissy-kissy 'love you' mode of relating. André began to visibly react under the strain of dealing with this new liberated Leon. Heart problems that had been a feature of his earlier life, before he had even met Nina, came thumping back. He began to clutch his chest and look faint every now and again, particularly when Leon was laying some of the 'truth' stuff on strong. On repeated occasions, Nina pleaded with Leon to stop upsetting André as she was sure his heart was going to give out.

'I'm not in control of his physical health,' he told Nina. 'Pills and doctors do that.'

'But you *are* a doctor,' she begged, the sheer terror in her eyes betraying the deep devotion she felt for her husband despite their lack of sexual union.

'Not his,' my father answered curtly and, I could swear, with a little grin on his face. The tables had turned and he was getting great pleasure, I could see, from this power switch whereby he no longer felt he had to be the solicitous and humble servant and could, instead, reign terror and chest pain over the ruler's palace.

Something was going to burst. Either André himself, like a blown-up balloon, or the whole of Nirvana thrown up into the air and exploding into thousands of tiny fragments of precious art objects, washing-machines and broken television sets. The moment of reckoning came sooner than any of us expected. Just days after our walk in Golden Gate Park, my father suggested a cinema trip. He wanted to take me, he said, to see his favourite film of all time which he thought I would enjoy as well. The film was *Les Enfants du Paradis* with Jean-Louis Barrault. It was showing at a small cinema club in a part of the city I had never been before. It was a cinema for devoted film buffs only, there were no frills: no popcorn stand, no ice-cream or soft drinks on sale and no cartoons before the main feature. We just bought our tickets from a guy in torn jeans who looked a bit like Che Guevara and took our seats in the tiny auditorium. Leon and I made up two thirds of the audience. The only other person there was an old man with grey matted hair who looked as though he must either be an Einstein or a tramp. He was half asleep and slumped in his seat, so I guessed that he was most probably the latter and had come into the cinema to keep warm for a bit.

The film started with a soundtrack that sounded as though it might have been stretched through overuse. The picture, too, was a bit crackly but it didn't really matter. It felt as though the cinema had arranged a private showing just for us and I was aglow with the sense of honour and privilege of it all.

The children of paradise mentioned in the title turned out to be grown-ups (Jean-Louis Barrault, several other French actors and a beautiful woman with dark sunken eyes called Arletty) doing various street performances in Paris. It was about adults playing and living out fantasies to the point where it was impossible to tell what was real anymore. It was not a far cry from what I felt San Francisco to be. A place where adults can try out lifestyles and attitudes like a child tries out playground equipment.

The film was over three hours long and at the end of it we both felt a bit spaced and needed to walk around outside a bit before catching the trolley-car home. We talked about the film and otherwise said very little. My dad put his arm around me and hugged me close and I felt glad to be his daughter. When we got in it was after midnight and we were both starving. The house was quiet and André and Nina, it seemed, had both gone to bed. Dad got some cheese from the fridge and opened up some crackers from the cupboard. We sat at the kitchen table and crunched our way through half a packet without using plates, getting the crumbs everywhere. I went to the fridge to get out a carton of tomato juice and had just started to pour two glasses when I heard the sound of padded footsteps coming down the stairs.

It was Nina in her bedroom slippers and nightgown. Her head, which I had never seen before without the covering of a scarf or turban, was completely bald. She was holding a large piece of paper that had several bits of plastic stuck to it. When she got closer I could see that the bits of plastic were credit cards, the credit cards that André and my father shared. Well, they were André's credit cards really, but they also had my father's name on them. They were all cut neatly in half and taped in a broken column down the paper. At the bottom was a date, an ultimatum, an indication of the time Leon had left at Nirvana before he and his bags had to be completely packed and out of there. He had exactly two weeks.

'André asked me to give you this,' she said coldly to Leon. 'He was waiting up till midnight to give it to you himself but you didn't come back. He's in bed now, resting. It's his heart.'

Leon took the sheet of paper with the display of cards ceremoniously and angrily snipped in half. He took it and laughed, a nervous snorting chuckle. I was hoping he might have said something calming or explanatory about our late arrival back or even apologized for the mess on the table, but he just laughed.

'So, André's in bed,' he said wryly, after a long silence, 'in *his* bed I suppose, which has, no doubt, been split now as well. I imagine I am no longer welcome there either.'

'André is asleep in my room,' Nina replied, as cold as ice. 'He'll stay there for the night.' Then she turned dramatically like the Snow Queen. She gathered up the skirts of her nightie and swept icily to the foot of the stairs. At the last minute she turned and faced us again, this time addressing her words to me.

'We both wanted *you* to know, however,' she said, 'that *you* are welcome to stay here with us as long as you would like.'

A rough knife cut through me. I felt my gut churning with guilt and undigested cheese. When Nina had gone my father turned to look at me. I tried to read his face. Was he grateful to me for being there, was he angry that I had escaped André's wrath or was he simply looking to me for guidance as a disciple would turn to their messiah?

'I'm not going to stay here either,' I said, in hopes that this would be both a reassuring and definite thing to say in the circumstances. 'I have found a place, I think, where I can have a room for a few months while the person who lives in it is away.'

'I don't know where I'll go,' my father said pathetically. 'I've really got no place to go.'

I felt suddenly frightened by the tone of desperation in his voice. I had always imagined Leon as someone endlessly capable of re-establishing himself in new places, with new people and in new circumstances. The pathfinder. I was not so sure of my ability to do it for him and I was afraid that he might be suggesting I take him with me. 'The room I've been offered is very small,' I said. 'I don't think they've got any others.'

My guru status was slipping. My father clearly felt as though he had been slapped in the face and now the shock was subsiding and anger was about to take over.

'I don't fucking need your patronization, Francine,' he hissed through his teeth. An old Leon that I remembered from aeons before who could not stand being constrained by responsibilities or ties was starting to show through. Little droplets of spittle collected in his beard. 'You've spent your life taking things away from me so why should it be any different now? You, your mother and your sisters. All of you taking everything.' He waved the piece of paper, heavy with credit-card halves, in front of my face as though it might somehow confirm me as a conspirator in his impoverishment. 'Stripping me bare.'

His face contorted then and he began to weep loud audible sobs, coughing and spluttering like a little boy. I thought and even hoped that Nina and André might come to the top of the stairs again to view the spectacle, but my father was without an audience except for me. I sat like Judas accused and underneath the table my legs had begun to tremble. I dreaded the prospect of spending even one more night in Nirvana and I wanted to be able to flee unnoticed from this house of wails and sobs and torn hearts and credit cards. If I'd had the courage or the combination codes to break through the thicket of alarm bells and systematic locks that protected every portal of the house from intruders (or escapees), I would have run away then and there and spent the night without fear on the lively and open streets of San Francisco. Instead, I went up to my room and shut the door. It was after one o'clock in the morning now but in England it would be around eight. Melanie would already be at school or on her way, but with any luck Mom might still not have left for work. I dialled the number.

The phone at the other end rang several times before anyone answered. Finally a voice I didn't recognize answered the phone. It could have been Spanish. It sounded as though I had woken whoever it was up.

'Alma?' I said, trying to sound super-American and cheerful. 'I'm trying to get hold of Alma, please.'

'Who's that?' the voice said wearily, still half-asleep. 'Nobody here.'

'It's Francine,' I said. 'Who are you?'

'My name is Gloria Victor. I am using the house. The other lady is not here. She stays with her daughter. Her grandchild is very ill.'

What does she mean 'using' the house? Which one of the grandchildren is sick? How sick? I *am* her daughter.

'Oh. OK. Thanks.'

I hung the phone up. The receiver made a hollow clicking sound that hurt my ears. I curled up like one of those grubs that live inside potatoes or on compost heaps and felt like I would have to stay in this position until I hatched into something better.

I lay on the bed but didn't go to sleep for hours. I kept thinking about the twins and wishing I could be one of them. The sick one. With my mom there to take care of me.

In the morning I rang a number I had written down from the little notice in a health-food shop window about a room. Along the top in bold print it read, ROOM FOR TEMPORARY LET IN SHARED STUDENT HOUSE, and then, hand-written at the bottom:

> *I'm going to hike around Africa for three months. If you need a place to stay for a while I'll gladly exchange a crash in my pad for some cash in my bag!*
> *Ring me quick on 377 5781. Jenny*

A voice with a South African accent answered. 'Jenny?' I enquired.

'Yees, it ees. Who's that?'

'Ummm, well, you don't know me. Is the room still free?'

'Not free,' she said. 'Seventy-five dollars a month. And my posters stay on the wall. Are you interested?'

'Yes,' I said without hesitation. Someone else's posters might help me to redefine my existence. I needed somewhere to go. 'Yes,' I told Jenny. 'Yes, I most certainly am.'

28

'San Francisco,' was my answer to the man who stood beside me waiting to collect his bags from one of the luggage carousels at London's Gatwick airport. 'I've just come from San Francisco. How about you?'

'New Delhi,' he said.

'Wow,' I said in genuine admiration, 'that must have been something.'

'It was. Crowded and hot but, nevertheless, something. How 'bout Frisco? Isn't it far out?'

'It's a beautiful city,' I agreed. 'A really beautiful city.'

My bags turned up on one carousel then, and his on another, so I was spared any more conversation in which I might have to elucidate more about my stay in Northern California. We nodded our farewells and parted ways. I vowed not to get into another conversation about my trip with anyone for at least the next twenty-four hours. I need time to mull the whole thing over and shape it into something I could easily tell people about. Actually, I slept for most of the next twenty-four hours. I felt as if someone had whacked me on the back of my head with a hammer.

'It's Aunty Francine.' Cynthia was holding one of the twins over me while I dozed, cooing in their ear. I guessed it was Tom from the mini-dungarees but I could have been wrong. 'She's very, very sleepy,' she told the child in a sing-songy voice.

'No, I'm awake,' I said, still trying to adjust to the reality I was in.

The baby, my nephew or niece I wasn't sure which, was frightened by my voice. Maybe it had thought I wasn't real. Just a big toy lying there waiting to be played with.

'It's all right Katykins.' Cynthia rocked her. I could see now; the dungarees had a flower pattern on them.

'Shall I leave you alone, Francine? Do you want to sleep more? Shall I make some tea? Actually you've been asleep for nearly two days. Are you going to get up now?'

I rubbed my eyes. 'A cup of tea would be great,' I said. 'An English cup of tea. PG Tips or something. With milk.'

Cynthia rolled her eyes. She obviously thought I was crazy. Either that or too demanding. She went off to make the tea anyhow.

'You can leave Katy,' I yelled after her. She didn't hear me or didn't think it was a good idea. After all, I was still a stranger to them even though I longed to be family. Katy and Tom had lived a lifetime already without me.

'Was she the one who was sick?' I asked Cynthia when she brought me back a mug of steaming tea. The twins were sitting up together on the floor playing with rattles.

'Katy? No, what do you mean?'

'Gloria said one of them was sick.'

'Who's Gloria? Francine, honey, just drink your tea.'

She came and sat on the side of the bed and stroked my head. I felt for some awful moment that I might really be crazy. That none of it had ever happened.

'Mom didn't come to stay with you?'

'When?' Cynthia asked, giving me that look again. Half exasperated, half sympathetic. 'Yeah, she's stayed with me. Lots.'

'Oh never mind,' I said. It was going to be too difficult to explain. 'I probably dialled the wrong number.'

Cynthia didn't know what I was talking about but then one of the twins, I think it must have been Tom, started to crawl over to us.

173

'He's crawling!' Cynthia yelled. 'Oh my God, he's crawling. Look, Francine, can you believe it? Oh come on, darling. Come to Mummy!'

Everything else had shrunk into insignificance then. There was nothing else that was important. The world was just one sharp-focus lens on Cynthia's child. I watched her clapping her hands in encouragement as little Tom rocked back and forth on all fours wondering what all the fuss was about. I have never seen my sister's face so radiant or full of life. I tried to blink away my tears.

Cynthia was going to be around with the twins for a week. Mike had some business in Sussex and then he was going to drive back through and pick them all up and take them back up to Skye. Melanie would be back at four and Mom a bit later. Then we would all sit down and catch up on each other's news.

I would tell them simply that living with Dad hadn't worked out and then I would talk about my last few weeks, in Jenny's room, the one with the posters, and how she came back from Africa sooner than expected. I would say how much I loved the cafés where you could go and listen to music and poetry and sit in a dimly lit corner sipping a glass of sweet lemon iced tea, and I would tell them about Fisherman's Wharf where you could get a bowl of clam chowder and watch jugglers and street-mimes recreate the feel of Covent Garden. I would tell them about the giant pretzels that come out hot and coated with rocky lumps of sea salt and sesame seeds and make you thirsty beyond belief. I would tell them about Golden Gate Bridge and the people who go there seeking new ways out of old lives and end up plunging themselves into non-existence. And I would remember silently Leon and the park we walked in with the green and the trees and the wide open sky where all of the world for one moment seemed to be contained in a single ray of sunlight. I would think of Nina who wrapped me up in a second skin when I was having so much trouble inhabiting my first. I would remember it all but tell only some of it. The rest would be secret and maybe with time and distance I would be able to shape it into the kind of memory that

I needed it to be. I just thought if I could hold on to it in my head for long enough I might be able to build up a picture where Katy and Tom and Dick and Harry and whoever else is on the scene by that time, have both a Grandma *and* a Grandpa who knows and loves them, and Cynthia and Mel and I can talk about the past without flinching or feeling as though we come from entirely different planets.

At dinner that night the conversation centred mainly around Tom's crawling. Katy too, apparently, had stood for three seconds by herself while holding on to her soft rabbit. Cynthia was sorry Mike hadn't been there to see it but Alma said it didn't matter, there would be other achievements of theirs he would be there to witness. Melanie had exams. Did I know anything about the English Renaissance and could I help her with her paper? Katy and Tom threw pasta at each other and I was shown how to work the new dishwasher and where the cups and plates were being stored now that the old cupboard had been taken away. Stories about my San Francisco trip were relegated to the back burner and there was relief more than surprise that I had very little to say about any of it. It was enough to hope that now, back at home, I might fit in with the changes and not try to dominate the table with my old ways. Francine who always has to do things differently. Francine the attention-getter and the family-meal spoiler. Francine Weitz who remains incomplete even now that her search for completion is over. Getting back to the womb is always a harder thing to do than I ever imagine it will be.

THREE

29

Different voices trailed around me like multicoloured ribbon draped around a maypole. There were pocket-sized flashes here and there where I thought I recognized the person who was speaking, but even those brief moments faded into the wider blue oblivion. The bed I was lying on was high up off the ground. Not as high as the bunk beds that Cynthia and I first shared in our bedroom in Seattle when I had the top one closest to the ceiling where a fluorescent poster glowed green and pink in the dark with the word LOVE written in giant bubble writing. Not as high as the diving board I jumped off of when Sophie Tomlinson dared me to at the Sunnyside Recreation Centre and I lost my nose plug and the top of my bikini came off when I hit the water. The bed I was lying on was just high enough to make me feel as if I was floating. It felt regal and powerful being that much off the ground and even though I was lying down I seemed to be just about even with the faces of the people around me.

Thinking about Cynthia was odd because it almost felt, with thoughts alone, as if I could conjure her out of my mind and into the room with me. Like one of those out-of-body experiences. There was a woman whose face I kept seeing. There was some-thing awfully familiar about her but I think she must have been a nurse. It was always possible, of course, that Cynthia was a nurse and I didn't know about it, but I didn't think the woman with the pinched face and grey hair who spoke so quietly and earnestly to the people around her could really be Cynthia. Cynthia wouldn't be that old. It was hard, really, to know how old anyone would be now. I knew I had to get the facts straight in my head so I spent quite a lot of time in this place with my eyes shut because it was easier to think like that. I tried the memory test on myself, partly as a way of making sure that I could remember things, but also as a way of trying to work out what my most recent memory was in the hope that it might give me some clue as to just where I was and how far I'd gone.

The memory test is an old one. I think I have been doing it since I was about seven years old. Around that time I hit my head in the playground at school while swinging on the parallel bars. I had just learned how to grip the bar with one knee and propel myself three hundred and sixty degrees to upright again. I hit my head on a piece of concrete that was jutting out where they had cemented the poles into the tarmac. Mrs White, the teacher who was on playground duty, had to call my mother and the ambulance because there was so much blood. I had stitches and everything, which I know because of the scar they left, but most of all I remember a kid called Sherry Lewinson telling me that I would have almost certainly lost at least a million brain cells with a blow that hard. I didn't know how many brain cells I'd started out with, but a million seemed a lot to lose all in one go. In the ambulance on the way to the hospital to get my head stitched up I tried to invent some kind of way of testing how well the brain cells I had left were still serving me. I figured if I had already lost a million my thinking would be somewhat impaired, but there was nothing I could do about that now. At seven, losing a million brain cells did not seem a huge price to pay for having mastered the one-kneed-swing-around-the bars, nevertheless I was concerned to know I was still functioning at a fairly OK level. I did the usual sort of running through of simple sums and general knowledge questions in my head, all of which I got right if I recall correctly, and then I invented the memory test. I tried to remember what the first thing was that I could ever remember. I made myself not cheat and decided that anything that I might have been told about or shown a photograph of that had happened when I was a baby was not allowed because that wasn't real memory, only replayed anecdote. Lying there with a wet bandage on my head and a vague sense of the ambulance lights flashing and siren sounding overhead, I surprised myself by realizing that the earliest clear memory I seemed to have of any event was my fourth birthday party just some three years previous. It was a bit alarming to think that I couldn't really recall in full anything that had happened before that time but I figured that my life before four must have been what the million brain cells I'd zapped away on the concrete earlier had been holding on to. My fourth birthday party, a modest affair with no real drama attached, therefore became my first point of reference. The place to use as a starting post for any future memory test. A place to go back to. A secure foothold and proof that I had lived then and was still living now.

So I did that, with everyone standing around talking and that man sitting there in the corner and doors opening and closing and me way up there on my mighty bed throne. I did the memory test and tried first to remember my fourth birthday party. It was summer and there were about six of us, including Cynthia, standing out on the lawn by the side of the house, throwing a ball around in a circle. Cynthia seemed to be leading in some way even though it was my birthday. My mother wasn't out there with us so maybe Cynthia had been put in charge. I remember only wanting to throw the ball to Patrick, a little boy who lived next door. I can't remember ever having been terribly interested in him apart from at that birthday party, but I do remember catching a ball he threw to me and then sending it back with great directedness through the air towards his outstretched hands. Cynthia was yelling the rules at us and apparently it was not Patrick I should have been throwing the ball to, but a little girl called Lucy standing on my right who was wearing a green plaid party dress with a huge satin sash tied in a Pollyanna-type bow behind her. Another boy at the party, whose name I can't remember, was teasing me because I was only four. Four-year-olds can't throw balls, he told me and they can't catch them either. He, apparently, had already had his fifth birthday which clearly made him an expert at throwing and catching and gave him the authority to call everyone else around him 'babies'. Cynthia, who must have been six at the time if I was four, took great pleasure, I remember, in stopping the game to inform this little squirt that actually she was a whole year older than him, which put her absolutely out of the baby category. She asked him whether he knew how to do anything else apart from throwing and catching balls, like skipping backwards with a rope, for instance, which is what she had just learnt how to do. She definitely put him in his place and re-established her own authority but I don't remember her defending any of the rest of us.

Francine. I heard my name being called. Or maybe it was just one of the many words that were being spoken around me. A sound adrift, floating around with all the other dusty particles in the air. Maybe I was in a room, inside a place, with many Francines. Each one of them elevated like I was, high above the rest of the world, lying with eyes shut tight, trying to remember what they knew and struggling to understand where they were. Francine. I heard my name again but this time it definitely wasn't being called. It was being spoken about. There were other things being said. Cracked voices, hushed whispers of conversation. '. . . couldn't have seen . . . nothing wasted . . . hours and hours . . . I'm so afraid . . . could take away her chances . . .'

Whispers of conversation like a patchwork quilt. I shut my eyes together even more tightly and set to putting all the little patches together to try to make them into something whole. First there was some sorting to do. There were many different colours and textures. It was important, clearly, to know which ones went together and which ones belonged apart. Coloured voices and so many words with different shapes and textures. *Afraid*. That was a kind of icy blue. Flimsy and full of static, like nylon. The kind that catches on bits of skin and nail when you run your fingers over it. *Wasted*. That's sort of grey muslin, not quite square and a bit frayed at the edges. Stained and useless.

As time passed there were certain things I could be sure of. I knew now that I could tell if it was a man or a woman talking. I knew, also, that I could tell if I had ever heard the voice before. If it was a stranger's voice it glided over the top of me, smoothly like a hummingbird. If it was a voice I knew, a voice I remembered or vaguely recognized from somewhere inside of me, it grated like nails on a blackboard. The sound of it sent shivers through me and made my spine tingle so much that I wanted to roll around until I found something hard I could rub my back against. But I couldn't move. That was the one thing I was absolutely sure of. Apart from the decision to shut my eyes there were no other choices I could make about my physical position. I had tried but it was impossible. There was no sense that my body and I were joined together in any way at present. Just my eyes. With them I could choose. I could open them and see, or I could close them and listen. Either way it was like clutching at straws. Only bits, patches, little pieces of information. I was determined to find a way of putting them all together.

30

'It's possible of course that she will never be able to have children.'

I was awoken mid-sleep by the sound of hushed voices. A man and woman in earnest conversation. I opened my eyes and tried to judge who they were and what they were talking about but from where my bed was placed I could do neither. I could make out shadows and the chair in the corner where the man who waited sat, but I could not see the couple in conversation. I turned the words over in my mind. I wondered if they meant that children would no longer be coming to this place, together with the rest of the throng, to stand around as I lay there trapped and unable to shoo them away. Or perhaps they meant something more sinister. Perhaps, like the witch in Hansel and Gretel, I was being referred to as someone who would wish to devour children and he was simply saying I shouldn't, or couldn't. That children would be bad for my digestive system.

'Oh my Lord,' a woman's voice sounded. 'She could always adopt, I suppose. She would have so loved to . . .'

Or perhaps the having of children was being talked about in the much more conventional sense of bearing them. And it was being pointed out that I couldn't. Bear children, that is. On reflection this did not surprise me because I knew in my present physical state of only being able to exert energy through my eyes, I would surely be defeated by the task of having children, whether that meant spawning them or tolerating their presence round my bedside.

The woman's voice cracked as she spoke and then broke off altogether into silent weeping. I had begun to hear people's tears more loudly than anything else they had to say in this place. The woman's voice I did not recognize at all. It was clear she had great feelings about the issue of whether the person being spoken about would or wouldn't have children by whatever means. The man spoke again. This time in gentle, reassuring tones. I pictured him as being large and God-like with a white beard and flowing robes. I closed my eyes for the full effect.

'Mrs Jenson, your daughter may still have eggs that are uncontaminated by the treatment she has been receiving. I'm afraid I can't let you decide on her behalf but, if it were discussed with her and she chose to, we could arrange to have some of her ovum removed and frozen should she wish to try for children by some artificial means in the future.'

Frozen eggs? I pictured them sunny-side up on a plate with hash browns and a couple of slices of bacon. *'Waitress, these eggs are frozen!' 'Oh, I'm sorry, madam, it's just a yoke!'* I smiled to myself and drifted off again into my own reverie about truck-stops and roadside cafés where you could order frozen eggs, scrambled, with pancakes on the side in huge stacks that came with a choice of thirty-three different flavours of syrup.

I must have been musing audibly, or else I really had found my own joke so funny that I had managed to laugh right out loud, because the man who had been offering his sympathies and reassurances to Mrs Jenson came rushing over to my bedside and began talking to me in a loud, panicked tone.

'Mrs Weitz . . . Mrs Weitz . . . Francine! Can you hear me?'

Mrs Weitz? Had I married my father? Or, had I managed to find, out of the other three Weitzes in the telephone book, a man I could marry that wasn't already some distant relation?

'Francine. Hello, can you hear me? Open your eyes if you can hear me and you understand what I'm saying. Can you speak? Can you speak to me? Say anything. Francine . . . are you hearing me?'

I was. Very loudly and very clearly. In fact piercingly so. I wished he would speak just a little more quietly when he was standing so near to me, or perhaps move away again to where he was with Mrs Jenson, when it was much easier to hear what he was saying without the noise of it going straight through me.

'My God, I think she has some of her senses,' he said with a huge bear-faced grin when I opened my eyes as he had suggested. He leant right over me with a tiny little pocket torch and shone it directly into my vision. I shut my eyes again immediately. Was he trying to blind me into submission?

I must have fallen asleep again then because all I can remember after that for a while is a dream about having babies. Thousands of them, all frozen. Babies born from cold metal ice-trays, clinking out on to the floor in little piles and then scooped into silver buckets like the sort they use for keeping champagne cold or the kind you see on counters at cocktail bars. Mother ice-trays delivering scores of frozen offspring to be piled into containers and then picked out one by one and dropped into drinks with a plastic stirrer, paper straw and a fancy tooth-pick umbrella. In my dream I was both one of these mothers and a person waiting to be served a drink in a moodily-lit cocktail bar, watching as drinks were mixed and little ice babies were separated from one another and put into large glasses to be stirred into the exotic concoctions. As the babies left their melting brood and struggled to keep afloat in their new surroundings they came to life and let out their first cries. At first just a small cry but, as more and more ice-cube kids thawed into audibility, the chorused sound of their crying became almost unbearable as it rose and rose into one single, piercing, high-pitched wail.

'Francine!' I opened my eyes as the wail of my dream merged with the insistent whine of the person standing over me. This time I recognized her absolutely as my sister. I felt something that hadn't moved for some time stir inside of me. A movement triggered by the sudden familiarity of her face and voice, but most particularly her eyes.

'Francine, it's Cynthia. Melanie's here too. We're all here.

Can you hear us? The doctor said that you might be able to now. Do you know who we are? Francine, it's us.'

Melanie's here? My God. Melanie, my baby sister. Melanie with the curls and the rubber-band earrings? There she was. She was wearing earrings now, this tall elegant lady. Large hoop earrings with beads threaded onto the gold wire of the hoop. She looked a bit like a movie star. Or someone who had once been a movie star and now basked in the past glory of it all. She was a bit taller than Cynthia and now peered over her shoulder to smile down at me as well. How had they suddenly risen so high and I, so low? What had happened to my throne bed, the one that towered above the rest of the things and people in the room. The one which let me be an observer of the proceedings rather than a participant. What had happened to all of that? I tried to close my eyes again to see if that would help to bring back the drifting feeling, but Cynthia's voice was too close and too insistent.

'Cyn . . .' I spoke the name to myself. My lips would move now and I could make the shape with my mouth but no sound would come out. Though I tried to release it, Cynthia's name stayed locked with all the others inside some ancient cupboard in my closed and secret attic.

'Francine, darling.' She smiled a warm grandmotherly smile. The endearment sat comfortably on her lips as though she had practised it many times before. She was a proper old lady, the kind you get in storybooks. She had a neat grey bun and wore a soft knitted shawl around her shoulders. I thought I could smell bread baking and vanilla flavouring when she leant so closely over me like that. Cynthia had obviously followed all the instructions and come out the way she was supposed to. A recipe old lady. By the book. Melanie, on the other hand, looked harder, coarser. She was more elegant than I had ever remembered her. More self-assured but with a crusty edge. She didn't have the soft lines that edged the corners of Cynthia's eyes and mouth but then she didn't have many lines at all as far as I could see. Her face looked evenly drawn and without blemish, almost like a painting. Perhaps it had been painted on. Carefully drawn perfection over a foundation of pancake and blusher. But their eyes, the eyes of both my sisters, hadn't altered. Nothing had changed about the browny glow, the deep dark centres that reached back like tunnels into all our lives. The ever wide and open doe-like roundness that always gave a hint of pathos even when they were smiling.

'Mmmm . . .' I wanted to say Melanie's name as well. I pushed the sound out but didn't seem to be able to get past the hum of the first letter.

'Shhh,' Cynthia stroked my head. Her hands were rough and papery. Her fingers were thin. 'Shhh, my darling Francine. We thought you'd never wake up.'

Wake up? I'd been pretty much awake the whole time as far as I could remember. Apart from occasional dozing perhaps, during which time I had my dreams, but otherwise there really had been no rest whatsoever in this place with its constant comings and goings.

'Natalie and Brian are here.'

She might as well have said that Mork and Mindy were here. Or Marks and Spencer. She might as well because I did not know who Natalie and Brian were, even though I could tell by the way Cynthia spoke to me that she thought I should have done.

'They're in the canteen getting something to eat. Brian can only stay a short while. He's due back East for a very important conference.' Cynthia smiled again, only this time like a little child bursting with pride about a picture they had painted or a story they had written, hardly able to contain the delight at the knowledge she possessed about Brian, whoever he was, and his business affairs.

Melanie seemed to know that I might be having trouble on this one. She leaned forward, even closer, hoop earrings jangling against her cheeks and spoke with very elasticated lips. I guess she thought that if I wasn't able to hear what people were saying to me I might just be able to lip-read.

'Natalie and Brian are your children. Two of them. You have a third. Poppy. Poppy's about to have a baby so she can't be here. You're a grandma, Francine. Natalie has two beautiful children.'

'Melanie, she knows all that.' Cynthia tried to brush Melanie away from her shoulder as if she were a fly buzzing too close.

'For goodness' sake. You know all that, don't you, Francine? They're your children, for goodness' sake.'

> *. . . Your children are not your children.*

'She can't hear us, Cynthia, she really can't.' Melanie seemed disappointed with my unresponsiveness. She was deflated too, no doubt, by Cynthia's shove and it appeared she wanted to pull her away from me too, now.

> *They are the sons and daughters of Life's longing for itself.*

'Don't be ridiculous. She can hear everything. She tried to speak just then.'

> *They come through you but not from you,*
> *And though they are with you yet they belong not to you.*

Leon was the first person to introduce me to the words of Kahlil Gibran. He gave me a copy of *The Prophet* for my twelfth birthday. The last birthday present I think I ever had from him. He gave me the complete works of Lewis Carroll as well and I read the whole of *Alice in Wonderland* to Melanie as a bedtime story over a period of about a year. But *Alice in Wonderland* disappeared with lots of other stuff Leon took when he left. I saw the book years later in a box together with other things in storage when Leon was living at André's house in San Francisco. I was going to ask him about it then. I was going to tell him that he had given that book to me as a present and that I would really like to have it back but by that time I figured I was too old for Lewis Carroll and his drug-induced nonsense. I figured that if my father wanted to have the book that was OK and if I should ever want to read something of Lewis Carroll's again I could always find it in the library.

> *'Twas brillig and the slithy toves,*
> *Did gyre and gimble in the . . .*

I wanted to say it so Melanie could hear. So she could remember with me the nights we spent being lost in Wonderland with Alice. I wanted to, but the words were stuck like the past in some dark pit too deep to see or reach down into.

My children did she say? *Mine?* I thought I had begun to piece things together but this bit didn't fit. Were they frozen children, these children of mine? Miracle babies? Why was everyone panicking a minute ago about my having them at all? Melanie and Cynthia had both said that I have children. Three of them. I don't like the name Brian at all and can't think why I chose it. Natalie has a pretty and mysterious sound to it, however, and Poppy is quite nice. Red and expansive. Poppies though . . . isn't that where they get opium from?

. . . *Did gyre and gimble in the* what? Silently I pushed the words around in my head looking for the missing one and wishing I still had the book to see them written down. They sat literally on the tip of my tongue pushing against the inside of my lips that were clamped shut like a garage door that won't open.

'*Wabe,*' I said finally. My lips and mouth felt dry. They stuck together as I finished the word. I wanted to say it again but couldn't. Cynthia said it for me.

'Wabe?' she looked terribly confused. I wished I could have done something for her. Offered some kind of explanation but my jaw had stopped working again and my lips were plastered shut like two rubber tyres melted together in the sun. 'Can you say it again, dear. Francine, darling. What did you mean by "wabe"?'

Ask Lewis Carroll, I wanted to say to her.

> *You may give them your love but not your thoughts,*
> *For they have their own thoughts.*

Ask him, not me. He wrote it. And ask him for me, while you're there, why the borogroves were mimsy and whether mome raths can ingrabe as well as outgrabe. I always wanted to know and Leon took the book away before I could study the whole thing properly.

You may house their bodies but not their souls,
For their souls dwell in the house of to-morrow,
which you cannot visit, not even in your dreams.

I never did get it out again from the library. I just have to rely on memory now. I'll just have to rely on my poor old memory for everything.

You may strive to be like them, but seek not to make them
like you.
For life goes not backward nor tarries with yesterday.
You are the bows from which your children as living arrows
are sent forth.

'She's tired now, we should let her rest.'

Cynthia bit her lip as if she were about to cry and Melanie tried once again to pull her away from my bedside. She even looked towards the man in the corner as though he might be able to help. I attempted one last time to push some words out, anything that might make sense and substitute for communication. I wanted to say, 'No, Melanie, it's all right. I'm not tired. I've rested enough, too much. That's the problem. I'm not tired at all.' But all I managed were the beginnings again. The beginnings of a sound. A word, perhaps. The first sound, the sound that a baby makes for the first time. Mama, mama, ma, ma. The beginnings of Mother, me, mine, Melanie, masticate . . . mmmmmm.

'Mmmmmm . . .' I breathed again.

'Mmm.' Cynthia and Melanie turned to each other and joined in my murmur.

'Mmmm,' I said again until we were a chorus of Mms. Unwittingly and unintentionally joining together into a unity of mumbling agreement, a sorority of sighs, a trio humming softly in perfect discordant harmony. Each part completely together and connected to the rest but not really knowing or understanding one another at all.

31

Many years ago I went looking for Leon. Way before I found him I was looking for him. I think, perhaps, I have always been looking for Leon. Looking for my father. Most of my looking was secret. Furtive. I knew I would be told off or disapproved of if people knew I was looking. 'He's not worth it' they would say. Or, 'Don't torture yourself', or even, 'If he really wanted you he'd come looking himself'. That was the worst one. People telling me that Leon disappearing and making himself so difficult to find was a measure of his not caring. I wanted to believe it could be a thousand other things but not that. I wanted to believe that he had been banished by some law or terrible reason he was protecting me from, maybe because he loved me and he didn't want me to be hurt or scared. I wanted to believe that his absence from my life was as much a torture for him as it was for me. Besides, I knew, or thought I knew because Leon had told me, that love between two people didn't necessarily depend on those two people being together. He told me that even if one person has nothing to give another person, even if they will never see one another again – if they are destined to be absent from each other's lives forever – there can still be love between them. Leon the scientist. Leon the doctor. He knows things because he has the evidence to prove them. In this case

I think his theory may have been founded on inadequate testing procedures.

Where are these children then? These arrows from my bow. I seem to have been waiting an awfully long time today for anyone to show. There is no one here except him, the one who waits. Both of us waiting and long empty silences where my children should have been. Natalie's the tall one, the pretty one. She's kind, too, but not so as she would let herself be taken advantage of. That's a quality that has to be admired in anyone, particularly one's own daughter. The ability to be generous and to give of oneself without being totally trampled or completely devoured in the process. Natalie's got the right balance. She goes out suited in armour thick enough to keep her safe but not so thick as to be impenetrable.

Brian had to go. Unfortunately. I liked having him here, holding my hand and talking to me. He's not lumpy like his name sounds but more like a feather. Fair and wispy, almost beautiful. He has a faraway look about him, not unreachable so much as unfathomable. He's the sort of puzzle, though, that you could sit with for hours, days even, without losing interest. The sort that makes you want to go on and on trying to solve it. But Brian had to go off to some important meeting with some important people. He'll be back. Poppy came in yesterday, or last week sometime. A while ago, anyway. She had my grandchild with her. Luther. 'He's old,' I told her. He reminded me of the man in the corner who was not here today. How'd she manage to give birth to such an old man?

'Babies are always wrinkly,' she said.

But Luther's not just wrinkly, he's old. In a nice way. He's old and wise and he looks as though he's been around for a very long time. People like that are reassuring to be with. They make you feel safe. You know that nothing would shock them because they've seen it all anyway. I wouldn't mind having Luther by my side day and night instead of this nurse they've given me who does nothing but sit and knit and watch the television. The television has nothing of interest for me except for those little numbers and letters they show in the top left-hand corner every so often. I believe if you watch them carefully enough and for long enough they spell out a message. I haven't quite worked out what that message is, but I'm memorizing the numbers and letters that come up so that one day I will.

Once I found him, or traces of him, in a house full of cats. It was a bit scary but I thought it probably served me right because Mom had told me not to go. 'Forget him,' she said, 'He's forgotten you.' And then, when I wouldn't listen, she yelled after me from the doorstep, 'What good is it going to do you?'

What good? I don't know. I was fifteen. I was thin as a rake and I dressed in black for everything, even bed. It was as though I was in constant mourning. I felt I was lacking in everything; friends, food (I was starving myself then), fathers. I begged my mother for some clue as to Leon's whereabouts. An address, a phone number, anything. Mom said she didn't have anything. She didn't know where he was or what he was doing. She said she hadn't heard from him at all and I was stupid if I thought he was going to welcome a visit from any of us even if she did know where I could find him. Eventually she got so fed up with my pressing her for information that she gave me the name and address of the last solicitors she had dealt with concerning the separation.

'You can ask them,' she said wearily, 'where they sent the papers of correspondence to.'

I left Mom alone after that. I didn't bother her anymore for leads as to where I could find Leon. I believed that she really was telling the truth about not knowing where he was or what he was doing and I found that thought profoundly disturbing and sad. Even if you hate and despise someone, if you've put your genes together and produced mixtures of yourselves in your children you should at least have an inkling as to their whereabouts. If only to preserve a sense of order and connectedness about the past and your children's future. Otherwise it's as though it never happened. The knowing of that person, the being with them, the meeting of bodies and souls – it's as though it's all a picture that can be rubbed out, washed clean and thrown away without trace.

The solicitor, as it happened, was not much wiser than Mom on this matter, as he had not been successful in any of his attempts to elicit a reply from any of the correspondence he had sent on behalf of my mother to my father, but he gave me the address he had been trying anyway.

It was a Battersea address. I was surprised. I had expected something further afield. Tanzania, perhaps, or Ethiopia. Even Bath, but not Battersea. I toyed with the idea of taking a friend but as I said before I didn't really have any so I went alone, in black, to the address the solicitor had given to me, neatly typed by his secretary on the gold-embossed stationery used by the firm. The house, unfortunately, was not quite as gilt-edged as the paper its address was written on. As I approached it from the bottom of the street I could see that number 17 looked pretty derelict. A couple of windows were completely missing, leaving an open entry on the ground floor, and others had been boarded up round the back. The door, which was splattered with graffiti inside and out, swung open on rusty hinges in the late April breeze. There were cats everywhere. The cat is not an animal I would normally associate with my father. He never, as far as I could remember, seemed all that interested in pets of any description although he used to tell me stories about a dog he had when he was a young soldier stationed in Germany. Anyway, whether he liked them or not there were cats going in and out of this place, through the glassless windows and the door that looked as though it never shut and through any other cracks and crevices they could manage.

This was not a place for people who did not like cats or were indifferent to them. This place was overrun with the creatures and had little else going for it. As I approached the house, with some trepidation as I was uncertain what I would discover there about Leon, I wondered also whether cats could smell fear the same way dogs could and might respond accordingly.

Cynthia was very old. Melanie was not all that old. This difference I could tell as I watched the two of them arranging flowers at the foot of my bed. I guessed I must be somewhere in between. The person, it turns out, who everyone was so worried about whether or not she would ever have children or should get her eggs frozen, died yesterday. She was a young woman called Sally, aged only thirty-two apparently. She had cancer – leukaemia according to Cynthia. She had come out of some isolation unit and on to the ward in the bed next to mine about three weeks ago, around the time I had the stroke. Unfortunately we just missed each other. When she was not so ill and could have been a friend to me I was in no state to reciprocate and now she goes and makes her exit just as I perk up and we might have been able to give each other some company. Perhaps she wouldn't have wanted it from me anyway. Do thirty-two-year-olds mind about associating with people that are old? Do they have any interest at all in conversing with someone more than twice their age? I don't know, I guess I need to ask Poppy that – she looks to be about thirty-two herself.

I wanted to ask Cynthia if they ever got as far as asking Sally if she wanted her eggs frozen and what she might have said. I wanted to know if, even in death, Sally might be able to get what it was that she wanted. But I was still only able to put one or two words together and Cynthia fretted so much when she didn't quite understand what I was saying so it was really better to stick to yesses and nos. There were actually quite a lot of things I was needing to know now but didn't quite have a way of asking. I needed to know things about myself and my situation, but I wasn't getting the right clues. Not one of the people who came and swarmed around my bedside each day could tell me, and I had still not deciphered the code on the television set.

Was I married, for instance? Had I found a man who was willing to stay with me longer than a few months or even years? If so, who was he and what was he like? Was he still around? I hadn't noticed any husband-like visitors coming, giving me flowers or chocolates or kissing me on the forehead, or whatever else it is that concerned husbands of that sort of age might do. But I suppose Brian and Natalie and Poppy must have a father. Perhaps not the same one, granted. It's difficult to tell by looking at them whether there could be any discrepancy in their parentage. They all have a substantial bit of me in them and a good part of themselves. Whether there is anyone else sprinkled in there and who that person might be I just don't know. I suppose it is always possible that they came from frozen eggs. Perhaps I had once made a decision like Sally might have done, although I found it hard to imagine who might have encouraged me to do so. Certainly it would not have been my mother worrying about my future chances for procreation as Sally's mother had done. Mom, I can imagine, would have very possibly thought it would have been a blessing to go without the burden of children around you. They are, after all, not easy things to deal with and create endless complications in an already difficult life.

The conversation between the doctor and my mother might have gone something like:

Doctor: 'Mrs Weitz, I'm afraid your daughter may not be able to have children.'

My mother: 'Thank God.'

Most of the cats dispersed quickly as soon as they caught sight of a human approaching. I wondered whether it was really possible that anybody apart from the cats lived in this place at all. Just as I was walking up the weed-strewn path to the free-swinging door I saw a small black man walk through from the back of the house and perch himself inside one of the windowless frames at the front of the house. He was smoking a small, hand-rolled cigarette which I assumed to be a joint. I thought of the hookah-smoking caterpillar who Alice takes advice from in her adventures in Wonderland.

'Excuse me,' I said, 'do you know a Leon. Leon Weitz? Does he live here?'

'Upstairs,' the man answered me in a beautifully lilting West Indian accent. The house, cats and all, took on a magical glow. He was here, my father really did live here. The man gestured for me to go inside in a kind of stoned but friendly way. I stepped through the doorway and into a large central entry hall with wooden floorboards, facing a rather elegant staircase. That is, it would have been elegant had there been a few minor improvements. The banister was missing and there were little sharp tacks exposed on either side of it where the stair carpet had been before. The smell of cats combined with stale smoke and a rather sweet perfume which got stronger as I climbed the stairs.

The perfumy smell turned out to be incense. A single stick had been left burning in a smallish room at the top which was, without question, where my father was staying. He was not there but traces of him lined the room like breathing shadows. A pair of faded pink corduroy trousers were folded over a hanger next to some beads made from painted seeds. The trousers I recognized as ones he had bought, when he was with me, from a market stall in Camden. We had both bought a pair and secretly I worried that it might be inappropriate for a father to be wearing pink trousers the same as his daughter, but the stallholder, who was dressed entirely in crimson velvet, assured us they were unisex and that there was no limitation on the age or relationship of the wearers. They were 'People Pants', he told us.

A couple of dog-eared journals with my father's initials, L.R.W., written on the front cover were lying on a small table by the single mattress in the corner. I wanted to tuck them under my arm and sneak away, carrying a bit of my father with me before the shadows came to life and I might have to face my real father in person. But my fear of punishment and my belief in the privacy of journals was too great, so I left them untouched on the table where they lay. Instead, I went around the room fingering the items of clothing and other bits and pieces I recognized as being his. I buried my face in a plaid shirt that hung, unironed, in the corner and smelt his fatherly bearded smell.

'If one person who is in love with another goes to a faraway place so that those two people will never ever get to see each other again and they still worry and care about what happens to the other one even though they can't give each other anything then that is love.'

My tears made a wet patch on the material. I tried to shake the shirt out a little to help it dry. I figured my father must be intending to come back soon, judging by the incense that had been left burning here. He would be coming back expecting to find the room empty and peaceful the way he had left it. A resting place where he could be alone with his thoughts and his journals and his incense. I felt a sudden urgency to leave. I did not know what I would say if I really did see my father and I thought perhaps the black man downstairs might be ringing the police as he had not actually given me permission to enter the house. I pictured several wild cats downstairs patrolling the front entrance, ready to pounce with claws out, as I tried to steal away. I gritted my teeth and dashed down the stairs catching my canvas sneaker on one of the tacks as I ran, ripping an 'L'-shaped tear into it. I saw a telephone in the hallway and memorized the number. Breathless, I dashed out the door without looking behind me to see if the same man was still perched on top of the window ledge. 'Irie,' he shouted after me. 'Jah lives!'

Jah lives. God lives. He is everywhere. Our Father. Our Father . . .

Forgive us our trespasses . . .

Everywhere and nowhere. In heaven and in hell. I wonder if God likes cats?

32

'It burns, it burns, it's burning!'

'Breathe, Francine. Don't forget to breathe. Look at me and pant. Like this, like a dog. Pant, pant!'

'Ouch, ouch, noooo.'

'That's a girl, there you go. See, here, feel it. It's here. Can you feel it? That's the baby's head. There you are, a beautiful round head.'

Just a head? Where is the rest of it? Did I do all this work just to have a head? Ouch, no more, I can't take any more . . . whoops. Oh, what was that? A waterfall? My God, it's a baby. Shiny. Rounder than I expected. I thought they were supposed to be shrivelled. Like prunes. It's a girl. I knew it would be. A perfect girl. The most perfect, I think, that has ever been constructed. Of course. There had to be a point to it all. Otherwise why would anyone . . . perfection. I'll call her Natalie. The name means birth. Perfect.

'Well done, Francine.'

'Well done, darling.'

There were two people. Two people there in the room with me. Apart from the baby. My baby. My Natalie. There were two others. One was a woman. A very kind woman with a hat on. A cap. One of those little caps that waitresses wear in short-order coffee bars. Or maids in old-fashioned parlour rooms. Or maybe a hat like nurses wear to keep their hair from falling on their patients. Nurses with clean hands and starched dresses, and little white hats like this one. The woman who was with me must have been a nurse. Or maybe a midwife there to help me with my birth, my Natalie.

The other person was a man. A man without a face. At least I could not give him one in my memory. Everything on his side had gone a bit blurry. It was like trying to see something through a steamed-up window. Reach back as I might I could only retrieve an image that was cloudy and without clarity. It was like trying to remember a fact for an exam. A fact that you can just about see the edges of but can't quite pull to the front of your mind in order to use it to complete your answer. Perhaps he was a doctor, this man. A doctor there to watch over in wonderment and authority as the nurse helped me to perform this most primitive of rituals. Or perhaps he was someone else. Someone else in my life that I can't quite place now. Someone who would have expected, like me, to receive Natalie, shiny and round and perfect, joyously into the world. I closed my eyes and went backwards. As far as I could go. Backwards into long tunnels and corridors without doors or windows. I did the kind of searching that is best done with eyes shut. The seeking out of a man's face. You could never do that by simply looking. It would be like trying to see God. It's no use even trying.

'Mother. Mum!' A man's voice filtered into my reaches. I knew its sound like paper rustling in the wind. A sound so familiar that you hardly know it's there. I grew up with the sound of this voice.

'Brian,' I lifted my arms. Both of them would respond now to my inward commands. Slowly my body was remembering the training, the lifetime of drilling, it had been put through. I did not even have to think about it. At least not very hard. 'Brian, my son. You're back. You came back.'

'It was only a conference, Mum. I was always coming back.'

'Natalie's been born,' I told him. I wanted him to know. I was crying then, but they were tears of joy.

'Natalie?' Brian seemed surprised. Well, of course he would be. When she had been born before he was not there for me to tell him. He had not yet been born himself.

Yanks Go Home! The message was printed in white. Huge white painted letters on the sides of bridges covering the road, buildings, the inside of tunnels and everywhere in children's playgrounds. Of course I knew what it meant. I knew it wasn't a message for me, but somehow I wanted it to be. I wanted to go home. To have a home to go to. The trouble was, I was neither sure enough of who I was to believe that I was a 'Yank' nor did I really believe I could call America, or anywhere else for that matter, my home.

Melanie started to say 'Pass the butt-ah' at the dinner table. Not long after we had all arrived, in our red-checked shirts and unmistakable American accents, Melanie had started to change and say things like 'Ta' for thank you and 'never mind' if she was upset but didn't want anybody to know. None of us in our entire lives had ever said 'never mind' to Melanie before. 'Forget it' or 'don't worry' but never 'never mind'. Nor had we ever pronounced the 't' in butter. It was *budder* with the accent on the 'r' at the end.

Melanie was trying to be English. Melanie's quest in life was to be accepted. If that meant changing the way she spoke and the words she used then so be it. The trouble was, if none of us were Yanks, how could we ever accept the invitation to go home?

'Grandma sends her love.'

Grandma? Me? I'm a grandma. What other grandmas do we know? Wait a minute. I can work this out. My son is referring to someone as Grandma. My son's grandma. The grandmother of my son, of my children. Their grandmother. My mother. My mother sends her love?

'She's alive?'

'And kicking, like you will be, Mum. Just you wait and see. We live long lives in our family. Yours is not over yet.'

My mother, alive? But she must be ancient. I feel old enough. What about . . .? I didn't dare, did I? Could I ask him?

'What about Grandpa, Brian?'

'Grandpa?'

'Yes.'

'Who *is* Grandpa, Mum?'

33

The telephone number from Battersea was easy to remember
because it spelled BAT-BALL if you thought of it in terms of
letters on the telephone dial instead of numbers. It was a few days
before I dared to try ringing it. I needed to collect my thoughts
and work out just what I was going to say.

I had already told my mother that the lead from the solicitors
had been no good and that I had not managed to track down the
whereabouts of Leon. She seemed relieved.

'Good,' she said. 'So maybe now we can just forget it, hm?'

My mother said 'hm' a lot. Sometimes it made me think she
wasn't bothered or hadn't been listening to what I was saying
but sometimes, like this time, the way she said 'hm' was quite
comforting. Sort of soft and gentle like someone is when they're
pretending to be cross with you but are really just concerned. I
remember her using that same tone when Melanie got lost in
the supermarket. We were looking everywhere. Cynthia had to
cover the frozen foods department and I went into confec-
tionery. My mother scurried frantically around all the rest. In
the end a description of Melanie and what she was wearing was
read out over the Tannoy and some biggish lady wearing a coat
with a fake-fur collar and pink lipstick carried her to the front
check-out. Melanie wasn't even crying and it was a little while
before I could tear myself away from the candy counter to

come and be part of the reuniting, but I do remember Mom holding Melanie and kissing her all over and saying in a gentle but very firm voice, 'Don't you ever, ever, ever run off again. Not ever, hm?'

I didn't forget it though. Neither the house in Battersea nor the telephone number in the hallway. A few evenings later, when Mom was in the bath and Cynthia had gone out with friends and Melanie was asleep, I dialled BAT-BALL and waited. I must have waited about twenty rings before someone answered. I recognized the voice on the other end immediately as my father's.

'Hello?' he said.

I was struck by the ordinariness of it. I had never thought of my father as someone who did things like other people. Like answering the telephone with a simple 'hello'. I had expected something else. I'm not sure quite what it was I had expected but 'hello' seemed too normal under the circumstances.

'It's Francine.'

I hadn't wanted to shock him. Or to confuse him. Perhaps he knew several Francines. Would he know which one of them I was? He might even have been expecting an important call from another person who also had the name Francine and he would be totally disoriented to find that I wasn't her.

'Your daughter, Francine.'

I wished I hadn't said that bit. 'Daughter' also sounded strange. Too ordinary. It was not the right way to describe our relationship but I really wasn't sure of how else to confirm just which Francine I was. There was complete silence at the other end. He hadn't said anything since 'hello'. I couldn't even hear him breathing. I felt I needed to explain myself, reassure him that I wasn't spying, but I didn't quite know how.

'You weren't there,' I said finally. 'When I came over. I came round. I was looking . . . you weren't there so . . .'

More silence. I couldn't even be absolutely sure he was still there. I heard Mom letting the water out of the bath. She would be out soon.

'I'm sorry for disturbing you,' I said finally.

My father hated feeble apologies. 'Sorry is a cop-out word,' he used to say. 'Only sorry people say sorry.'

'Umm,' I needed to say something else. Something else that would get a reaction. A confirmation that he was listening and that he knew who I was. Some indication that he at least had some idea where the phone call was coming from. The last of my mother's bath water slurped down the drain, making a huge suction noise like somebody choking. A lump had risen into the back of my throat and I was afraid that even if I tried I wouldn't be able to say anything else. My mouth and tongue moved into position to say 'sorry' again but I stopped myself, or my tears stopped me because I started crying then in huge, held-back bursts that felt like someone punching me from the inside. I tried to make the crying sound like laughing but then I got worried that he might think the whole thing had been a prank call and phone the police to trace my number. My mom came out of the bathroom without a towel on, her hair dripping. I hated that. Why couldn't she wrap a towel round herself or a dressing-gown and another one around her head so it looked like a turban, like other people did? Seeing her body there, naked, made me stop choking for a moment and I managed a very quick 'bye' before putting the phone back into its cradle.

'Who was that?' Mom yelled in a kind of stage whisper so as not to wake up Melanie.

'Wrong number,' I told her. 'They wouldn't say.'

34

And the fifth grasshopper jumped right over the sixth grasshopper's back and the sixth grasshopper jumped right over the seventh grasshopper's back and the seventh grasshopper jumped right over the eighth grasshopper's back and the eighth grasshopper jumped right over the ninth grasshopper's back and . . .

'They were only playing leapfrog, They were only playing lea-eap-frog, they were only playing leapfrog and . . .'

'The tenth grasshopper jumped right over the eleventh grasshopper's back.'

'No. No, Brian, it's the ninth grasshopper jumped right over the tenth grasshopper's back.'

'It is not.'

'It is, isn't it, Mum. Mum?'

'Yes?'

'Isn't it . . .'

'I don't know where you were in the song. I wasn't listening that carefully. I was looking at the view like you kids should be doing. This is Yellowstone National Park, where Yogi Bear comes from. Aren't you even interested?'

'I'm hungry.'

'Natalie, you can't be hungry. We only stopped an hour ago.'

'Me want someping to eat.'

'OK, Poppy, we'll get something. Just wait a bit and we'll stop and get something.'

'Just because Poppy wants it.'

'No.'

'I want it too. I'm really hungry.'

'You are not, Brian. You're only saying that to copy me.'

'I am not.'

'You are, isn't he, Mum?'

Well, I don't know. How could I know? How could I even pretend to know without copying someone else who thought he knew everything. Copying is the highest form of flattery but believing you know everything . . . assuming omniscience. That's the highest form of arrogance, surely, and deceit. No one knows everything. They only pretend they do to hide what they don't know. To avoid ever having to admit they're wrong. That's not godliness, that's evil. And why did we believe him when he said he knew everything? When he told us that his way was the right way, the only way. Why did we follow when his way took us further and further away from everything we had been sure of before. Real knowing must be about coming home, not going away from it.

'How much longer?'

'Don't whine, Natalie.'

'Someping to eat.'

'OK Poppy, OK.'

The car in front had a Wyoming number plate and three kids in the back. It was a stationwagon and they were all facing out the back window, pressing their noses against the glass and making faces. It's very disconcerting to be stared at by someone else's children. Especially when you know that you are being expected to give some sort of reaction. That's the bit I find hardest. Knowing how to react. Do you smile, wave? Make a funny face back at them? Or do you haul your own kids up to the front so they can save you the embarrassment?

I turned to the man next to me to see if he would know what to do but when I looked I couldn't see his face. He had one, I'm sure. Everybody has a face. Most of the time those faces stay like stamps in your own mind so that you hardly have to look at them to know who they are. We memorize faces, more than any other feature. We only have to see them once to remember them. We see a face once, in the street, on the television, in our bed, and we remember it. It becomes part of our own history and we connect, every time we see that face again. Like the pieces of a puzzle, patches in a quilt. Every time.

'Francine?'

'Leon?'

'Who's Leon?'

'It's her father.'

'Mum?'

'Brian?'

That face again. So many faces.

35

Could be days, could be weeks in this place. They don't care. They don't give you a clock or a calendar to measure the time against. I haven't even got a mirror so the only way I can tell how old I'm getting is to look at the faces of those around me. Just about everyone has a name now, at least one I can remember. Cynthia, Melanie, Brian, Natalie, Poppy . . . except that man in the corner, the one I don't know. He sits there waiting and I can't quite see his face. That doctor with such a serious look about him, that's Dr Peacock. They didn't tell me what his first name is, but I think it might be Luke. Luke Peacock. I've no way of knowing but the two sound right together when you say them in your head.

I'm getting better. They all say so. I can turn my head and if my top arm is in the right position I can turn my body too. Sometimes right over. Depending on my mood, I can get out whole sentences without stopping and still be understood. Sometimes I like to say something and for it not to make any sense at all. It's a way of being heard without having to explain yourself. Cynthia doesn't like that, it makes her feel worried and uncomfortable. She thinks that everything I try to say must have a meaning. I used to think so too but lately I've realized that it's not always like that. Sometimes it just doesn't.

Like this morning. They brought in my breakfast, which I can eat now provided someone feeds me and the pieces have been cut up quite small. It was porridge first and then bacon. I didn't mind the porridge but I knew I didn't want to have the bacon. Even cut up small it takes a long time to chew and I wanted to save my energy for something more important than that. I told the nurse who brought it that I didn't want it. She offered to cut it up into tiny little pieces to make it easier for me but I realized then that it wasn't just the size of the pieces. I really just didn't want the bacon. She got a bit worried and asked if I wanted to have anything else instead. I didn't really – the porridge was fine – but I let her go through the list of options to satisfy a need to get it right in her and a curiosity in me. When she had gone through all of the alternatives and I had said no to each one, she eventually just sighed and took my tray to leave.

As she was going I wanted to say something. I was grateful for her concern and her attempts to find something to take the place of the bacon, but it wasn't really 'thank you' that I wanted to say. I was also happy to have someone spend a bit of time with me running through lists of ideas and possibilities. That was what I spent most of my time doing on my own but it was nice to have a partner in the process. I was a little sad that she had given up when she did and was leaving with my tray. I would have liked us to have stayed longer together, wondering about what it was I wanted and eliminating the available choices. All of these things, I suppose, were in my head when I opened my mouth and shouted what I did after her.

'Line king, no spillius plog. Lint and linnefer trackle umfire!'

She stopped in her tracks. Everything stopped for a moment as though my words had acted like a 'pause' button on the universe. Perhaps it is simply lack of understanding that stops action and confusion that stops thinking. I didn't know what my words meant either but I quite liked the sound of them. The nurse turned in the doorway and faced me. She didn't say anything but I could tell she was running the words through her head, jigging them about to see if they came to rest anywhere she could find a meaning. When they didn't she just smiled and the man waiting smiled too, and then the nurse turned around again to shut the door behind her.

It's quite a comfort knowing that it wasn't only Lewis Carroll who could dream up nonsense words and put them someplace where they are going to get heard. Good to think, too, that even if I never get that book back it is possible to construct one's very own wonderland without it. Natalie and Brian and Poppy. All three of them. They all once had nonsense words of their own. I had thought, when they were young, of compiling a kind of dictionary as a record but it seemed wrong to try to give their made-up words a fixed definition.

'Amenway. Amenway!'

'What's she talking about?'

'It's just a word she uses sometimes. I think it might mean church.'

'Church, why?'

'I don't know. We'll have to ask her when she's bigger.'

'Did I used to say Amenway, Mum?'

'You did.'

Sometimes I tell stories of things I remember and then they just become stories and not things that happened at all. Frozen moments pasted together for others to see, like photographs in an album. Little snippets from time that tantalize and tease with their clarity but always waver, just in front, just out of reach, never to be recaptured or relived completely.

When I saw Melanie later on that day I knew what it was I wanted to say to her. What it was that I had been wanting to say to her for days, weeks even.

'Luvvity,' I cried out when she was within earshot, but at first she didn't hear me or, at least, I couldn't be sure that she did.

'Luvvity, Mel. Luvvity, luvvity.'

She crinkled up her face kind of half smiling because she thought she should. She didn't remember, or wouldn't. She didn't know that this was her word I was saying. A word that she had given to us and that now I was giving back to her. She didn't know or couldn't, maybe. It made me think that maybe words are only transitory, like names and faces. Maybe they only stay for a short while on the person or the idea they are first meant for and then they move on and take up other positions, other homes, always moving so we can never be sure of where they are at any one time. The possibility that there could be such uncertainty in the world of words and people was a sudden comfort. We, none of us, knew quite when or how things were going to happen.

'Luvvity, Mel. Melanie, luvvity.' I stretched out my arms and pulled her to me. She smelled of wet roses and woollen underwear. I held her there for a long time, my little sister. I held her close and breathed her name. An old name that had once been hers and then moved on to other people, other places, other homes. 'Melanie, my baby,' I said. 'My baby, my darling baby.'

The man in the corner smiled.

36

It was a Wyoming number plate so I guess those kids just felt right at home and figured they could do whatever they wanted. They kept on making faces at us out of their back window and there was no getting away. We were bumper to bumper in a huge jam of people waiting to get into Yellowstone. We didn't even want to get into Yellowstone. We'd have been happy enough to drive alongside it and just get a general picture of the place, but we must have got steered off into the wrong lane somehow. The two boys looked to be about seven or eight and there was an older girl with a sharp nose and braces on her teeth. She appeared to be the big sister but was obviously not very hot on discipline. In fact, she seemed to be egging them on, encouraging them to put on a more and more daring and disgusting show for their captive audience. At her whispered bidding, the two boys began picking their noses and then letting the contents swing from their fingertips like a bit of dried glue. Both of the boys were missing their front teeth which made them look evil rather than cute. They had freckles, too, which always seems to go with menaces. Freckles and missing teeth. I'm sure in any other context it would have seemed adorable.

Poppy had finally piped down about getting something to eat and seemed to be drifting off to sleep. Natalie and Brian were still bickering in the back and although I wasn't consciously tuning in, their fighting was working on me like a dripping faucet. I was at the wheel now and hadn't adjusted the rear-view mirror so all I could see if I looked in it were my own two children's faces twisting and flexing like the kids in the car in front of me. I was mesmerized for a moment by the hidden stories in the faces I was watching in the mirror. Parts of myself that had gone missing and turned up in the features of my children. Natalie's eyes flashing with anger, but large and sad behind the fire. Dark corridors of passion. Brian's smile, teasing and reflecting unashamed delight at his ability to wind up his sister. I couldn't take my eyes off the finer details of their faces. A constellation of tiny moles danced in the bottom left-hand corner of Natalie's right cheek. Markings she'd had from birth that were a mirror opposite to mine in the top right-hand corner of my right cheek. The Big Dipper and Little Dipper. There was a dimple just by the corner of Brian's right eye which made him look smug and too certain of himself. It was my mother's look, a look which I inherited and then we used in defiance of one another. A look which communicated our unwillingness to budge, ever, over anything.

My head jerked forward and I felt the car crunch. Natalie and Brian both screamed, Poppy cried out in her sleep and then fell unconscious again and the man on my right stirred ever so slightly. The children in the car in front stopped making faces and stared at me in horror. The back of their car looked badly dented. I wondered whether the impact of my car hitting theirs had stunned the little urchins into behaving or whether I had actually managed to impale them on some fraying bits of metal. I rested my head on the steering wheel and closed my eyes. I think if you can resist the urge to rise to the general level of hysteria and stress around you for long enough it will sometimes dispel itself. I kept my eyes closed until I heard Brian asking Natalie if I was dead, but when I opened them the car in front was still as badly damaged. There was water spouting out of the front of ours like a fountain and through the spray I could see the children from the car in front together with their parents standing on the road by the side of the car yelling in my direction. A minute later a policeman arrived. A Wyoming cop, quickly followed by a second. Big burly men dressed all in blue, with guns in holsters riding their hips like some fancy-dress cowboys.

'Ma'am?' The policeman stuck his head inside my open window. I stared at his neck in disbelief. It was thicker and more muscular than I had ever imagined necks could be. More like the trunk of an oak tree than a support for the human head. 'Are you the driver of this car?'

No. No, I just sit here and look pretty. The driver is off having his tea-break. The driver is somewhere else, operating the whole thing by remote-control. I just sit here watching the water spray like a fountain out of the front. Must be the radiator. What did he mean?

'Yes, officer. That's right. I'm driving this car.'

'Well, you sure did a good job of driving it into the car in front, now didn't you?'

What was this, an exercise in stating the obvious?

'I guess so,' I said.

He glanced with disdain at the front of our car which currently resembled a geyser. 'You're not from around here, are you?'

'From Wyoming? No.'

'From America. Your accent. That's not a US accent, now is it?'

So when he said *around here* he meant as in around the Nation. The whole thing. He meant, 'you're not one of us, are you?' I felt the need to defend myself and have a stab at belonging.

'Well, yes, um I mean, no. It was once, sort of,' I said. I couldn't be bothered to explain further.

The policeman couldn't be bothered to ask any more either. His partner, the other boy in blue, had gone over to talk to the family from hell. Our one, the one with the thick neck, was look-ing longingly in his direction. The other family may be monstrous but at least *they* had Wyoming licence plates. I felt sorry for our cop. I tried to make his job easier for him.

'Would you like to see my driver's licence?' I asked.

He sprung back into action and pulled out a pad from nowhere, with a pen poised ready to write.

'Why yes, ma'am, I would. Can you show me your documents, please?'

As I leaned across to open the glove compartment, I heard a muffled murmur from the back and guessed that Brian was about to ask me for a mint which he did every time he saw the glove compartment open. For as long as I can remember I always kept mints in there somewhere. I could see in the mirror that Natalie had put a hand firmly over his mouth to stop him from speaking. The policeman craned his elephantine neck with some difficulty to peer at my children lined up on the back seat. Natalie pretended to be wiping something from Brian's mouth and moved her hand away as she shot the policeman a winning smile. I fumbled around in the glove compartment, trying to find the envelope in which I had put our passports and driving licences and just about everything else important and official that we were travelling with. The cars trapped behind us had begun to hoot with frustration, as we had become something of an obstruction and they could see that the traffic in front had managed to start moving again. The policeman waved on the impatient drivers behind us with some authority and continued to wait somewhat impatiently himself for me to find what I was looking for.

'I can't find it. I can't find it! Oh my God, where is it?'

I became aware of a rustling sound getting louder as my hands reached, searching. Underneath the cotton sheet I could feel the paper that they line the beds with to make them easier to clean if you are sick or don't manage to call for a bed-pan in time.

'Francine, calm down. It's OK. What can't you find, honey? What is it you're looking for?'

As quickly as it had made itself real, Wyoming and the policeman with the thick neck faded almost to a speck in the distance and there was Cynthia, again. Calming and soothing. Where did she come from?

'My driving licence. The policeman needs to see it . . . needed to see it. He . . .'

'What policeman, honey?'

It was no use. Cynthia never quite understood me when I needed her to. I really wanted her to this time because it seemed as if she was part of it in some way. She might have had something to tell the policeman in Wyoming herself. But the moment had passed and Cynthia couldn't have been any other way and it was all right anyway because when I looked, the other family with the kids appeared to be gone too. I couldn't see the mirror any more either and the faces of Brian and Natalie and Poppy asleep in the back had vanished with it.

'It's because I was watching them. Brian and Natalie. It's because I was watching them that we crashed.' Cynthia tried hard to follow me but still looked terribly confused. I always seemed to be the cause of her confusion.

'Maybe Poppy took it. The envelope with all the documents in it. Do you think she could have opened the glove-box all by herself?'

Cynthia just held my hand, trying to smile and saying nothing.

'I don't really want to go to Yellowstone,' I told her finally. 'I prefer the Grand Canyon.'

Cynthia was squeezing my hand just a little too hard but I didn't want to say anything more so I closed my eyes and bit my lip to see if I could stand it until she decided to let go of her own accord. Then, out of the silence, a response to something that I had said light years ago, I heard a man's voice speak.

'You're not going anywhere, Mrs Weitz, until you show me that you can move those legs.'

It was that Dr Peacock. Luke. That doctor that always seems to be there just when I am beginning to lose true sense of myself. Well then, maybe for Luke Peacock I would learn to move my legs again. And maybe just to show the good doctor I *will* go to the Grand Canyon. I'd rather walk down the side of it than take one of those helicopters over it, though. I'd rather have my feet on the ground and know what's what. Besides, helicopters have this habit of just hovering and I can't stand that. I need to know where I'm going and get there. Not just to hover like a humming-bird, suspended in mid-air doing nothing.

'She's been dreaming again, Doctor. Just some dreams.' Cynthia tried to console herself with her explanation. It was better than feeling confused.

Cynthia was wrong though. I haven't had any dreams for a while. Not real dreams that help to make sense of how things are and rehearse how things could be. Only backwards dreams that show me how things were. I wouldn't even call them dreams necessarily. Thoughts maybe, memories. Little clues to the past.

'We were on our way to Seattle,' I told her. Maybe if I started at the beginning she would understand better. 'Me and . . . the kids.'

'Yes, that's right, Francine. You took all three of them to see our old house. On Ivy Street. Poppy went too. She was just a baby.'

'We were on our way to Seattle, through Wyoming, but he wasn't there.'

'Who wasn't, Francine, honey. Who wasn't there?' She turned to Dr Peacock apologetically. 'She was dreaming. I think she needed to find a policeman or something,' Cynthia explained. She wasn't being helpful. Luke, however, the good doctor, nodded as though she was and put his hand on my forehead. His touch was soft and leathery, like an old armchair. Rough and smooth at the same time.

'*He* wasn't,' I tried again looking into both of their bemused and benign faces and knowing that they would never understand. 'Dad. Dad wasn't there. I looked, we all looked but . . .'

Cynthia's face froze. This took me by surprise. I had expected another non-response. Something stark and non-committal. Suddenly I felt less like I was struggling to explain the unex-plainable and more like something had planted itself, without my even wanting it to, inside me. An old thing, a feeling, something big that is still part of me. Cynthia pinched her lips together tightly and I could see the little lines standing like a picket fence on her upper lip. Little lines like Grandma had, all around her mouth. Little lines standing to attention and guarding the lips lest they be asked to speak and remember, too. Tight shut mouth pulled together with barbed wire. Cynthia would not speak another word until I had erased the words already spoken. This I knew from a very ancient set of rules between us. She would not speak until I had found a way to change the subject and pretend that I had never mentioned the other in the first place.

37

The man who waits is not there today. I looked for him when I woke up but the place where he sits, the chair in the corner, is empty. I thought about asking someone but it would seem silly to be so concerned about someone who just sits like that, waiting. Waiting is such a patient thing to do. This hospital is filled with patients. All of them patiently waiting for something. To die, to live, to remember, to forget. Perhaps he will come later. Perhaps he will come when they bring the trolley with the green teacups and the folded newspapers. Perhaps he will be there then, sitting, watching and waiting patiently.

I could not be patient when we got to Seattle. Ivy Street, the street where we had lived, was too changed. Our house had been painted a different colour and was covered with trailing vines of blooming wisteria. When we lived there we had ivy clinging to the red brick walls. Ivy like the street, like the world we lived in, clinging tight and suffocating. The wisteria felt oddly English and trivial and mocking. I imagined the flowers to be laughing at me in their blues and purples and lacy whites. Laughing at me for expecting to come back and find things unchanged, just like I had left them. Poppy and Natalie and Brian were not impatient like I was. They were happy to stay and explore and when the lady called Mrs Robinson answered the door which used to be mine and invited them in to have a look around their mother's 'old house', they went in eagerly. He went in too with a wide-eyed child's curiosity. It was only I who hung back. Only me who could not go through the rooms looking and remembering with such emptiness.

I told him, when the children were busy looking around the garden and Mrs Robinson had gone to make some lemonade. I told him then that I would be back soon. I tried to explain before Poppy came up and pulled him away into the garden to have a look at some 'big red girl flowers'. She had found her namesake in the crop of poppies that flopped languorously in the sun with their papery faces and limp stems leaning gently on the backs of their stronger stemmed cousins growing around them at the rear of the house. The poppies had sprung up from nowhere one summer when I was about six, next to the peonies and purple irises in the flower bed that my mother had once watched over with a kind of tenderness and care which I have never seen in her since. Now my little Poppy gazed with the same watchfulness.

I needed to tell him that it was a journey I would have to make on my own, but Poppy had already grabbed him by the hand and I knew as I watched them wander off down the path together to where Natalie and Brian had also discovered an ant's nest inside a crack in one of the paving stones that it would be all right for the three of them, and that he would be there taking care of things for as long as I needed him to be. They would be able to see his face even if I couldn't and he would watch over my Natalie and Brian and little Poppy. He would look around Seattle with them and find a few museums, a cheap hotel, some places to eat. I could rest assured that they would be well looked after and that they would have a good time, just like I must have when I was their age.

38

'. . . We are born alone and it is alone we die . . .' Some priest-like person was delivering a sermon to the woman in the bed across from me. He spoke in a sing-songy, elegiac kind of way that made me think he didn't really believe, himself, what he was saying. Of course it isn't true that we are born alone. There is someone with us from the moment of our conception, if not in spirit, definitely in body. We could not be separate from our parents at that point even if we wanted to. And dying . . . well. I'm still wondering about that one. I think perhaps dying is the one time in our lives we have permission to retreat absolutely and completely from the company of others, bodily that is. But even being dead does not make us separate. In death we become cemented forever in the thoughts and memories of others. Even if it is only the ward-nurse or the hospital priest who eulogized over our dying body that remembers us.

Travelling alone to San Francisco from Seattle I didn't know whether my father was alive or dead. I didn't know whether the Leon lurking inside my head was a real presence or a distant memory. The man who sat next to me on the airplane was a Pakistani. He wore a white cheesecloth top and loose silky trousers. He smelled of patchouli oil and Indian spices and it made me think of plaster-statue gift-shops and newsagents. He struck up a conversation with me. It was only a short flight so we barely had time to become intimate or awkward in between the complimentary drinks, peanuts, the perfume and cigarette sales and announcements from the pilot. His name was Rudi and he was, I found out, a swami master bound for the Golden Gate City to address devotees in a Buddhist monastery hidden somewhere behind the trolley-cars and Rice-a-roni. His lecture was on 'Love and the Holy Spirit'.

Rudi only had hand-luggage with him, an embroidered cloth bag with a rope tie, and in my haste to leave I had not remembered to pack anything so I had only my handbag to take with me when I left the plane. We walked together as far as the outside of the airport terminal where Rudi hailed a taxi to take him to his monastic lodgings and I got onto a bus heading for the city.

My first instinct was to go straight to Nirvana, the house where Leon had lived with André and Nina all those years ago. But I knew that if I did I would not find what I was looking for. Leon had left Nirvana the same time as I did and I assumed that the passage of time would have meant that Nina had also left, not only Nirvana but this earth, and perhaps André, with his weak heart, had followed her. If not Nirvana then where? Castro Street had always been a favourite place of mine when I had lived in the city before. I liked the colour and the hustle-bustle that made this area feel as though it was always at the centre of a Mardi Gras. But the bus I was on did not go to the Castro and before I could think my way through all of the other possibilities the bus had reached its destination, Golden Gate Bridge, and I felt myself drawn like a lemming towards the opening doors together with the throng of others.

'In life, every soul has to withstand great pressure and to be well tested . . .' the minister at the bedside opposite droned on. Mrs MacGregor, the woman for whose benefit he was delivering his sermon, looked either bored or dead. Perhaps they are much the same thing when it comes down to it. Being dead is just a sort of permanent state of ennui. A complete and final disenchantment with life and all those who live it.

'. . . Every life is an important piece of work towards the

common goal of complete harmony. When life breaks down before the soul has finished its journey and work is left unfinished there will be other lives so each soul can take up the road again and follow the path of light. We are all but steps along the way to ultimate fulfilment.'

I think Mrs MacGregor would have liked to have seen herself as something a little bit more special than a step for just a moment before she died. As far as I could tell she had spent most of her waking hours (and probably sleeping, for that matter) as something to be stepped on by others. She had five children of varying ages who never spent more than twenty minutes with her at visiting times and never all at once. During the time they spent with her they did not waste seconds on enquiring how she was or checking if there was anything she needed or wanted that they could get for her. They came only when they needed something from her. Usually what they needed was money. Mrs MacGregor kept her Bradford & Bingley chequebook in the drawer of her bedside table for these very frequent requests. If it wasn't money her children wanted it was permission to do something they would have felt too guilty doing without her blessing. Maggie, Mrs MacGregor's eldest daughter, came often to ask if she could borrow clothes belonging to her mother (and, by implication I guess, to ask whether she could have them all when Mrs M was gone). Maggie had her mother's body, full-figured and robust, as it had been before illness had pulled and pinched away the gentle rolls and curves and left only sharp edges in their place. Now Maggie MacGregor wore her mother's clothes and seemed to have taken the very colour from her cheeks and painted it on to her own.

I have seen Mr MacGregor only twice in the whole time I have been here, though of course he may have come at times when I was not conscious enough to know who was visiting whom and when. The first time I saw him was when his wife arrived on the ward. He moved her in, so to speak, carrying her bags for her and walking with some haste, looking at his watch all the time and saying he couldn't stay because he had left his car on a meter which was ticking away and the time was going to expire at any moment. Of course that was nothing to the meter that was ticking away on poor Mrs MacGregor's life but the angel of death who watched over her was less of a threat, I guess, than the traffic wardens that milled around outside, waiting to throw their clamps upon the likes of Mr MacGregor.

The second time I saw Mr MacGregor was when he came in wearing a suit and tie and a flower in his buttonhole. The smart attire was clearly not for his wife's benefit, however, as I heard him telling her with unashamed excitement that when he'd left her he was going to go out to dinner with one of the nurses he had met and befriended while visiting the hospital. He said he had wanted to let Mrs MacGregor know so that she wouldn't fret over his happiness or loneliness whilst she was not there to look after him herself. Perhaps, like his children, he needed Mrs MacGregor to absolve him of any guilt he might possibly suffer for his infidelity. He explained in great detail the restaurant they would be going to, the excellent house wine, the lobster main course, the floor show that accompanied the dinner and the dancing afterwards. Mrs MacGregor simply smiled sweetly, telling her husband how pleased she was that he was managing to get out and enjoy himself. I'll bet the closest Mrs MacGregor had come to a lobster dinner with this man was at the local Chinese takeaway where the only show was *Coronation Street* blinking silently from the telly behind the counter. Mrs MacGregor had stopped blinking altogether. It was hard to imagine in her silent darkness that her soul was about to take up the road again to follow a path of light in this life or any other.

'You are the holiest of spirits. You are immortal. You are radiant and divine beings. Children of God! Live in your wonderful spirits and allow nothing to bind and limit you!' The man stood on a soapbox at the edge of the bridge on the San Francisco end. He had what looked like a golden eagle sitting on his shoulder, attached by a metal chain connecting the bird's foot to the man's belt loop. I wasn't sure whether the eagle was supposed to be a symbol of the free and glorious spirit of mankind or of

226

animal captivity but I stood and listened to the soapbox preacher a moment longer while I breathed in familiar San Francisco smells and tried to think where to go and what to do next.

'Do not be tempted by material things. Do not be led by the evil seductions of possessions and more possessions until these things you thought you wanted begin to possess you. Live freely, simply, breathe the air that is yours unquestionably. Children of God, children of the light. Possess the world you inhabit and the life you have been blessed with. No less and no more than that.' I checked out the label on the jeans which hid behind the belt loop the bird was currently clamped to. Fiorucci. Perhaps they came with the job. The man reached out a hand as smooth and elegant as the jeans he was wearing to take mercifully the many small items being passed to him from converted members of the small crowd that had gathered. The soap box made a handy container for the handfuls of jewellery, mobile telephones and wadded billfolds of which these unfortunates needed to divest themselves.

Another small crowd had collected towards the middle of the bridge on the right-hand side – the side that faces in towards the city. I wondered whether there was another golden-winged preacher at the centre of that one. I watched a woman walk out of the crowd carrying a briefcase and wearing high heels and a rusty-red coat that matched the girders of the bridge. She looked solemn and shook her head slowly as though trying to rid herself of a thought. A wispy silk scarf that was anchored around her neck by a brooch of silver wings danced about her cheeks and brushed her mouth, painted with lipstick the same colour as her coat. As we neared each other she moved the scarf away with her hand and smiled.

'Number five hundred and twelve,' she said earnestly as though this numeral should hold enormous significance for both of us.

'Number five hundred and twelve?' I repeated, thinking that if I kept on saying it I might eventually understand the true meaning of this figure.

'About to be,' she said. 'Unless someone does something to stop it.'

I looked over again to where the small crowd was gathered and thought I could just make out a single head that was higher than the rest of them. A head cloaked in a dark hood which precluded any possibility of seeing the face. I thought fleetingly of the *French Lieutenant's Woman* on a windswept Cornish coast and then of medieval executioners. My final thought before I left the crowd I had been part of and went to join this new one was of angels and the fluttering of gold and silver wings.

'Seems crazy saying "life goes on" and "I've got to go to work" but it does and I do,' the woman's words gave strange voice to my need to move on in one direction and hers to proceed in the other.

'Right,' I said. 'You're right, so do I . . . I mean, I agree . . . well, thank you.'

As I watched her walk away, she pulled the wide collar of her red coat up around the back of her head and ears and I was struck by a pain and fear so deep I had to close my eyes for a moment to steady myself. With my eyes closed I felt very small and I knew then what the hooded figure on the bridge really reminded me of. It reminded me of myself. Or, at least of a character in a book I had once identified with. Little Red Riding Hood. Little Red Riding Hood, a young girl so naive and bent on seeing good in people that she couldn't even see her own death coming.

When I was six, Cynthia and I took part in a summer reading scheme at the library. The brief was to choose and read at least eight books all the way through without any help from a grown-up and write a short paragraph about each one. I chose six versions of *Little Red Riding Hood* and because there were no others of that title stocked in the library I did not read any more than these six. Cynthia read twelve different books and was awarded a certificate with added stars on it for the extra reading she had done. I did not get a certificate but was sent a polite note from the library explaining that the object of the scheme was to encourage children to have a wide and varied reading repertoire and they suggested some other titles to me like *Snow White* and *Cinderella* as they figured I must be interested in fairy tales. In fact it was not fairy tales in general that interested me, just this particular one, a story of a girl and a wolf.

Then a hand rose up from the audience and the questioner asked the speaker, 'What do you mean by love?'

And then he, whose face before had been veiled and hidden from view, lifted his head and there fell a great stillness. But the questioner had not finished and spoke again, piercing through the silence with her asking.

'Can there be love without any incentive? Can there be love without wanting something for oneself out of love? Is it possible to love and not be loved back or even could it be that we are loved without ever having loved ourselves?'

The master's eyes grew big and his lips parted, showing two great rows of gleaming white teeth. The silence grew also until it became almost unbearable and the questioner began to shrink and cower for fear that she had asked the wrong question.

Finally, as though God himself had heard her question and knew her need to be answered, the great man spoke: 'Love that appears to come from outside ourselves is merely a reflection of the love of the Holy Spirit that resides within. Love is an inward beauty which flows from the heart and the river of the soul which goes beyond life itself.'

'Rudi?' I called his name boldly aloud, wanting desperately to be picked out from this throng of disciples as someone who had some special connection with the man even though I knew in my heart that he had only been a passing acquaintance.

'Who's Rudi, darling?'

Cynthia. It was Cynthia. Still trying to understand. I knew then that I couldn't have been there with the others listening to Rudi speak, for Cynthia would not have been there with me if I was. The sermon I was hearing was the farewell address to Mrs MacGregor. We were all there to witness it: Cynthia, Melanie (looking rather smart in a rust-red skirt and jacket outfit that reminded me faintly of . . .). The man who waits was back, but he had moved forward from his corner and was standing next to Natalie and Brian who were sipping coffee noisily from polystyrene cups. I saw Poppy, too, with her peasant blouse unbuttoned halfway down her chest to let little Luther nestle his head right to her very centre so he could suck out the nectar, the pure opium pouring straight from her source.

I saw everybody but when I looked again Mrs MacGregor wasn't there. Her bed was empty and it was only mine that people were standing around. Even the preacher man seemed to be saying his prayers, delivering his eulogies in my direction. I wanted to laugh and tell them I didn't believe in all this and besides there was somebody who far more urgently needed my attention. The hooded figure on the bridge was going to be number five hundred and twelve unless somebody . . . unless I found a way to do something about it.

'Stop!' I shouted.

The preacher man stopped giving his sermon. Melanie took a step backwards and Natalie and Brian stopped sipping their coffee. Cynthia let go of the grip she had on my fingers and little Luther looked up drunkenly from where he had been buried. The man in the corner moved closer and smiled. On the bridge the crowd stood still. Watching and waiting in both directions. A small path opened up so that I could walk unfettered towards the figure, hooded and cloaked, facing away from me with back poised, ready to jump. Everyone was silent but I could hear my own breathing and my heart beating inside of me as if it were the roar of the mightiest ocean. As I moved steadily and quietly and easily through the crowd I began to realize that I was closed in from all sides. All faces were turned in towards me, waiting and watching to see what I would do. Like a crowd in a Greek stadium, seated on all sides but watching and waiting with one breath, one gasp, as slowly, slowly, the condemned man is released into the lion's lair.

As I moved closer I began to see what I had not been able to see before. The hood and the cloak were empty. The wind that was blowing out from the bay teased the material up and around the emptiness that was underneath, waving it gently and laugh-ingly in my direction as if to say, 'you've been fooled, there's nothing here . . . no one'. But through a crack in the crowd, just at the side of my vision I could see what had happened. There had been someone at some time who wore the cloak from the inside. Just as there always is. Even a knight's shining armour, that stands like a mausoleum after the man inside has perished and shed his metal skin, once shielded something real.

The figure that had been cloaked and hooded and hidden from all view had crept out quietly and nakedly and was moving quickly over to the other side of the bridge which was where I always thought he would go. It didn't seem right at all that he should want to die like all the others, facing inwards towards a city shaken by earthquakes and where thousands before him had already left their hearts. Better to be looking outwards towards the sea where there are all sorts of possibilities. Old lives and new ones waiting to take shape, acres and acres of ocean, tide beating against tide, waiting for futures unknown and huge salty torrents of waves ready to embrace the present and wash away the pain and sorrow of the past.

In his nakedness I could see absolutely who it was. My own features, my own eyes stared out from his aged face, tired and worn but unmistakably related to my own. His gaze was steady and slow and so insistent that I could not resist, one last time, the cruel invitation to join him in this, his final descent.

The empty cloak hung like a scarecrow on the city side and the crowd waited with held breath as I approached it. I had only a split second – the time it takes for a person to blink or to jump or to stop breathing and thinking for just a moment in order to catch up with the last breath or thought they had – I had only this short time to make my invisible escape and join my father on the other side. If you leave a place fast enough, so fast that no one or nothing has seen you leave, then people will believe for that same stretch of time that you are still there. That is what hap-pened. I saw the crack in time and my father's nakedness and I ran or rather, shot, like an arrow, like a bolt of lightning towards the man I had been seeking all my life. I ran to catch him or go with him before he made himself one with the ocean, the sky and all the other intangible things around me that I can never quite reach and never quite get close enough to touch. I ran so I could be with him and know him like one drop in an ocean can know another and in that split second we were absolutely together, climbing the railings of that bridge the colour of sunsets, the colour of blood, the colour of red earth deep in the centre where ancient truths lie buried.

He said my name softly so only I could hear it. Francine. And I said his, Leon, and then we were both weightless and falling. My eyes were shut so I did not see when or how he hit the water. It could have been before or after I felt the icy cold of the wet splash hit me. The water did not close around me as I thought it might, taking me under and holding me there, forcing me to breathe in its wet saltiness until I was part of it completely.

Instead I felt as though by some magic I might have been suspended and held in mid-air just above the surface. I was aware of water on my face, running from my eyes and cheeks, but when I reached out to taste it with my tongue it seemed fresh and clear like mountain springs, with only the tiniest trace of salt which could have been left over from a tear that had been waiting too long for its turn to be cried. I awoke to find smiling faces towering over me and the woman with the briefcase emptying a bottle of Evian over me as though I were a plant that needed watering.

'Did you want to be number five hundred and thirteen?' she asked me. 'We only just managed to hold your legs before you went.'

I wanted to say lots of things. I wanted to ask her why she had come back. I wanted to apologize for making a spectacle. For causing her to waste perfectly good mineral water on waking me out of my daze. I wanted to know if I had been dreaming or if what I had imagined had really happened. 'Did he jump?' I asked finally, needing to know only that. 'Has he gone already?'

'She,' the woman said, gesturing to the opposite side of the bridge where the cloak had been and now wasn't. 'Belle. She wanted to go. You can't stop someone if they really want to do it.'

'Belle?'

'*Was* Belmont once upon a time. Used to be a man, but he decided to try being a woman. She, or he, couldn't get used to being either.'

'The cloak,' I whispered.

'Yes,' said the woman. 'She'd been up there a long time. Someone gave it to her to keep warm. A passer-by. It's over there now,' she pointed to a little dark bundle lying where the crowd had been standing over by the railings. 'Belle jumped without it. I was going to try to . . . do you have a coat?'

I had begun to shiver as my hair and shirt were still wet from the baptism I had received earlier. 'A coat?' I needed to repeat her question for myself because something about it had begun to reverberate inside of me and shake my body in a way that I knew was nothing to do with being cold. Then, as though she had always meant to do it, the woman reached for the brown flannel cloak and wrapped it around my arms and shoulders. For just a moment as she did so I had a flash of someone else, another woman who had also given me a coat to wear and offered a hand when I thought I was drowning.

Someone was rubbing my arms and my feet. I could hear my skin rustling like brown paper. The sound was inordinately loud. I wanted to cover my ears but someone else had my arms and I was unsure as to how to get them away. I could hear Cynthia's voice, and Melanie's. Natalie and Brian, Cynthia's Katy and Tom were there too. Alma, my mother, who looked like a painting of herself, was over in the corner watching. The preacher man, the one giving the sermon, was standing next to her. He was too far away for me to hear what he was saying. I could hardly even see his . . . the man with no face. The man in the corner . . . where had he gone? Where was the . . .

When I finally managed to adjust my focus. When I could finally look and see what was closest to me rather than that which was so far away that I would never see it in its entirety. When I finally managed to do that I could see that he had moved closer, inward. It was he who was rubbing my arms, my feet. His hands that were causing my skin to sing with this loud brushing sound. A sound that was loud enough and brash enough to wake the dead. He was close enough for me to see his face properly for the first time or perhaps I had never stopped seeing it. It was a face I knew better than myself, a face I recognized almost as though I had been part of its very creation. It was a father's face, of course, because he was a father. My children's father. Father to Natalie, Brian and little Poppy.

'You went cold,' he said. Gently. His words, his eyes, his hands rubbing and rubbing the life back into me. So gentle.

'Yes,' I answered him in a whisper.

'I've been waiting for you,' he explained.

'I know,' I said. 'I've been trying to get here.'

Cynthia had moved away and had her arm locked through Melanie's. She looked happy but confused. I think I shall always be a source of confusion for Cynthia. Natalie and Brian were debating whether or not to go for another coffee and Poppy was trying to unlatch Luther who had fallen asleep at the nipple. Alma, my mother, looked more like me and more beautiful than I had ever remembered her. A nurse was standing behind me sponging my face. I could taste with my tongue the clear fresh water dripping from the sponge.

He held my hand and sat close to me, smiling.

'It was a bit like drowning,' I said to him. 'You know, life going before your eyes and all that.'

'I know,' he said. 'Was I there, in that life?'

'Eventually,' I said. 'Thank God, thank God, eventually.'